Cathie Dunsford is director of Dunsford Publishing Consultants which assesses, edits and sells feminist and general texts from the Pacific to the publishing industry globally. She taught literature at Auckland University for seven years, was Fulbright Post-Doctoral Research Scholar at the University of California, Berkeley, for three years, and has directed the NZ Writers' Conferences and read and lectured in Europe, UK and USA. She currently teaches Creative Writing and Publishing at Auckland University. She regularly attends international book fairs. She has edited four collections of NZ literature and her own writing appears in anthologies published in New Zealand, Australia, USA, Germany and the UK. She has been on the Editorial Board of the *Lesbian Review of Books,* USA, since its inception.

Other Spinifex Press books by Cathie Dunsford

Fiction
Cowrie
Manawa Toa
Ao Toa
Song of the Selkies

Anthology
Car Maintenance, Explosives and Love and
Other Contemporary Lesbian Writings
(co-editor with Susan Hawthorne and Susan Sayer)

THE JOURNEY HOME

TE HAERENGA KAINGA

CATHIE DUNSFORD

Spinifex Press Pty Ltd
PO Box 212
North Melbourne, Vic. 3051
Australia
www.spinifexpress.com.au
women@spinifexpress.com.au

First published by Spinifex Press, 1997. Reprinted 2017

Edited by Janet Mackenzie
Typeset by Lynne Hamilton
Cover art © 1997 Jacqui Young
Cover design by Spinifex Press
Text artwork © 1997 Cathie Dunsford
Printed in USA

National Library of Australia
Cataloguing-in-Publication data:
Dunsford, Cathie, 1953 - .
The journey home = Te haerenga kainga

ISBN 978-1-87555-954-1

I. Title.
NZ823.2

Acknowledgements

The author gratefully acknowledges the New Zealand Arts Council: Creative New Zealand for their support of New Zealand authors and in providing a grant to enable the completion of this novel.

My grateful thanks also to: writers Susan Sayer and Beryl Fletcher for their detailed feedback on the text in progress and for their commitment to my work. Susan Hawthorne and Renate Klein for comments at all stages of the text development and for their commitment to getting our South Pacific texts into the northern hemisphere. Michelle Proctor for editing suggestions at early draft stages. NZ writers Noel Virtue, Whiti Ihimaera and Keri Hulme for their support for my first novel, *Cowrie*. My Whanau, without whose support I could not write. Sue Hardisty, Export Sales, Spinifex Press, Melbourne, for promoting overseas sales. Michele Karlsberg, Spinifex Publicist, USA, for outrageous promotion of *Cowrie* in the USA. Jo Turner for her efficient editorial management; Janet Mackenzie for her astute editorial comments; Jenny Nagel at Addenda for New Zealand promotion and publicity; Libby Fullard and the Spinifex team for their support and Jacqui Young for the cover art. Sara Fuller, for breaking through colonial barriers to promote our South Pacific work in the UK, for the London launch and UK promotion of *Cowrie;* and for her total belief in my writing and the power of fiction to change old ways of thinking. Starfish Enterprise, Edinburgh, for organising *Cowrie* readings for the Edinburgh Festival, 1996. Helen Benton, Bob Ross and Penny Hansen at Tandem Press, New Zealand, for *Cowrie* and *The Journey Home/Te Haerenga Kainga* and for their support for New Zealand writing. Rawinia White and Marewa Glover for allowing their work to appear in this book.

Darkness. Chaos. Words lash her like branches, ripping at her skin, thorns tearing her body. She must climb higher, get away. The wind whips her from all four directions. If only she can get to that top branch. Will it hold her weight? Below, voices. Girls screaming. She imagines her mother climbing, reaching out for her. But at the point of contact, she turns into a pine nut. She yells. The sky collapses and she is crunched into the ground.

"Come on Cowrie, move that big puku of yours. We wanna dig a pit for the hangi. Fat lotta good you are, lazing around in the morning." Eruera grins as Cowrie wakes to see him dangling a flax kete full of pipis over her face. The sweet, salty water runs like tears down her cheeks, drops softly into the black earth below.

"Thanks, bro. Just what I needed. What time is it?"

"Well, you missed sunrise 'cos you sure as hell weren't with us digging for pipis at dawn."

Today is the opening of the new marae and Mere will be needing Cowrie to help put up the tukutuku panels. They worked until dawn finishing them, and Cowrie collapsed into sleep where they'd been weaving the final strands. Mere left her there, knowing she'd be woken by the boys after the gathering of pipis, and warned them to leave her alone.

"Eruera! Hone! Come back here and get those pipis into water. The buckets are by the wash-house." The boys reluctantly obey Mere, carrying the kete of shellfish between them. Cowrie staggers over to the hose to douse her face with cold water.

"How come you're up so early, Mere?"

"What makes you think I went to sleep, eh, Cowrie?" Mere grins.

Cowrie hugs her. "Jeez, it's good to be back home, Mum."

"So Aotearoa is your home, then. Not Hawai'i?" Mere teases.

"Both now. I miss Koana, Nele and Peni. Keo's big jelly belly, Paneke's voice and steambath. But Aotearoa will always be home. Te whenua. Whanau..."

"Yeah, and kai moana. That's what really brought you home, eh? The gifts of the sea—pipis, tuatuas, paua, smoked kahawai and mullet... I know you, Cowrie. Puku comes first, eh?"

Cowrie grins.

"So where do we start hanging the tukutuku panels?"

"They're up already. The aunties did a ritual at dawn and we decided to hang them then. You were so out to it, we didn't want to wake you."

Cowrie looks deeply hurt that she'd been left out of the ritual but Mere adds, "And, my little mottled Cowrie, we've named one of them in honour of you. Haere mai." Mere takes her hand and leads Cowrie to the brown and cream weaving on black painted sticks strung together with flax. Underneath, Hawai'i—Aotearoa: Te Haerenga Kainga. The Journey Home.

Tears surge like a tidal wave from the crater of Cowrie's belly, surge, hang swollen behind her eyes. Mere holds her close, croons into her ear. "Be calm, my little turtle. You've worked hard for this. The new

2

marae welcomes young and old, Pacific and Pakeha. You're a symbol for us of the directions we're heading in. We embrace the traditions of the past—but we are also a part of the wider Pacific, the world, and we have a vital role to play in its healing. We must honour that whakapapa, let it feed the present, nourish the future."

Cowrie tries to speak, but cannot. She holds her mother close, letting tears fall onto Mere's cloak, feeling the soft kiwi feathers touch and caress her face tenderly.

Dusk falls as the ritual opening of the new marae ends with a feast for the manuhiri provided by local Maori. Kuini and Cowrie are unpeeling layers of pork, chicken, lamb, kumara and cabbage as kai is lifted from deep within the belly of the black earth. Through steam, men's faces sweat while they heave up each layer from its ritual placing and carry the woven kete over to the makeshift kitchen under a bright canvas awning. Women arrange plates of kai, while kids duck in and out taking new trays of food to lay on the long trestle tables.

Once everyone is seated, karakia is offered to bless the food and waiata sung to carry the blessings over the top of the giant mamaku, through the rainforest and to every Nga Puhi home of those present and absent. Tables sigh with delight under the weight of the food. Steam from the smoking hangi hangs around the edges of the trestles, then billows up between the laughter. They are in a giant cavern filled with hope, dreams inscribed around the cave walls, in the hearts of the new generation.

"Great to have you home again, sister," Kuini whispers into Cowrie's ear.

"Choice to be home, Kuini, especially up here on my own turf."

"Our own turf, thank you! Remember I'm Nga Puhi and Tainui."

"Yeah, best of both worlds, eh? How could I forget?"

"Hey, I'm still gettin' used to your Hawai'ian whakapapa, so no worries. How come you never told me about it until last year?"

"I didn't know much. Except what Mere told me—that I was left at the Rawene Orphanage with an old box of tokens—and I just followed the trail from there."

"Does it change how you feel about us here?"

"No, except that it's made me wonder if we're silencing others like us around the Pacific. What about the Samoan and Nuie Islanders our cuzzies are married to? And maybe there are other Hawai'ians here in Aotearoa?"

"You'll get heaps for daring to challenge biculturalism—but go for it, Cowrie. You always were a boundary breaker."

"C'mon you fellas, what's all this heavy rap? We're here to celebrate the new marae. Save your voices for waiata after dinner. We'll be singin' till dawn and we need you for the poi dances," It's Rawinia.

"OK, aunty. Keep your potae on! We'll be there," replies Kuini, laughing.

They eye the kumara and Cowrie reflects on how much she missed the bright purple yams while in Hawai'i. She slices down the belly of the kumara, using her fingers to part the inviting yellow flesh, then smothers rich creamy fresh butter over the warm, soft interior. Her mouth fills with moisture in anticipation of taste. The kumara is about to enter her mouth when Kuini bursts into laughter and whispers in her ear, "You are a very sensuous woman, Cowrie, but you don't need to let all the rellies know you're a dyke in one go." Cowrie bites into kumara to prevent it spluttering on to the table, then grins sheepishly.

After dinner, there is dancing and singing around a crackling fire lit with kanuka felled after a recent storm. The children are put to sleep in the whare nui and some of the weary mothers join them when the kitchen has been cleared. People from neighbouring Tai Tokerau iwi settle around the flames, ready to laugh, cry and celebrate.

Some of the older children enact a play that tells the story of Maui, who first caught the great fish, Te Ika a Maui, the North Island of Aotearoa, and raised it from the ocean depths in his sturdy canoe. The waka is made from children's bodies laid around Maui in the shape of a canoe. Others create waves surging up, threatening to drown Maui as he struggles to lift the island to the surface of the water.

Later, a group of adults recreate the demise of Maui, who was crushed to death by Hine Nui Te Po, the goddess of darkness and death, when he attempted to enter her body, rape her, to secure immortality for man. Kuini has organised this drama and some of the men giggle in embarrassment, as if caught in the act. Cowrie wants to smash the brown bottles in their hands, force them to face up to the fact that Maui is still alive and well and raping today. Te Aroha Terry, who has worked longest in this field, reckons that every second Maori woman has been raped, assaulted or interfered with. And these men still act as if it's some kind of joke. Lucky the women have Hine Nui Te Po.

Kuini knew her interpretation of the myth would cause a reaction but she wanted to keep the challenge alive, remind the men that they could not just act as they felt all the time, take from their women to fire their own strength and egos. One of the drunk men yells out, "Go, Maui, fuck her now. Get her while the going is good." At the moment of his cry, Kuini closes her thighs, crushing the face of Maui before he can enter her cave, and someone throws a wet log on to the fire, making a whooshing sound emerge from its belly. Mere quietly moves around the edge of the flames and orders the offending voice to disappear and not come back again. He starts to protest, but the men take the bottle from his shaking hands and escort him away.

The incident is over in a flash, hardly noticed by some, but Cowrie's face is flushed with anger, and her will is urging Kuini to finish the act. Maui lies contorted in pain, as life drains from his tuatara limbs. Hine Nui Te Po rises from the ashes, strengthened by her act of defiance. The women clap, cheer, and some of the men's voices join them. One fellow nearby mutters something about that bloody Duff fella starting this all off with *Once Were Warriors* and how men couldn't have fun any more. Aunty Rawinia turns to face him, looks him in the eye and states clearly and strongly, "Hine Nui Te Po was around long before that bloody Duff fella and she's always given us women strength and courage. You men had betta just watch yourselves, because we have the power and support to crush any of you who enters us wrongfully, or even thinks about it." Hone shrinks from her stare, hoping his mates will support him. But they have mysteriously disappeared.

After the storytelling, they sing waiata and soon the disturbance is forgotten among the excitement of the new marae. Cowrie puts her arm around Mere, hoping the incident has not upset her too much. "You OK, mum?"

Mere turns to her, smiling. "Never fear, my little turtle. We women have always had the real power, the inner power. Now the men are starting to come to us to find out what is missing from their lives, to discover how to reclaim the fire in their spirit. They thought that to be warriors they had to conquer women, treat us like dirt. But now they're realising it is we who have true strength, who possess the secret of continuing life. It is we who will heal this planet and only those men willing to listen will survive."

Cowrie stares at her mother. She'd never really seen her as a feminist. Mere would shrink from the term. She'd say it was Pakeha privilege, a white woman's word. But between the different words lies the truth. Hine Nui Te Po is living proof.

Kuini arrives for a hug and they leave to plot for the writers' hui and finalise the speakers and sessions for the next few days. They work till late in the night and sleep in peace on the sand dunes, away from the snoring and spluttering in the whare nui where everyone else is spread out.

She drew another woman giving birth. The small creature dived from a tattooed vulva, its arms outstretched grasping at the world, a solid scream escaped its open mouth. Tihe Mauri Ora! The mother held in her hands a decorated weaving stick—tool of her trade. Below her Miria drew the child grown, half woman, half reptile, her tattooed breasts symbolising the past and her mystic limbs the unknown future—who will she be?

The women at the writers' hui draw in a breath, waiting to know what Miria's decision will be. The marae is alive with words as more women give voice to their dreams.

Marewa continues.

Miria wanted to draw the woman's future. She would draw her free. Free from violence. Free to stand, not at the base of the poupou holding up the iwi, but side by side with her whanau— all linked somehow, all together again. Miria closed her eyes and visualised the painting—the carved brown women had come to life. They were singing and waving. In their hands were, not weapons, but bracken fronds. Her hand jerked madly over the page in a race to catch the fading image.

The eyes of the women listening are willing the speaker on, wanting her words to affirm their own experiences. A baby cries outside the window as a woman passes, on her way to the tukutuku workshop. No one notices, they are so involved in the story.

She would paint this vision of a people who might have been had their soul not been cast in wood and enshrined in Pakeha museums. She would paint a vision—her dream of a people who might be free again one day—if only on canvas, and when and if Miria could find the time.

There is a hushed silence, then cries of "kia ora, Marewa, kia ora!" as the writer who has finished her story sits down on the woven mat, shy at the applause.

Rawinia reads a story about a family who used to come to their creek to catch eels. At the time, she didn't know how to eel, so "when the bait wasn't taken I just kept putting more on until the only thing that would take it was one mighty big eel. Sure enough, I struggled by myself to land an eel that weighed in at 9 pounds 5 ounces before it was smoked and eaten by Wiki and her family."

She pauses, sighing, and adds, "You know it's never bothered me till now that I never got to taste that eel. It's not strange that I didn't. After all, I wasn't supposed to in the first place. But still, it's something you can't do nothing about and leaves an ache that doesn't shift for the knowing."

Everyone is silent. Grief-stricken, her aunty reaches to hug her. It's time for a break.

Cups rattle in the kitchen as the women drink gumboot tea and eat anzac bickies, eager to discuss the stories that they've heard and add more of their own. In the afternoon, Patricia Grace and Bub Bridger read from their work, answer questions and support the writers. The hui ends with readings from all the participants and one of the women presents them with a carving of a creature—half woman, half reptile, with tattooed breasts symbolising the past, and limbs inscribed *Marama,* moon, to invoke the dreaming of the future.

"So, where to now?" asks one of the younger women.

"It's in your hands, your souls," offers Cowrie.

"Na, I meant let's not let it end here. Let's go down to the beach and do a ritual to call up the spirits to support our future work."

Some of the older women are not sure, knowing full well what the spirits might say if invoked unwillingly.

"Haere mai. We need a ceremonial ending," adds Mere, who has come in for the final session. "Let the tamariki lead us this time. The rest of us have been working so hard to make this happen."

Seventeen-year-old Irihapeti grabs a stick of toe-toe, hoists it high above her head, yells out "Follow me, wahine toa!" and begins marching toward the sand dunes. The kuia laugh and gesture everyone to go with her.

A line of writers, thinkers, dreamers, women who by night change nappies and at dawn prepare kai o te ata of eggs and bacon to sustain their men and children through the day, march over the dunes with toetoe branches flying wildly above their heads. As if moved by one energy, they build a gigantic sand castle in the shape of a sea egg, and decorate it with shells and twigs, like mother turtles covering their young for the long months before hatching. They dig a moat around the kina to protect it from invaders and wait for the tide to complete their work. As the first trickles of water enter the moat, they cheer.

Kuini breaks into waiata, "*Wahine ma, wahine ma, maranga mai, maranga mai, kia kaha*" urging the women to gather round to celebrate their togetherness. Gradually all the voices in the circle surrounding the egg join in, some high, some low, some in between, some in descant. Water creeps up over the moat to the base of the egg, but stays lapping the edges, as the women keep singing. Toetoe from the top of the sandy kina flap in the breeze and a fiery orange sunset flames up the faces of the women, young and old, fat and thin, Maori, Pakeha, Samoan, Nuie Island, Yugoslav. Kuini glances over to Cowrie. The new era they dreamed has already begun.

Korero at the end of the week's events celebrates the opening of the marae. The final hui reveals that many on-going projects have emerged from their time together. In accordance with custom, each speaker is heard and no one can interrupt until he or she is finished, allowing people to listen more carefully, although there are always a few old codgers wanting to hear the sound of their own voices drone on. Mere and the kuia have subtle ways of urging them to be succinct.

The elders have spoken. Irihapeti rises, tentatively, stretching up to her full height. Cowrie remembers her body lit by fire, toetoe in her hand like a taiaha, her warrior face, at the beach ritual the night before. The younger Maori women who have grown up through kohanga reo programmes, knowing their language and their place from an early age, have turned out to be so strong and proud.

Irihapeti speaks first in Maori, then in English for the mixed group. She acknowledges the mountain she was born under, the river she grew up beside, the canoe which brought her ancestors to Aotearoa, her iwi Nga Puhi, her elders, the tohunga and kuia, and the kohanga reo that nurtured her. She honours the traditions that shaped her wairua, her spirit. By now, everyone is prepared for her to make a challenge because she has so carefully and respectfully laid her ground. After a few more feathers are stroked, she launches her waka into unknown and choppy seas.

"While I have been proud to be a part of this week and am excited by the waka to be built by the men, the results of the women writers' hui and all the other workshops, I want to speak for myself and for other silenced voices on the marae and in our communities. You may have noticed an incident on the opening night during the enactment of Maui and Hine Nui Te Po's story..."

There is coughing from a few of the older men, and a general stirring of muffled voices. One of them looks about to speak, but knows he cannot interrupt. Mere shoots him a stony glare and he recedes visibly.

"I was one of the group who invited our Nga Puhi-Tainui sister, Kuini, to bring her theatre group to perform for us. I want everyone here to start asking themselves what this story means to us, as Nga Puhi, as women, as men. You all know that the treatment of women by men in New Zealand society has got so bad it has even been taken up by the media and the police, and that means it has reached epidemic proportions. Every night new stories blare out in the media. It's a Pakeha disease also, but the focus is often on us. Where it's estimated one-third of Pakeha women have been assaulted, raped, physically or psychically abused by adulthood, in our culture it's estimated to be over half—and that's from Maori specialists working in the field."

More coughs, embarrassed looks. But everyone is riveted on Irihapeti. Some of the older women disapprove. The younger men throw sharp glances at each other. But everyone is listening.

"I realise now is not the time and place to deal with this at length, but I want to say that the endorsement of male aggression that we've all seen signs of this week, that we women have discussed among ourselves, is linked to the wider problem. It's time we addressed these issues out in the open and it's time we began to educate our mokopuna not just in te reo and tikana Maori but in how to treat each other respectfully again. If we don't, all the rest is lost, useless knowledge."

"Kia ora." A lone voice from the back. Then others. Even some of the men.

"I suggest that we make a commitment to set up a group to discuss how we can best address these issues and empower that whakahuihui with resources from our combined iwi funds to implement a programme of education. It's a long, slow process and it needs to be on-going. We are challenging centuries of mistrust and abuse and we need commitment to developing lasting programmes to deal with offenders and victims. The offenders must be brought before us all, to deal with the problem effectively in our own communities. The Pakeha justice system of throwing offenders in prison to learn new crimes is no use to us. We have to develop our own system of making offenders responsible to their victims and the whole community, facing their crimes and going into training that lasts as long as it takes for them to understand and change their ways. Kia ora. Thank you for listening."

There is mumbling and some applause. Then Piripi, one of the young iwi negotiators and a scholar, rises to speak.

"Kia ora, Irihapeti. I totally support your words. But I suggest that when we make this commitment, it must be made by all of us and that all of us agree to go through the programmes, not just the young, not just the men, and not without the elders. Some elders have been known to rape in this land. They should be stripped of all mana and made to face the consequences like the rest of us. I will give time to help establish this group and make sure we men take responsibility for ourselves in this, so that all the hard work does not return to the women, as so often in the past."

There are nods of support from the women, young and old, but grim faces from the paepae where the elders sit.

Mere makes sure she is next to speak. "Tena korua, Piripi, Irihapeti. I'd like to suggest that anyone interested meet in the kohanga rooms after the hui and I will make sure that we take up this challenge issued by our mokopuna. Can I get an idea how many of you are interested?"

Cowrie surveys the marae. Only a few hands, most of the older women, many of them victims themselves, at first. Then, gradually, some of the younger women, and a few of the men. Enough for a good start.

The korero lasts an hour. Afterwards, the meeting in the kohunga room establishes a working group and Cowrie and Kuini are selected as resource people for the project. Later, they stroll to the beach for fresh air and inspiration.

"D'ya reckon it'll work, Cowrie, or be another token effort that results in the status quo?" Kuini pulls at some marram grass in the dunes, kicking off her jandals to feel the warm sand beneath her feet.

"If Mere stays as facilitator, then there's no show that they'll back down. She's good at this work and has been doing it in the community anyway, just without all the support that she'll now have. It's great, Kuini. And I'm rapt that Irihapeti issued the challenge, that it came from the younger wahine this time."

"Whad'ya mean, sister? You're only in your twenties. You reckon you're over the hill now?"

"Na. You know what I mean. I've issued such challenges before but 'cos I'm mixed blood, then I don't get taken as seriously. I reckon if Mere wasn't so respected, I wouldn't get listened to at all."

16

"Well, it's not easy being adopted. But I've always sensed a real respect for you here, especially now you've made the effort to check out your true whakapapa. That counts for heaps here, as you know. As for the rest, there's always distrust of us women who prefer to be with women."

"Yeah, but some people don't like mixed blood either. I don't fit their stereotypes. I'm dark but I don't look fully Hawai'ian or Nga Puhi. Too much Pakeha mix."

"Well, who the hell hasn't got that mix, eh? C'mon, Cowrie. I'm Tainui, Nga Puhi—but there's wild Irish in me too. My grandfather had a bit of a fling about the time my mother was conceived and my real grandmother is part Irish, part Scottish."

"Really? Why didn't you tell me before?"

"Well, whanau don't talk about it much. In honour of the grandmother who raised my own mother, birth mother to my uncles and aunties. But I've heard grandfather tell his mates about it, after a few whiskies when all the trawlers are back home and the fish gutted. I used to hang out with Dad down there in the waterside sheds, and I heard a lot I probably shouldn't know now."

"I'm rapt you told me, Kuini. Mahalo."

"No worries, kid. Time we hit the breakers. Beat ya to the surf!"

Kuini flings off her lavalava and races down to the edge of the ocean. Cowrie is close behind. Just as Kuini enters the water, Cowrie launches her body into the approaching wave and disappears. Kuini stands, still adjusting to the cold. She watches Cowrie dive under the waves, breast-stroking to reach the next one. She remembers her letters from Hawai'i, thinks how like a turtle this woman is, so at home in the sea.

The night before the opening of the marae, a kuia dreamt that a ghostly white bird with a huge wingspan flew over, nearly touching the poupou, as if trying to communicate with their ancestors, or bringing a message back from them. She described the flight of the bird in detail, how it came up from the ocean, over the dunes and circled the marae three times before swooping down beside the poupou then gliding away on the wind. The bird was a kotuku, a rare white heron, whose nesting place is further south at Okarito, Ngai Tahu country. The elders met for korero and decided the bird was a symbol from their ancestors that they should be working together, iwi to iwi, instead of fighting over the fishing quotas. That they'd name the new marae Te Kotuku o Hokianga, that the bird was hokioi, a fantastic dream bird, a sign of hope.

Eruera, Hone, Piripi, Matiu and Hemi are working on the design of the carving to grace the top of the marae—a white heron in flight. Kuini is now back in the Waikato and Cowrie misses her daily. They send parcels each week. Cowrie tests the claims of New Zealand Post to get a fastpost package to the receiver the next day. She prepares freshly smoked kahawai she'd caught that morning, covers it in ice packs and sends it in one of the prepaid bags the locals scored when their only post office was closed down as part of a plan to reduce rural delivery services. The dairy in the township handles mail. Only it is five days before the kahawai arrives at Karioi and Kuini says it's pretty ripe but tastes delicious! The post office admonishes her to tell her relatives not to be so stupid as to send fish in the mail. Kuini replies by sending a frozen kumukumu—red gurnard—she'd hooked in her kayak off Karioi. It arrives just in time for dinner.

Today she is teaching at kohanga reo. Cowrie feels restless. She longs to return to her studies, but not at Auckland University. She has applied for a scholarship to do her thesis at the University of California in Berkeley. She'd half thought of attending the University of Hilo, Hawai'i, so she could see her cousin, Koana.

Cowrie guides one of the tamariki to complete her painting of a large red mouth covered in bugs. Maata's mother was beaten to death last autumn and she is still recovering from the shock. She may never be fully healed. Suddenly, Anaru grabs Maata's crayon for himself and Maata bursts into tears, sinking into a heap on the mat. Cowrie reaches for the child. She is screaming, her eyes in panic. Anaru is surprised. He'd only borrowed her crayon. But Maata is in terror and Cowrie knows why. How can she explain to this boy that every time Maata is violated, the memories of watching her mother being beaten regularly, then finally beaten to death, come rushing back to her. She holds Maata close to her body, rocking her gently, crooning familiar waiata into her ear.

Gradually, the panic subsides and Maata relaxes in her arms. She gazes at Maata's face, her large black eyes, and sees her own childhood fear of abandonment, common to other adopted children she's met, in the muted panic there. She bends and kisses the child gently on the cheek, tasting the salt tears that have left their mark on her skin. Her heart cries.

Matiu arrives with the mail. There is the expected letter for Cowrie from Wellington, with the "NZ-USA Educational Foundation" plastered all over the top. Her throat dries and her voice, still singing to Maata, crackles in response. She lays the child gently on the mat beside the other children and holds the letter up to the light. Yes? No? What does she want? What does Mere want? What is her future role? Should she stay here now? Where she belongs. Or take up an opportunity she may never get again? Mere wants her to take it if it comes, just as she urged Cowrie to find her Hawai'ian family.

She carefully opens the seal and unfurls the letter, her eyes glancing over its contents. Thank you, very many applications, sorry we have had to turn down so many fine scholars, only so many places for Fulbright travel grants... She sighs, figuring she was meant to stay. She turns the page. "You have been accepted for a scholarship and a place awaits you at the University of California, Berkeley, to complete post-graduate work in Pacific women's literature. You will need to check you have the relevant US visa and will depart on United Airlines UA 821 on August 20, leaving time for you to get settled before the new term..."

Shit! Only six weeks away! I've got so much to do before then. Cowrie wants to scream with joy, but dares not wake the tamariki. Instead, she visualises herself walking up Sproul Plaza, ascending the very steps where the freedom of speech movements of the sixties were started, and smiles, wondering what the nineties will bring.

Na'alehu
Hawai'i

Aloha Cowrie,

Ela and I are looking forward to seeing you again. Have you heard about that scholarship yet? We may be visiting the mainland soon to attend the court case to make sure we get to keep Ela's kids and Chad does not take them back to Texas. Nele and Peni get on so well with them it'd be a terrible shame and the six of us make such a fine family these days.

Mahalo for those news clippings of the struggle to reclaim land in Aotearoa. I have joined the Kanaka Maoli—Hawai'ian Sovereignty Movement—and am organising a retreat for the women to discuss specific issues of importance to us. Paneke and Ela are involved as well as Pele Aloha, who is recording some of our oral herstories for the movement archives.

we are holding it at a village near the sacred pond I took you to. Remember that day? I still picture you diving for that oval ochre stone you gave to me. I wear it next to the cowrie shall on the woven flax necklace you made for me. So you are still close to me, to all of us. Peni and Nele often speak of your adventures

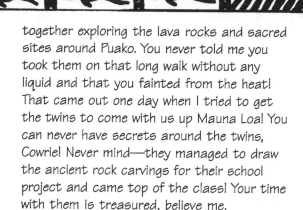

together exploring the lava rocks and sacred sites around Puako. You never told me you took them on that long walk without any liquid and that you fainted from the heat! That came out one day when I tried to get the twins to come with us up Mauna Loa! You can never have secrets around the twins, Cowrie! Never mind—they managed to draw the ancient rock carvings for their school project and came top of the class! Your time with them is treasured, believe me.

I'm enclosing some clippings from our land marches and the latest hula celebrations at Volcano. Diana Aki sang for us and sends aloha to you. Let us know your plans soon. Maybe Ela and I could stay with you a few days at Benny's apartment an route to Texas? We'd love to see you—then you could visit us on your next trip back home to Aotearoa. You know you are always welcome here, Turtle.

Malama pono,

Koana.

Cowrie replies to Koana's letter on the plane, inviting her and Ela to stay in Oakland. Below, thick fog and patches of vibrant ocean. Then the spires of the Golden Gate Bridge emerge from the mist. She spies black shapes moving, like watching ohelo berries descend into the Kiluaea crater until they are no more than distant dots, as the evening traffic crawls home to the Marin headlands. The plane arcs around and catches the sun gleaming off the steel struts of the Bay Bridge, Treasure Island spanning its belly. Between, the glistening calm ocean, triangular sails, Ghiardelli Square and Pier 39. Cowrie can taste the seafood already, smell the familiar sea air spiced with the festivity that marks out this city as magic.

Emerging into the terminal, she looks out for the San Francisco film-maker whose studio she is renting. Hardly likely to be that woman in army gear, standing there with an icecream. Who'd come to meet someone at the terminal in this heat with an icecream to eat and one for the poor sucker arriving, melting all down her hands, on to her dungarees. To her amusement, the spiky-headed woman approaches Cowrie.

"Hi! Welcome to San Fran. D'ya like chocolate or strawberry? I have both. We await your tongue."

Cowrie can hardly believe her ears. "Are you Benny Anvil, the film-maker?"

"Why sure, honey. Didn't they send you my mug shot? Want left or right? I like my left profile best. What d'yer think?"

"Either will do me, Benny. I'm exhausted. And chocolate's my fave, thanks."

She returns to her Californian mode easily, the relaxed pace a contrast to the uptight British stance of people back home, except on the marae. Benny looks like good fun, and after the hard work of the past six weeks, tying up ends at Te Kotuku, she is ready to relax before term begins.

Benny is surprised at the weight of her case.

"Watchya got hidden in here, babe? Rocks?"

"Well, no, heaps of books actually. Here, you take the backpack. It's lighter. I'll lug the case."

"You'll what the case?"

"Never mind, Benny. Just lead the way." Cowrie chuckles. This could be fun. They walk through a maze of passages.

"Let's take the lift," suggests Cowrie.

Benny stares at her.

"OK. The elevator."

"Right, babe. You got it."

Benny stalks out of the lift and heads towards a large pre-war BMW motorbike which could be a Harley for all Cowrie knows.

"Now ya see why I wondered about the case, huh? Well, I'll stuff it on the back and wind these ropes around, but you'll have to stay tight 'cos the backpack will need to hold it all down. But if you move, we lose the lot, and in this traffic, that's suicide." Benny grins at her mischievously.

"I can't believe this, Benny, but let's do it."

Benny organises the load, tells Cowrie exactly where to place her butt and then hops on the front, kick-starting her baby into gear. Cowrie yells something from the back. Benny says "what" and Cowrie yells "helmets". Benny turns her favourite profile towards her passenger and says, "You wanna ride, honey? Or you wanna walk?" Cowrie gathers helmets are not a part of Benny's gear, but gets in behind anyway.

They zoom off at a reckless pace for a car park. Benny weaves between the parked cars until they reach the attendant, then chucks him some notes, wound together with a rubber band. She half turns to Cowrie and yells into the oncoming wind, "Helps to keep 'em banded so ya don't have to waste time stopping," then shoots into top gear down the freeway, home.

There are few city sights that inspire Cowrie as much as watching the sun setting over Golden Gate with her swinging steel ropes glowing orange and her tall spires shrouded in fog. She is a magnificent creature rising out of the mist, a taniwha of modern imagination, spanning two worlds and carrying people from one borderland to another. Benny points out the place where the recent earthquake split the Bay Bridge. Cowrie saw it on television, especially the motorist who kept going, innocently, flew too close to the sun, his car suspended on the edge of the ravine dropping down to the hungry sea below.

Zooming off the bridge, Benny makes a dash across five lanes of freeway to reach the first exit in time. Cowrie closes her eyes after lane three. They motor up to San Pablo Avenue then through a maze of Oakland Streets until they reach Grove and 46th, now Martin Luther King Junior Way. Cowrie remembers the district because of the fabulous Genova Deli, always packed with people, and five or six Italians yelling numbers and slicing salami, doling out lascivious, fat artichoke hearts and making buns to die for. She reminds herself not to call lunch rolls buns since they mean buttocks here and she's got into trouble before on that one.

Benny's bike splutters and dies in front of a derelict building with eight freeway lanes snaking above them. Green and orange paint hangs off the window sills and the front windows are covered with bars. Over the road is a corner dairy and further down a laundry.

"Welcome home," yells Benny, as if the motor is still on. "You grab the case, I'll take the pack and show you how the keys work." Benny goes through a system of unlocking six latches. Cowrie vows she'll never choose to live permanently in a country where she has to do this. She laughingly thinks of home, her little cottage with Mere and how the once used key is still rusted in the door. The large frame swings open revealing a substantial film studio set up with an editing suite and developing rooms, workbenches, cameras, lights and hundreds of mail-out forms. *Amazon Films: We'll come in your face* reads one. Not exactly subtle.

In the back room is the living area, a small space with stove, desk, makeshift couch, stereo and bathroom to the rear. A vertical ladder leads up to the sleeping loft made of wooden planks with a mattress on top. Cowrie thinks of how many times she rises to pee in the night and figures she'll be very fit or very sore from a fall within the next few months.

Benny lights the gas and fills the kettle. "I s'pose you guys like tea, huh?"

"Yeah, gumboot preferably. You know, ordinary tea. Choysa."

"Lipton OK?" She hands over a box of teabags. Cowrie nods.

Benny tells her that she'll stick around for the next couple of weeks while Cowrie settles in. She sleeps over at her lover's house in Berkeley. Cowrie is relieved to hear that, looking at the size of the loft and the hardness of the couch. Then, Benny says, she's off around the States shooting a film about areas of power energy, "places where you get wet and feel like angel wings surround your naked body, spiritual places where strange and eerie things have happened." One of these, explains Benny, is in the desert where there are ancient rocks like Stonehenge, and once every hundred years the sun splices down and splits the core of the rock. "Real cunt energy, babe. Sends me spinning."

She rattles on for ages, is highly entertaining, but Cowrie is longing to sleep off the jet lag. She yawns and tells Benny she might take a nap if that's OK.

"Don't hit the hay yet, babe. We're off to a party in your honour. A bunch of local lesbian film-makers and writers. They want to meet the May-oree scholar. We have to go anyway, 'cos that's the only dinner we'll get." Benny grins.

Cowrie winces at her pronunciation of *Maori* and considers correcting Benny on her assumptions but decides to flag it. Benny means well, and since she's unlikely to sleep much anyway, she agrees to go to the party.

They arrive to a garden full of dykes from the Bay Area, and Cowrie is immediately high on the energy. She meets several local writers, musicians and film-makers, and realises Benny set this up so Cowrie would have some contacts later. She's grateful for the thought.

One woman, who has been staring at her intensely, finally slinks near to introduce herself.

"I'm Cloudlight Pink. I'm a therapist and you will probably feel lonely here at first and miss your friends. I specialise in grief and loss therapy and have sliding scale rates. But you need to book me weeks in advance. I'm in great demand. Here's my business card if you need me." Ms Pink then slips into the night air and is lost amid a new crowd of questioners. Cowrie is still trying to take in her name and approach when Benny saunters over with some ribs from the barbecue.

"You're lucky here, Cowrie. Most dyke events are

vegie affairs, no perfume and certainly no steak. Here, have some Southern barbecued ribs. Living in Oakland, you're in Black territory now. You should feel right at home."

Cowrie looks around. There are women with shells tucked inside their braids, others with short cropped hair and leather gear. Benny fills her in on their stories between every course, with added titbits of gossip concerning who has slept with whom, who's into chains and who's now celibate for life.

Just before they leave, a striking woman approaches who reminds Cowrie of her cousin Koana. She is tall and self-contained. She takes Cowrie's hand and places a bundle of stalks with a small shell attached in her palm. She leans down to kiss her cheek and whispers "Kia ora, Cowrie. I'm Peta Owihankeshni. Hinewirangi told me you were coming. Here's some sweetgrass to burn away any anxious moments of your stay, let you know we are here with you and welcome you to Great Turtle Island. I put a small abalone shell on the end to remind you of home. My address is on the card should you need me." She smiles warmly.

Tears surf up through Cowrie, hanging in waves about to break behind her eyes. She folds her brown hands around the sweetgrass bundle and bends over to hongi with Peta, who seems to understand that the rubbing of noses is a traditional greeting.

"Kia ora, Peta. I will treasure this taonga, this gift. And yes, I will be in touch when I'm settled in. You can tell me how you got to know Hinewirangi."

"We met at Big Mountain, Arizona. And it's a long story. But I've met many indigenous Pacific people through our networks and especially Women of All Red Nations. I even know a few words of your language, more than I know of my own, alas." Peta looks down with sadness. Cowrie knows how she feels, being raised without knowledge of her language, her true origins.

"Peta, I am from the Pacific, but I am also a part of Great Turtle Island. My grandfather, Apelahama, came from Punalu'u, Hawai'i. I was raised without my own language, but at least in a similar tradition. I would like to talk with you more about this."

"Yes, we will. I must go, but rest well and call me after the semester starts. I have a poetry collection to complete before then." Peta's soft voice touches Cowrie, remains long after she has walked past the flowering cherry trees and out the garden gate.

Cloudlight Pink is by now quite drunk and looks dangerously as if she is about to make another invasive approach with her bright pink and gold business cards, but luckily Benny sees her first and guides Cowrie back to the barbecue. "Time we got you to bed," she says, loudly enough for quite a few eyebrows to be raised. This is, of course, Benny's intention. She likes to be the centre of gossip and especially around her sexual prowess. But Cowrie knows she is safe because Benny will drop her off in the heart of Oakland and power out on her BMW to sleep with her safe white lover in a safe white neighbourhood in middle-class Berkeley, like so many other Amazons and political activists. She smiles, thanks her hosts and takes Benny's arm for the Grand Exit. They disappear in a cloud of steam billowing into the night air of a crisp Oakland summer.

Cowrie wakes with her bladder full and the bathroom a twenty-rung ladder away. She eases off the edge of the loft and slowly descends to relieve herself and light the stove for a cuppa. While making the tea, she suddenly realises there is no milk. Benny must have taken it with her. Not only that, there is no fridge. The living area is sparse, probably because Benny hardly sleeps here, she reasons, but surely she'd need a fridge during work hours. Cowrie hunts around the boxes and piles of film magazines, hoping she'll discover a small humming prize tucked within. No luck.

She gazes out the window to freeways snaking above the apartment, which is one of four in the building; the others are occupied by dyke artists, according to Benny. A sculptor and a writer above and a stained glass artist next door. There is a large verandah and a bay laurel in the yard. The sun is creeping over the top of the tree and through the slits in the freeway entrances and exits overhead, so she braves the garden with her milkless tea. A door with a wooden plank which slides into two holders either side of the entrance bars her way. Underneath, another lock and a third for good measure. Cowrie takes out the bulky key ring Benny left her and begins trying the largest keys. The third one fits, and eventually she releases the door.

Outside is an overgrown garden, wilted from toxic freeway fumes, with wistaria climbing across the old boxes and rats scavenging in the rubbish pile. Cowrie grimaces. Maybe she can clean it up, create a fernery so she can sip tea in the outdoors. But there will always be the roar of the freeway above, the fumes drifting down. She'll need to think about that further. Beneath the steady traffic noise is an intermittent humming to her left, behind an old disused wardrobe. Cowrie walks up the verandah to discover a huge fridge decorated with women's and peace symbols, and of course, one of Benny's fliers, *Amazon Films: We'll come in your face*. She laughs. In purple lettering, above mountains that look like nipples, are the words *Communal Fridge. Wimmin Only. Boys Beware*. The fridge door is padlocked.

Cowrie searches through her keys and finds one that fits. Eureka! Inside, four shelves, each with containers, and each marked with the apartment numbers. Luckily, Apartment One, her own, has milk. The same carton Benny used last night. Excellent. Cowrie reaches for the milk to top up her tea and rises into the mound of two naked breasts.

"Hi, I'm Lori. I guess you're Benny's new lady, huh?"

"Well, not really. I'm the new tenant."

"Oh, yeah, she mentioned a lady from Noo Zeeland was coming to stay. So how d'yer like the States, huh? Bit of a change from island life. I've got a distant cousin who lives in Australia also. She's a real bitch, actually, and she speaks like a dingaroo."

"You mean a kangaroo? Dingos are wild dogs, more like coyotes. And Australia is a different country, like Canada."

"Well, that's splitting hairs, ain't it, honey? I mean Canada is just the northern extension of the States. It's all America."

"Canadians don't see it that way, but originally it was all Great Turtle Island—so I s'pose you've got a point there." Cowrie decides it's not worthwhile alienating the woman she shares her fridge with. Besides, Lori looks as if she could be interesting. Stunning silver hair with a purple streak at the side and a wonderful lizard tattooed across her back, down over her butt and about to enter into nether regions. Each breast sports a rose with shackles around it. Lori notices her noticing.

"That's the symbol for our SM group. We're all roses shackled until we get to work with chains, find out what they're about. It's no big deal."

"And do you now feel free after all that working with chains?" Cowrie asks suspiciously.

"Well, honey, to tell you the truth, I like the chains so much I don't wanna be free no more." She bellows out a laugh. "You into SM, honey? Ever tried it?"

"No. I work with survivors in many fields, and I find I'm too close to the pain to want more in my private life, thanks."

"Well, how can you know if you don't try, huh?" Lori winks at her and unwraps some frozen chicken breasts to defrost in the sun.

Cowrie changes the subject. "You want some orange juice to marinate that chicken? I got some yesterday. It's great with fresh basil and coconut milk. Cooks up moist and delicious."

"Well, honey, why don't you just come and join us for dinner tonight and show us?" Lori offers. Cowrie hesitates, then realises she'll look bad trying to avoid it, so they agree on a time and Lori hands over the chicken so she can marinate it to her heart's content.

Back inside, Cowrie turns just one of the locks and places the chicken on the bench. Fuck. Now I have to find coconut milk. Wonder if the corner dairy has the canned variety. She dresses and ambles over, the only brown face among the blacks who stare at her, amazed she's in their neighbourhood. As soon as she enters, she remembers it's really a liquor store made to look like a grocery. The walls are lined with bottles of spirits. In the middle, a row of canned food, essential supplies like loo paper and stacks of wonder bread— pure white and crumples to the size of a nickel if you roll it up. She searches among the cans and eventually finds some coconut milk from Thailand, not Samoa. She doesn't know what refried beans are, but gets a can to try and looks for decent wholemeal bread. No luck. No fresh vegetables or fruit either. She picks up a copy of *Bay Area News* to check out the upcoming events.

Back home, she finds some herbs Benny has stashed away in the cupboard and adds them to the marinade. How do fellas without transport ever eat decent food if the corner store is full of junk food, canned food and liquor? Cowrie squishes garlic over the dish and covers it.

The evening with Lori and her lover, Squish, is revealing. Turns out that Lori and Squish are both from abused backgrounds and see SM as a way of working the abuse through, not perpetuating it. Cowrie isn't so sure. It's hard to tell where one abuse ends and the other begins, where pleasure and pain intersect. They debate the issues at length and agree to disagree. Eventually, they get on to white water-rafting—a passion they all share—and plan to make up a group to raft the Grand Canyon together, which Lori and Squish did a few years back.

"Awesome. Those rocks tower over you daily, reminding you of their dominance," says Squish.

"Yeah, a clit in every slit," adds Lori.

The chicken dish is a winner and Squish wants the recipe. She asks if there's any canned juice that combines the orange and coconut. Be good if all the herbs were in too. "You know, someone should do that. Bottle up your quaint South Pacific ways of cooking and release 'em on the American market. You'd make a fortune."

"Well, there's enough bottling of our country going on already. If you want the juices, you need to fly on over and have them fresh. And then leave again afterwards," Cowrie adds.

"Well that ain't real friendly." Lori wrinkles up her nose.

"True. But we've seen what has happened up here and we want to retain some of our 'quaint South Pacific' ways. Besides, there's nothing to stop you starting up a canned food business right here in Oakland. You'd do a roaring trade. You could can those Southern barbecued ribs just to remind the local kids of their own heritage when they get to the liquor store, stoned out of their brains, and forget what it was they came for."

"True enough, sister," Squish agrees. "It's a sad comment, huh? Anyway, try some of my famous pumpkin pie. That comes out of a can too, Cowrie, but it's as good as mom ever made."

They laugh and Cowrie accepts ginger herb tea, swishing it back, thinking of Paneke. In her head she hears Diane Aki's voice, sees Pele's crater and in moments is deep within her memory, wishing she were back on the Big Island, back with her family. After a few yawns from Lori, she knows it's OK to leave and thanks them for the dinner.

"Not a worry, little lady. You cooked it after all," bellows Lori, as Cowrie descends down the rickety staircase to her apartment. She hears the upstairs door close behind her and imagines Lori and Squish climbing into their leather and chains, which they proudly showed her, like war uniforms.

As she passes the purring fridge, Cowrie debates a late night juice, but then realises it is not worth the hassle of sorting through all the keys. Tomorrow, she will number and code them to save future problems. Now, all she wants is to climb up into the loft and stretch out in bliss.

Within an hour, she is breathing softly, calm and at peace. She is walking over a moonscape, avoiding flowing lava. Then suddenly, fire sizzles up her arm, catches her hair alight, and she falls with a thud on to the hardened lava. Through the heat waves, Paneke's voice soothes her as she completes a ritual to appease Pele, Goddess of the Volcano. Then she sees boiling

36

mud. Whakarewarewa. Mere is calling to her in the distance. She is dragging something up out of the mud. Cowrie cannot see what it is. She tries to look closer, but her vision blurs.

Telegraph Avenue, Berkeley. The sixties revisited with a layer of nineties New Age veneer. Bright tie-dyed T-shirts and socks, crystals hanging in rows, the sun glinting off them onto the hawkers' faces. Huge belt buckles with American eagles flying in brass, Harley shirts and gear next to beautifully crafted hand-made books. "The little lady makes 'em," the big, hairy-chested, gold-chained, leather-clad man tells her, meaning his partner who cowers shyly behind the books. Cowrie buys a journal for herself, and three more for Kuini, Irihapeti and Mere. Kuini will use it to write her poems, Irihapeti to record her dreams and Mere as a recipe book.

She compliments the woman on her exquisite artwork and the care she has taken with the binding. Her face lights up with pride. The man leans over, his breath smelling of beer, freely available from the roadside cafes, and slurs, "Ya don't wanna belt buckle for the old man, then?' Cowrie stares him directly in the eyes and says, "No, the books are for my three ladies actually. There's no old man," and saunters over to the crystal stand. Through the hanging shards of light, she watches his face grimace as he realises what she means and automatically puts a hairy arm around his "missus" and gives her a bear embrace, as if to claim her for himself.

Cowrie admits she finds belt buckles hard even to look at. She's seen so many of them emblazoned on to the faces, breasts and buttocks of women who came into the local rape crisis centre where she worked as a volunteer while putting herself through university. Even here, in the welcoming sun and vibrant energy of Telegraph Avenue, women can't be away from the reminders of abuse in their daily lives, by experience or as witnesses. It takes only the smallest symbol to bring the memories back.

Books. They've always been her retreat, inspirers in times of stress. She heads for Moe's where she can be immersed in floors of new and secondhand books, read all day if she wishes, and discover authors who never made it to the pages of the *New York Times, San Francisco Chronicle* or *The Women's Review of Books*. Cowrie spends all morning there, reading, taking notes, and choosing a few books to carry with her, prized treasures that will warm her candle-lit nights in the loft.

The UC Berkeley campus is much as she remembered it from her first research trip. Only the Reagan posters and Republican propaganda have been replaced by "Right on Hillary and Bill" posters and graffiti. One poster shows two gay muscle men posing together with Clinton's and Gore's heads superimposed. Hard to know whether it's Democratic Gay inspired or Republican FBI. But then she notices the same poster on the door of the Gay and Lesbian Studies Programme, and next to it is a wonderful photo of Hillary and Madonna dancing together. Only in America. Women's Studies, Film Studies, Gay and Lesbian Studies. Not a bad mix. Typical to see all the outsider groups together. At least Native Americans get their own department. They're celebrated now, often for the wrong reasons and more to do with the idealisation of their culture which has replaced the guilt for most Americans of how they are treated as tangata whenua. But at least Gay and Lesbian and Women's Studies are still present.

39

Cowrie had witnessed the horrific struggles here in the eighties when the university tried to oust the instigator of the Women's Studies Programme. She'd built it from nothing. Then they wanted to get rid of her, make UC Berkeley "the Princeton of Women's Studies" and bring in Big Names. She remembered arguing with a famous feminist historian that New Zealand first gave a whole nation of women the vote in 1893, whereas Seneca Falls did not represent the USA. The woman dismissed her views with arrogance and said it didn't count because a small island nation was insignificant in the larger picture. She discounted a nationwide suffrage movement which was to lay the foundations of the first welfare state in the world with a swift sweep of her hand. Throughout her time in America, Cowrie was to discover that this would continue to happen, despite more Americans travelling, even in feminist circles, where there was some dedication to understanding between cultures.

There is a tap on her shoulder. "Are you the Noo Zealand Fulbright Scholar attached to our programme?"

"Yes. How did you know?"

"Well, that ain't hard to figure, honey. There's a British looking flag on your pack and you're wearing slippers instead of Birkenstocks." She laughs, looking down at Cowrie's jandals. Cowrie blushes and points out the indigenous flag of Aotearoa next to the other one. The woman smiles and leads her into an office. There are two large armchairs and she gestures Cowrie into one.

"Are you willing to teach in our Gay and Lesbian Studies Programme while here?" she asks.

"Kia ora, I'd be delighted to do so. But preferably Pacific Lesbian Studies since that's my main area of interest."

The next hour, they discuss how a course in South Pacific lesbian writing could fit the wider programme and Cowrie finds Rita genuinely interested. Rita invites her to a storytelling workshop that Luisah Teish is offering locally, and Cowrie accepts, having seen the power of Teish on tour in Aotearoa.

Walking back down Telegraph Avenue, she notices the Hairy Harley Man's lips curl as she passes. Cowrie throws him the biggest, widest smile she is capable of giving and blows a kiss to his partner. She doesn't look back to see the response but sails on down the avenue, heading for Mama Bears Bookstore, glad to see that some of the secondhand clothes and book shops have remained despite the apparent yuppification of the district.

Cafe latte
Capuccino
Expresso
Jasmine Tea
Raspberry Tea
Hibiscus Tea...*gigantic apricot double blooms, like labia folded in around each other, wet with dew and inviting a hungry tongue to lap up their moisture in the hot Hawai'ian sun.*

"So whad'yer want, sister?"

Cowrie looks at the young dyke behind the counter, fascinated to see that waistcoats are back in fashion, minus all the dyke buttons of the seventies in Aotearoa.

"Hibiscus, thanks."

"Sure. Anything to eat?"

Cowrie is tempted to say hibiscus but realises the dyke won't have a clue what she's on about. She is actually longing for Vegemite, some kind of savoury flavour, so she eyes the croissants.

"Blue cheese croissant with sprouts will be great, thanks."

"Wannit melted?"

"Yeah. Ta."

The dyke swings around, gathers the croissant, plasters it in blue cheese, pokes it under the grill and tends to the hibiscus tea.

"Are Alice, Carol or Natalie around?" Cowrie asks, not wanting to disturb the young woman's concentration as she pours out the hot water.

"Who?"

42

"Well, when I was over here in the eighties, they established Mama Bears. I helped out with the painting. It was a really exciting time. The same women had also started up the first women's bookstore in America—A Woman's Place in Oakland—until the new politically correct collective chucked them out for being old-fashioned working-class dykes."

"Really? I've seen 'em about, but I only work here on afternoon shifts between my studies, so I'm usually gone before they come for the evening events."

"They are amazing women. Carol was one of the famous dykes in Judy Grahn's *Common Woman Poems*—you know *Carol with her crescent wrench*?"

The young dyke looks at Cowrie as if she is crazy.

"Was she into SM or something?"

"I don't think that was it. More a woman capable of fixing her own car."

"Oh." The young dyke looks disappointed.

"Judy Grahn was working on the final revision for *Another Mother Tongue* then and a small group of us workshopped and gave feedback on it, right here in Mama Bears Bookstore. Paula Gunn Allen held Women Warrior classes to reclaim our lost warrior selves, using Native American traditions. Beth Brant launched the first Native American women's anthology at the opening night of Mama Bears. This bookstore holds living herstories within its walls."

The young dyke does not seem to know the names Cowrie mentions, does not seem that interested.

"So what are you studying?" Cowrie asks.

"I'm in the Gay and Lesbian Studies Programme at UC Berkeley. Second year."

"Well, that's the group I'm teaching next semester. So you'd better do some homework," Cowrie ventures, smiling.

There is an immediate change of attitude. "Really? I thought you must be from Fat Lip Readers' Theatre and you were just putting on that accent to prepare for one of your shows. So you're the scholar from Australia. Pleased to meet you."

Cowrie is stunned. Not that she is called Australian. That's usual. US geography is from movies and she remembers the fuss when *Crocodile Dundee* came out here. That's about the limit of their Pacific knowledge. But it is not this that concerns her. It's some time since she has been singled out for identification solely on her looks as a large woman. Especially coming from a young dyke who has had all the opportunities Cowrie missed in her earlier years to understand these politics.

"So why did you think I was with Fat Lip?"

"Well." The woman blushes. "Isn't that obvious?"

"Do they have many other Pacific Island actors, then?" Cowrie asks, pushing her case.

"I'm not sure. No. It's not that. It's, well, you are rather chubby. Not that it isn't fine, but you really oughta get more exercise."

Cowrie is ready to explode. Just today she has walked from Grove to UC and the length of Telegraph, about three miles, and she'll do five by the time she has shopped and returned home. The usual per day for her.

"Well, here's some advice. You had better read *Shadow on a Tightrope* and everything else written since, before you dare set foot in my Lesbian Studies course," Cowrie whispers into her ear.

The young dyke stares at her in disbelief. Cowrie feels guilty. "Hey. That was a bit harsh, but it gets tiresome to have to defend myself especially in safe havens, where I least expect to. I won't hold it against you. What's your name?"

"DK."

Cowrie leans over to whisper in her ear. "Well, DK. next time you see a Fat Dyke, just try to imagine what it would be like to immerse yourself in the most erotic Georgia O'Keefe flower paintings, or Lariane Fonseca's sensuous photographs from *If Passion Were a Flower*. Imagine yourself floating on the ocean in a kayak, watching whales make love in the Baja Lagoon. The majesty, the beauty, the passion, the power. Imagine entering into the face of a gigantic wet hibiscus, savouring the moisture and moving your tongue up towards the tip which turns into an exploding frangipani bursting with the most fragrant, erotic perfume you are ever likely to encounter. Then think about whether you'd rather lie down next to a blade of grass."

Now it's DK's turn to be stunned. "Gee, I'm sorry. I never thought of it like that. So, what are you doing tonight?"

"Forget it, DK. I never sleep with students and I'm already in love with a beautiful Hawai'ian woman." Cowrie doesn't add that they can't be together because Koana is blood family. "Thanks for the thought. Save it for the next luscious large woman who comes in here."

By now, the late afternoon lull has been replaced by women buying books and sipping cappucinos. Cowrie takes her tray and thanks DK for her croissant. "It's lovely, ma'am. Melted to perfection."

DK busies herself behind the bar but cannot get Cowrie's words from her head. She waits until the night rush is over and buys a secondhand copy of Wolf's *The Beauty Myth,* which she'd been meaning to read anyway, but didn't really feel applied to her. She is thin, cute, spiky-haired and available. She never entertained the thought of ever sleeping with or being attracted to, or even being seen with anyone over 110 pounds.

She finds an interesting essay in an old copy of *Radical Voices*: "Obesity and Women—A Neglected Feminist Topic." She tucks the purple hardback into her pack and pays for both the books at the till. She doesn't know if she'd really bother if this foreign woman wasn't teaching the prescribed visiting scholar's course which all level two students have to take. Damn! But lucky she knows now. She'll do her research and get top marks. Or that's what DK thinks. And maybe she'll even score with a Fat Dyke, just to see what it's like. Wonder if there are Fat Dykes into SM? One did come to a meeting at FJ's but she didn't stay. They were all relieved. DK knows this isn't what Cowrie intends, but she's not going to be lectured to by some scholar from a far-flung island at the end of the world without a challenge.

"She's as wild and exuberant as her films," whispers Rita to Cowrie in between courses, as Benny returns to the kitchen to get more wine. It is Cowrie's farewell dinner for Benny. Rita wanted to meet the dyke film-maker, only Cowrie hadn't banked on Benny inviting Lori and Squish as well. She'd been nervous about how all the different factions would mix but so far the evening has gone well. Rita's partner Claudia works for the Oakland Housing Commission and has a great sense of humour. They are sitting around the big oak table which Squish has filled with candles of different heights and colours. Lori said it looked like some kind of weird religious festival but Benny was delighted at such a fuss for her farewell dinner.

"Make a large space in the centre of the table for my *pièce de résistance*," hollers Cowrie, peering anxiously into the oven. The guests scramble to clear the first course of artichoke hearts, and the chef returns with a huge oval plate containing the largest fish Benny has ever seen. Around the steaming fish—eyes and all, much to Lori's delight—are strange purple creatures, rather like yams. Squish can't bear looking at the eyeballs. "Yuck. Didyer have to leave them eyes in?"

Rita laughs. "Back in New Orleans where Claudia and I grew up, you'd get more than eyes, Squish. Claws, whiskers, tails, you name it."

"Yeah, babe. Y'ain't seen nuttin till ya had my gumbo. We'll do that next time." Claudia's deep bass tones sing with more than a hint of humour. She's clearly enjoying Squish's discomfort.

"What's in the belly, Cowrie?" asks Benny.

"This, my fellow Americans," says Cowrie, mocking a Little Rock Presidential accent, "is jen-yoo-eyen baked snapper stuffed with red peppers soaked in sharp feijoa wine with fresh sweet basil and garlic to flavour the coconut bread which binds it together."

"Orgasmic!" yells Benny. "Let me document this," as she reaches for her camera.

"And," continues Cowrie, "surrounding the baked snapper are real Noo Zeeland green-lipped mussels which I scored at the Berkeley Fish Market, where I also found a Latin American variety of our own kumara, or yam."

"Y'all sound as keen on eatin' down there as we are in New Orleans," adds Claudia.

"You bet. We are seriously into good food, especially what we catch and grow ourselves. That's part of the enjoyment."

Cowrie places dishes of asparagus and beans around the fish and a fresh salad made from eight different lettuces she discovered at the Berkeley Bowl Produce Barn. "I have to admit, you've got a greater choice of food up here and it kills me to see Pacific produce cheaper than at home!" she admits. Cowrie offers a karakia for the food, then, "Come on, dig in!" There is no hesitation in doing so. Over dinner, they discuss the food traditions they grew up with and are amazed to find such variety. Lori and Squish are relaxed around Benny, and Rita opens out much more than on campus.

"So, Benny, what do you have planned for your next film?" asks Rita.

"I'm on tour filming places of energy which different cultures have identified as vital to their existence. I'm finding it fascinating that many of these places have since been marked out by pagans and are used as women's ritual sites yet often they haven't explored past connections."

"So you reckon it's more than coincidence, then?"

"For sure. Convinced of it. But I want to let the places and the groups speak for themselves, let the viewer decide."

"How will you convey this on film?"

"That's my biggest challenge. I want to show the spiritual energy and the eroticism of the landscape and that'll be through camera angle, the slow shoot, the right music."

"Like in Barbara Hammer's *Pond and Waterfall*??"

"Yeah. I've always thought that close-up intensity shot in a pond at the lip of a waterfall to be her most erotic film ever, much more than all the cunt shots in her other films, actually."

"I agree," adds Lori. "There's delicacy and sensitivity there."

"Thought you were more into the close-up body parts myself," grins Squish.

"Well, I can enjoy both."

"Ya old softy." Squish cuddles into her lover warmly.

Benny tells them about the film she made to document Lori's most infamous sculpture exhibition, which was an eighties protest against nuclear armament during the Cold War. She gets the stills from a cupboard and they pore over Lori's organ pipes turned into nuclear weapons, each installation a shock. Squish wrote the poems and did the research that accompanies the works.

"How would you like to come and speak to our students about this?" asks Rita. "I could get you a speaker's fee and maybe we could show the film if Benny is agreeable."

Lori's face lights up. "Sure. Love to. Whad'yer reckon Benny?"

"There's a copy in the studio. Make sure the projectionist is up to it. And take along plenty of Amazon Films fliers."

"Here's my school and home address. Call me next week when I've had a chance to check the schedule and we'll organise it. Cowrie, your class would be interested, right?"

"Yeah. Lori never mentioned her sculptures before, but come to think of it Benny did tell me a sculptor lived upstairs. I'd like to see your more recent work too."

"You were so busy goggling at our SM gear the first dinner we had we hardly got time to mention our other activities. But I've got an exhibition coming up at Wimminspace Gallery in Santa Rosa. Squish and I can drive you up for the opening if you like."

Cowrie blushes, knowing she's been caught out. "Thanks, Lori, I'd love to come."

"Me too. What about you, Claudia?"

"Sure, honey. It'd be a welcome break to get ouda da city."

They make plans and agree to meet at Santa Rosa the following weekend. The dinner party ends with Benny showing the documentary and two other short films she's made recently. After farewelling the others, Rita and Claudia offer to stay and help clear up. Cowrie accepts gratefully. Drying dishes, Rita explains that she fears some debates concerning the predominance of postmodernism and theory are surfacing in some of the courses and wants to know where Cowrie stands.

"Well, it depends what the students want really. There needs to be a broad approach, but I have to admit I'm personally damned sick of postmodernist theory overtaking the primary work of the writers themselves. I find it reactionary and elitist."

"So I gather I can't depend on you for support then?"

"I'll support what the students want. Obviously a range of approaches are necessary but we need to bear in mind the history of women's studies and the growing dislocation between the actual lives of women outside the universities and what is theorised inside. I still see the necessity for radical writing and radical action."

"Hmm. I thought you might."

"So where do you stand, Rita?"

"Personally, or as head of the department?"

"Are they different?"

"Afraid so. I have to try to please all factions."

"You seldom get change or satisfaction from doing that."

"An occupational hazard, Cowrie. Sometimes I wish I'd stayed a teacher in a small town rather than becoming an administrator in a large university. I was more effective as an activist and at grassroots level."

Claudia throws her arms in the air. "You think you got problems? There you are discussing university politics and I'm working with the homeless in Oakland, not far from your doorstep at UC. None of your theories or writers are gonna affect my lot. Not even Alice Walker. Ain't no books in these houses, ain't no money to buy dem even if they could read dem. It's estimated a third of the local population's illiterate."

Rita and Cowrie are brought into line fast. Over coffee, Claudia tells them tales of real-life Oakland and both of them are silent, knowing she is right, and that their work is a very small part of the full picture.

51

Cowrie returns from UC, several weeks later, to find a note dropped through the letter hole in the front door.

Kia ora, Cowrie (not bad, huh? I've learned a few words from my Pacific sisters!). Haku. I hope everything's going well for you. My niece, Uretsete, is in your class at UC. She's enjoying it. She's the first apart from me to be openly gay in our family. It's not easy, culturally, as I'm sure you know. Divided loyalties. But we can talk more about that in person. What are you doing this Saturday night? Katsina tells me there is a wonderful film about Hawaiæian land rights and the tricks the US Government played on them in taking over Hawai'i. It's called Act of War. Since Haunani Kay Trask is a leading force in the research and making of the movie, it promises to be great. Wanna come with us? Call me tonight if possible. I'm at home collating research papers for the upcoming Indigenous Peoples' Conference. We'll be there en masse this year.

Aloha, sister,
Peta.

Cowrie intended going to a reading at Old Wives Tales. Most of them are great and the salads at Artemis up the road are well worth the trip over to the lesbian district on Valencia Street. However, she does not want to miss seeing Peta again, or the film.

She walks through the studio to the kitchen, places her books on the sofa and lights the gas for a cuppa. So Uretsete is Peta's niece, eh? That figures. Not only is she stunningly beautiful, but she has an extremely sharp political mind and is more tuned into Pacific issues than even the Black American women, many of whom have been separated from their own lands and languages for so long they find it difficult to see te whenua and te reo as crucial for identity and survival. The two women from Trinidad have a closer empathy for the issues since they were born on an island and also under a British colonial system. And as for DK. Well, she's still trying to chat up the one other large woman in the class!

The kettle sings and Cowrie grabs it to prevent the screeching, then makes tea in the new teapot she bought today. She couldn't stand teabags any longer and found a store in downtown Oakland's Chinese district with ceramic teapots, decent leaf tea and authentic jasmine. She pours hot water into the pot, swills it around several times to heat the clay, then pours the water away. She puts three spoonfuls of tea carefully in the teapot, pouring the remaining boiling water over the leaves. Damn. No tea cosy! That's unheard of here. So she wraps a clean tea towel gently around the pot then turns the pot 360 degrees three times. That's Mere's recipe. The tea always

53

tastes better. She allows it to draw for one minute, then pours it over the milk in her cup. Now this is where the experts disagree. Some, like Mere, swear the milk must go first. Others say that's barbaric and of course it must come after the tea is poured. Cowrie can't bear to see the milk oozing through the tea, so she opts for the former school of thought.

As she raises the cup to her lips, she pauses. Help me Pele! This is unbelievable. Am I so inculcated with British colonial habits that I carry them over into my life, even after analysis of every aspect of our colonisation? She sips the tea. Not half bad. Much better than Lipton. Indian Darjeeling from a Chinese store in downtown Black working-class Oakland made in colonial style learned from a Maori mother in Aotearoa and now transported to Oakland, California, USA. I guess the world is becoming smaller, the global local. She moves to the stereo and puts on a tape of Moana and the Moa Hunters. Maori women's music to remind her of home, then turns it low to be able to concentrate on the phone call to Peta.

"Kia ora, Peta. It's Cowrie. Mahalo for your wonderful invitation. I'd love to come."

"Haku, Cowrie. Great! The others can't come now because there's an extra meeting for the reservation committee, but I'm still available. The movie is at the San Francisco Cinemathique in the city. D'you want to do dinner as well?"

"Sure. Any suggestions?"

"Well, there's a real good seafood cafe nearby that isn't too expensive. I'd like to treat you as my guest."

"I'd love to accept. Mahalo. What time shall we meet?"

"The movie is at six, then we can do dinner about 7.30, giving us plenty of time to talk, so let's say a quarter of five."

"Great! See you then. And thanks for thinking of me, Peta."

"I haven't thought of much else since I first met you, Cowrie," Peta finishes. "See you Saturday."

After she's put the phone down, Cowrie lets out a whoop of joy. She turns up Moana and dances wildly, energised by Peta's words, glad the feeling between them is mutual.

That night, she dreams she is in the Kiluaea Crater. Flames sizzle up her arm, engulf her head and there is no Paneke to rescue her. She faints, but the fire embraces her entire body, lifts her from the lava and flies her into the pit of the crater belly, where Pele is still erupting. She looks down into the boiling red cauldron, feels her body sweating with fever. Flames lick her, touching her soft skin, almost sensuously. She loses consciousness, seduced by the heat, and enters the heart of sacred fire.

"What a powerful film," exclaims Cowrie, throwing her popcorn carton into the waste basket as they leave the cinema.

"Yeah. At first I was surprised at the low-key documentation, given the strength of Haunani's politics, but that was a feisty move to draw in the widest audience. Incredible how those businessmen and politicians colluded to take over Hawai'i."

"Familiar story, eh?"

"Yeah. Let's go for a stroll."

Peta takes her arm and leads her down to the waterfront, beside the trawlers and fishermen washing down their boats for the next day's catch. They walk in silence until they come to a pier. "Come, Cowrie, there's something I want to share with you." Peta guides her up the pier, beyond the buildings to the very edge of the wharf. Cowrie notices a familiar oily smell, then hears the sounds. She looks over the edge, and there, right in the arm of San Francisco Bay, is a colony of seals. Her eyes open in amazement. They nudge and cuddle close, making the most obscene noises, music to Cowrie's ears. She remembers first seeing the seals at Jenner, up the Russian River, after a gay mardi gras at Guerneville. But in her heart she is back at Akaroa, Aotearoa, in the water with the seals, diving and playing.

"Mahalo, Peta. This is the most magic treat you could provide. I've been missing my sea creatures."

"I thought as much." Peta takes her hand. "May I,

Cowrie?" Cowrie nods, and Peta holds her hand cupped in both her own, as if it is a precious gift. Her fire flames through Cowrie, who remains still, earthed, touched by Peta's thoughtfulness, this gesture of warmth. The harbour below is dark and alluring, draws them both in thought. Cowrie looks over to the lights of Golden Gate Bridge in the distance. Peta watches the reflected colours of the fiery water on her face and whispers, "Would you like to know about our Rainbow Bridge?"

Cowrie smiles. Peta continues "My mother is Chumash and our people come from Santa Cruz Island off the coast of Los Angeles. We are created from the seeds of a Magic Plant sprinkled over the soil by our Earth Goddess, Hutash. Her partner is Sky Snake, the Milky Way. He makes lightning sizzle from his tongue and so gave us the gift of fire that we could cook and stay warm. But this meant more of us survived and soon Santa Cruz Island was bursting with people. Hutash was like you and I—she liked time alone to think and create. So she imagined into life a Rainbow Bridge stretching from the highest peak of Santa Cruz to the tall mountains of Carpinteria on the mainland."

Cowrie takes in her breath, imagining Hutash sending a rainbow thought that becomes real. She remembers how the Hawai'ian grandmothers thought into life a bamboo shoot that would carry Turtle Woman to her island. Peta looks deep into her eyes, then back out to sea.

"Once Hutash created the Rainbow Bridge, she told us to cross it carefully and fill the world with people. So we began moving out from small island life onto Great Turtle Island. But like Golden Gate, there was some distance to the ocean below and fog embracing the Rainbow Bridge. A few looked down, lost their balance and fell into the water. Hutash was afraid they'd drown and she turned them into dolphins so they could swim away. To this day, dolphins are still our sacred friends."

Cowrie whispers "mahalo, Peta" in her ear, brushing her cheek gently. Peta kisses her lips. Her tongue is moist, fiery, soft. Sea laps the pier and flames flicker through every cell in Cowrie's body, licking her sensuously. Fire whooshes through Peta and sizzles Cowrie's wet tongue. Cowrie takes Peta's hand in both hers, earthing the fire. She draws a deep breath, then settles back to tell Peta of Laukiamanuikahiki and how her own journey kept intersecting with this Turtle Woman, in her dreams and her life, when she went in search of her grandfather Apelahama's family at Punalu'u on the Big Island of Hawai'i. How the turtle survived the tsunami and swam back out to sea, floating at the tip of the waves before they broke. How her own childhood dreams were haunted by being smashed on the beach like a coconut in the crashing surf until, like the turtle, she realised she could swim back into the approaching wave. How the journey taught her to pay attention to her dreams.

"Since then, Peta, I have listened carefully to my dreams and I learn from them, create out of them. I believe that we can imagine into life rainbow bridges strong enough to carry our people across to safety."

"Yes, and turn them into dolphins if they fall off," Peta smiles.

"But with these dreams we need action, we need to ground them in the knowledge of our experiences or they just remain floating, indulgent."

"Ah, yes, my lovely Turtle, but remember that dreams can be breathed into life. Ask Uretsete about that in class sometime."

"I will."

"So what's for dinner? Turtles, dolphins, prawns?" Peta jokes.

"I think I'd prefer vegetarian pizza after tonight, Peta, if that's OK."

"Yeah, I thought you might." Peta laughs and leads the way to Pizzeria Plantation, a new Italian-Pacific Gay Cafe where hungry people eat pizza surrounded by tropical gardens that produce bananas and taro under the solar glasshouse eatery. It was dreamed into life when Michelo Luigi met and fell in love with a gorgeous Samoan, Fale. By having the courage to follow their instincts, they made it into one of the most popular cafes on the waterfront.

New York

Hi there, Cowrie. Hope yer haven't burned
down the apartment yet with that fiery
volcano goddess you carry in your heart. Get
a load of this postcard willyer? A queer
statue of liberty. Check out the symbol on
her crown, her slinky leather garb and
especially the spiky stud glove. Enough to
turn any girl on! As for the erotic fire
erupting from her torch. Slay me now.

Queer culture is alive and well in this city.
None of that Bay Area political correctness.
I've a feeling you wouldn't like it. But for
me—a film-maker's dream. The visuals are
dynamic. I reckon Lori and Squish should
move on out here. They'd be in SM Paradise!
Throw them a kiss or two when you can,
Make sure yer stick this card up on our
communal fridge. That'll excite the hell out
of 'em. No words needed!

Had a letter from the landlord. Reckons he's
upping the rent. Fat chance. I sent him a
picture of some local punks and told him to
just try. He knows we'd have the Oakland
Housing Commission on the doorstep in a
day! Make sure you keep in with Rita. Never
know when Claudia's position at the
commission might come in handy. if the
landlord tries on a deal, just write back to

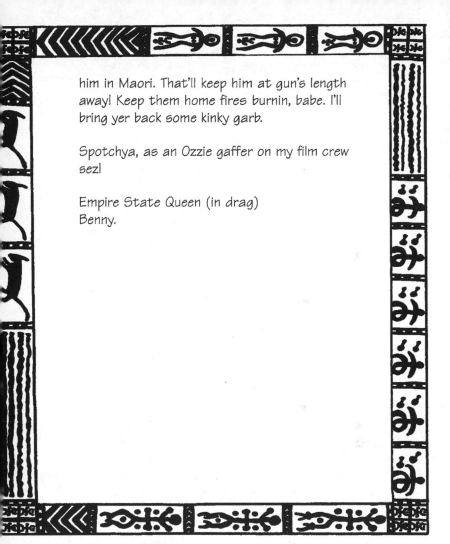

him in Maori. That'll keep him at gun's length away! Keep them home fires burnin, babe. I'll bring yer back some kinky garb.

Spotchya, as an Ozzie gaffer on my film crew sez!

Empire State Queen (in drag)
Benny.

Cowrie chuckles, not sure if Benny is getting into queer culture or whether she's just after the dramatic visuals. She sticks the postcard on the fridge, glad, for once, that the humming monster is outside and not gracing her kitchen.

61

"I don't see what the big deal is," cries Tanya, brandishing a copy of *On Our Backs*. "Why are you all so judgemental and uptight? Shouldn't we be encouraging each other to explore our fantasies, shake off patriarchal domination?"

"Get real, Tanya. It's more a perpetuation of heterosexual conditioning. Like, when was the last time you got it off without being whipped or chained? That's how we are raised to think by the patriarchy. It sucks."

"I agree, I find it offensive to play games with acts of imprisonment and oppression. By implication, you are making fun of the history that led to us being exterminated *en masse*. And that includes all of us here, whatever our tribal origins, because 600,000 gays and lesbians were slaughtered in the death camps too."

"Oh, get a life, Ruth. Honestly, does everything have to return to your heritage?" Tanya slams the newspaper onto the desk in irritation.

Ruth looks at Uretsete pleadingly, knowing that she is probably too shy to support her, but their traditions are both being attacked in this refusal to acknowledge genocide.

Paula stands up. "I'm sorry, but as a woman whose relatives come from Mississippi, and Ethiopia before that, I agree with Ruth. It's fine for you honkies to dismiss our different heritages, but we can't ignore them. They have patterned who we are and we don't want to forget lest our daughters have to suffer this again."

"Paula's right. My ancestors worked in the fields in chains picking damned cotton for you honkies and when you've walked in chains, worked in chains and slept in chains for generations, it's offensive to be told we should welcome getting back into chains for some kind of erotic pleasure."

"Haven't you read Irene Reti's paper 'Lesbian SadoMasochism and the Holocaust'?" adds Ruth, nearly in tears.

Cowrie knows it's time to intervene before anyone gets more hurt. But she lets the students speak from the heart after they've done their reading because so much women's studies these days is theoretical head-binding and she wants the students to feel passionate about the issues they are discussing.

"Has everyone had their say on this now?" she ventures. There is silence. "Right. I want you to really think about the issues that have been raised over the next few days and address them carefully in your essay for this semester. I want to see that you've done significant reading in the area and can support your opinions with research, documentation and experience."

"Wow. Like, you mean we get to do it *and* write about it?" chips in DK.

"Experience does not have to be taken so literally, DK. Your ancestral heritage may be a deep part of that experience, as Ruth and others have shown. But I want you to consider the effects of our discussions today and how you approach the issue from here. OK?"

There is a general buzz. The class expected the term paper to be on Adrienne Rich, but Cowrie will now save that topic for the following semester. She's sick of the SM issues dominating class discussions and interpretations; she knows the only way to deal with it is to give them all space to be heard but in a way where they really have to consider the issues thoroughly.

"Since you are clearly not into SM, how does that affect the way you grade the papers?" asks DK.

"Each essay will be given a number so there are no names on the final copies and I will share them with my lesbian colleagues, so that there will be three sets of eyes examining the arguments raised. Then, the final grade will be the average mark. Remember, this is only one of the four essays this year and you get to choose which three will count for your final mark. Does that meet with your approval, DK?"

"It's a good start. I'm looking forward to my research." She grins at Suzanne, the gorgeous fat dyke, and Cowrie hopes to hell this woman is too astute to become a part of DK's research. She noticed them together in Sproul Plaza yesterday. At least DK has got to the stage where she can be seen with someone over 100 pounds.

"Now, remember that you've still got to complete one of your essays on South Pacific lesbian literature. Are you enjoying the reading? Any questions?"

"Yeah, those dykes downunder sure are feisty," offers Ruth, her voice still shaken from her battle to be heard earlier. "And some of their work is surprisingly familiar, even though the language is different."

"Which ones touch you in particular?" Cowrie asks.

"The mother-daughter piece in *The Exploding Frangipani*. That could be my mother too, only she'd be throwing Yiddish words everywhere and eating while she was saying it all."

The group laughs. Ruth is quite capable of self-irony and celebrating her own culture in the process. Others agree. It doesn't matter whether they are from African-American, Jewish, Caribbean, Taiwanese or any other culture represented in the group. They can relate to a strong mother-daughter story, written about the expectations mothers have of their dyke daughters. They read extracts from the story, each one taking a line and cracking up laughing at the familiarity of the voice. It cuts across cultures and divisions, helps heal the barriers.

The students are enthusiastic about these lesbian voices from the South Pacific, annoyed they never had the chance to read them before. Cowrie explains that it takes time to go global, especially when you live in the States, where the centre of existence is perceived to be.

"When you're born on small islands at the very edge of the world, a stone's throw away from the Antarctic, then you read widely, if you read at all. We get books, newspapers, journals and TV from all over the globe. During the Gulf War, for instance, we saw differing perspectives on it according to the origin of the reports. You so often just get the US version, propaganda and all. Same with the US invasion of Haiti. It's more complex than you might ever imagine. Not just a case of US paternal brotherhood. So you need to read us, just as we need to read you, if we are to ever get any kind of balanced world view, ever have a hope of effecting change."

"But it's so hard to get news from outside here. We're inundated with thirty-eight channels in the Bay Area alone, yet the news is the same on all of them," complains Heta.

"Well, maybe you need to go beyond TV for your

news," says Ruth. "I bet you don't even know there's a Jewish Brown Bag Theatre group here on campus."

Most don't know, so Ruth gives them the details. Ellena suggests they network information, so they can at least find out what's happening in their own and each other's communities as a start. They agree, and Ellena offers to put all the details on her computer and print out the results as an ongoing newsletter, if the others are committed to providing them. Some local cross-cultural action at last. And, most importantly, from the students themselves.

Uretsete does not contribute to the SM discussion, but did have a lot to say about the connections with Maori and Aboriginal lesbian authors in the text they discussed earlier. Cowrie suddenly remembers Peta telling her to ask Uretsete about dreams being breathed into life. She specifically said to ask her in class sometime, so the context must be appropriate.

"Uretsete, I heard a Chumash story about dreaming a Rainbow Bridge into life and I wondered if you could tell it to the class—if you wish to, that is."

Uretsete is shy, but delighted to have an opportunity to get away from topics she finds difficult. She tells the story of Hutash creating the Rainbow Bridge and the class is utterly transfixed. "I was breathed into existence through music, just as Hutash dreamed the Rainbow Bridge. Naotsete and Uretsete were twin sisters who were sung into life by Thought Woman, long before the creation of the world. We exist in many different tribal contexts. In the Keres creation story, Uretsete is transformed into a male. But this is more about balancing the energies of the universe, about regenerative power than literal meaning. As a Native American lesbian, my naming is vital to my identity. It is a part of me, it signifies where I come from and where I'm going. I am proud to hold the balance of power in the palm of my hand, in the core of my heart."

The class is astounded at the beauty, grace and power of the story, of Uretsete's strong sense of self. Cowrie is humbled and reminded she needs to make space for each of them to express themselves more openly. She suggests that they do more storytelling as a part of their work.

"But we still have to get through all the course reading," DK complains.

"True. That's the constant pressure. OK. How many of you would be open to coming over to my studio and having storytelling sessions once every two weeks? I live within walking distance of campus at Martin Luther and 46th. We could make it on Thursday nights instead of *Hollywood 90210.*"

The class giggles, some of them caught out.

"As if we'd watch that heterosexist trash," states Ruth in disgust.

"Agreed. Then we can all make it?"

The group loves the idea and Uretsete offers to bring some sweetgrass to get them in the right mood for the first session and to honour her ancestors. She reminds them they are all guests on Great Turtle Island and should think about this respectfully. It's as if her shyness has been cast aside, as if by telling her story, she has sung herself and her ancestry into the hearts and minds of the class. The group really feels together, perhaps for the first time.

Peta knew all along this would happen. Peta the word weaver, rainbow bridge builder, fire eater. Peta is like a flame, always licking around the insides of her mind, heart and soul, sizzling the tips of her waves.

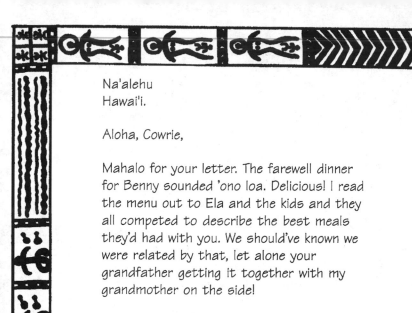

Na'alehu
Hawai'i.

Aloha, Cowrie,

Mahalo for your letter. The farewell dinner
for Benny sounded 'ono loa. Delicious! I read
the menu out to Ela and the kids and they
all competed to describe the best meals
they'd had with you. We should've known we
were related by that, let alone your
grandfather getting it together with my
grandmother on the side!

Thanks for the invitation to stay with you en
route to Texas. We'll leave the kids behind—
but nice to know you'd offered to look after
them while we went on. Meleana and Hale
are having them stay at Hilo and you know
how much Nele and Peni like sleeping
outdoors in the hut with Ika'Aka. So it's all
settled.

Last week we staged a land demonstration
up at the Kiluaea crater. It was led by Pele
Aloha and over three hundred Kanaka Maoli
turned up with flaming torches. Some of
them came from Oahu, Maui, Kauai, Molokai
and even 'ohana from Lanai. The rest were
locals. We surrounded the lip of the crater in
a circle and chanted pule, sang mele,
demanding the land be returned to native

control. It was kamaha'o. When the crater echoed the first chant, tribal elders want down with their torches and led the ritual chanting. We replied from the rim of the crater. It felt like Pele was answering our call each time it echoed around the cavern and the chants flowed back up the sides. Every hair on our bodies stood on end. The next morning we heard that the lava flow into the ocean was the most powerful in years. We've learned it's as important to strengthen our resolve and work with Pele as it is to stage protests at the doors of our colonial US offices here. I tell you now, nothing will stop us until we gain sovereign rights back over our land!

More about this when we see you. Flight details enclosed.

Malama pono,

Koana. XXX.

*Finally, then, to encapsulate the dis/course, dis/
cursively, framing the author in the no/frame
where end/less bound/less space occurs, we can
say, with [pen]ultimate assurance, the aut[her]
of this book, does not, in fact, retrospectively or
presently exist.*

Cowrie sighs. Well if the author doesn't exist, then
why are you, the critic, sitting on a big, fat salary,
creaming it with all this wankery, while authors
struggle to non-exist on little or no real wages just to
keep you, the critic, lavishly employed? Without the
authors, you simply would have no salary. Authors
should look at their own empowerment more closely
instead of propping up an industry that is so
exploitative. She slams the book shut and flings it over
the edge of the loft, letting it smash into the wall and
then plop as it lands on the hardwood floor.

"Aloha, angel!" comes a voice from below. "A bit
of pre-menstrual tension today?"

Cowrie chuckles. "Haku, Peta. Come on up. I'm
still in bed. Read until late last night."

Peta climbs up the ladder and snuggles into bed
next to Cowrie. "So what's up? I never thought I'd
see you throw one of your precious books into a wall."
She holds Cowrie close, looking into her eyes,
concerned.

"I'm sorry, Peta. I've never done that before. I just
feel so frustrated. First I was denied my own

languages growing up, so I learned the colonial discourse and mannerisms. I had to translate patriarchal language so it made sense to me emotionally, then decode heterosexist language and try to find terms that fit our reality. And now I find I have to start all over again with feminist critics outsmarting the boys at their own game. Under it all, the notion that the author simply no longer exists."

"Well, fuck that. I'm one poet who wants to be, has to be *present* in my own work. After centuries of annihilation, the last thing a Native American lesbian writer like me is going to be is invisible again. Time we sent these crits some infected blankets, muskets and alcohol. Give them back a bit of their own medicine for a change."

Cowrie laughs. "Or we could make them sign a treaty giving up their laptops and yuppy toys, their postmodern houses, built on the backs of starving writers, and then gradually make them beg for crumbs until they have no sense of identity or self-esteem left."

"What makes you think they had any in the first place?" Peta grins. She strokes Cowrie's cheek. "Now, my lovely large sleepy Turtle, how about I prepare some brunch? I brought over ingredients to make you an omelette: fresh tomatoes, mushrooms, shallots, artichoke hearts..." Peta kisses her in between each ingredient, spinning out the list. Cowrie is already softening to her embrace, feels the ocean surge beneath her, carrying her out to sea.

"I want your heart now, artichokes later," Cowrie whispers, kissing Peta softly, passionately. Peta's tongue enters her mouth, playing with her own. They tap dance, tongues flicking gently, softly, like dolphins playing in the waves, eyes open, always present to each other, always drinking in the nectar of other, affirming their soul bond. Peta can feel Cowrie floating to her touch, watches her enter her seascape world, taking Peta with her. Her tongue moves to Cowrie's nipple, sucking, playing, cajoling until the nipple hardens to her tongue, urging the fire to flame up through her loins. One hand cups Cowrie's breast as she suckles and dances her tongue around the nipple, her other surfs down, slowly, gradually, sensuously, to part the waves, enter turtle ocean.

Cowrie is floating out at sea, bobbing on the water, relaxed, giving herself up to the soft, tender motion of the waves. She hears Peta purring in her ear, whispering like the wind, her slender fingers parting the fur at the entrance to her underwater cave, entering her fleshy, moist cavern, sliding her fingers along the inside walls, wet and glistening with sap dripping from her centre.

The fire in Peta rises to meet the waves coming toward her, shuddering with their motion, surfing down over her fingers, her whole hand. Kissing Cowrie's body tenderly, she reaches into her hip pocket for Saran wrap, which she places over the cave entrance, her fiery tongue lashing the oncoming waves, drinking them in, wanting to drown in them, become one with them, soothe the hot flames within.

Cowrie feels Peta's tongue hot and wet, sailing the shaft of her clitoris, pausing to dance in the hollow of the wave just before it crashes. She stays there, tongue flicking, while the wave surges and expands, each new wave adding power to the next, until Cowrie is so full she begs for release. Fire rages through Peta's fingers as they enter Cowrie like a heatwave in full motion and lava sizzles as it hits the ocean where their currents meet. Cowrie's body arches like a wave curling to break on the beach. The ocean keeps surging, each oncoming wave meeting with the ripples flowing out into the calm sea beyond. She lies floating in Peta's arms, wanting to stay here forever.

Peta gazes into Cowrie's face. She loves her turtle friend like this. So soft, tender, calm, as if she is in another world. She kisses Cowrie gently on her closed eyes until gradually she wakens. This is the moment Peta likes best. Swimming in the ocean of Cowrie's eyes, seeing all the sea creatures float past as she re-enters her body. Her fingers remain within Cowrie, hot and wet, and she relishes being there, warm, moist and secure. Cowrie is floating, pregnant with sap, holding sacred fire within her moist cave.

"Mahalo, my darling, mahalo," Cowrie whispers, her hand gently guiding Peta's face to lie on her breasts. She kisses her hair, sliding her fingers over Peta's cheek, drinking in the joy. "You are like fire in my ocean. Your flame can stay alight even in water. I love you, Peta. I love you for being you. I love the work you do, the poetry you write, the beauty you bring to everything you touch. I love you being inside me. This is sacred." Tears well behind Cowrie's eyes.

Peta looks up. "And you, my sweet Turtle, deserve every inch of ocean magic my fire can sizzle up for you." They lie together, arms and limbs wrapped around each other, and sleep peacefully for an hour.

Cowrie wakes to the smell of mushrooms and onions sizzling in the frypan. She peers over the edge of the loft. There is Peta, humming quietly at the stove, flames licking the side of the frypan. She slides out of bed, backs down the ladder and wraps her naked arms around her friend, touching her softly while she cooks. Peta loves this, though she pretends to be very busy. She laughs and pushes Cowrie away playfully. "Later, O hungry one. You can eat this first and I might feel like letting you ignite my fire after we decide if we'll spend the rest of the day here or see that play at the Berkeley Rep."

"Oh, please, Peta. Stay here. I want to read your poems and play you some Maori music. I want to relax and drink in your charms. Then I will be ready to go out into the world."

"Well, lucky for you the play doesn't start until three. So we've plenty of time to do it all. Now get some clothes on so we can eat."

Cowrie wraps a lavalava round her waist and sets the table with the beautiful painted fish plates she found in a secondhand store on Telegraph. She gently places a poem she has written for Peta against the jar of poppies. She is nervous about sharing her work with such a fine wordsmith as Peta, but she wants to show her appreciation.

Peta turns to the table with the pan. She notices the poem, with Cowrie's ink drawings around it.

"So what's this, my sweet Turtle?"

"You need to eat first, and read later," says Cowrie, blushing.

"Well, now. Just like you wanted artichokes before sex, huh?"

Cowrie blushes even deeper.

"It's OK, Cowrie. I love teasing you. I will save the best for last."

Peta kisses the page and places it back under the poppies, savouring it for later. They slice into an omelette cooked to perfection, exploding with mushrooms and artichoke hearts, then split open Peta's home-baked cornbread to mop up the juices swimming on their plates.

New York.

Gidday and Howdy, Cowrie,

I'm learning all this new lingo from the Ozzie gaffer working on our film. Her name's Fig and she's a gorgeous soft butch. The only fruit I'd like to get my teeth into right now! But not sure what my girl back in Berkeley would say about that. So it's strictly professional as yet. We flirt like crazy on set, though!

Fig, LT and sky took me to a queer studies conference. What a mind-blow. The radical feminist network in Berkeley would freak out majorly at this scene. I'm really attracted to the glamour and range of choices, the drama of it all, but I'm a little concerned that it's largely amongst baby dykes and there seems to be so little knowledge of our herstory and the struggles to get us to this place.

Yet the film-maker in me loves it. Wish I had my BMW over here. It'd go down a treat with the femmes and notch me up a few credits with the soft butch crowd! The AF's [Achievement Femmes] are into major PD [Power Dressing] and accompany the SB's [yeah, soft butches] to work in sassy cut pin-striped suite and silk ties with

Madonna and Hillary emblazoned on them. Fig showed me a tie with Lady Di, hair greased down in soft butch style, in a sharp black silk suit and bow tie. Thought you'd love it as a dig at your British colonial education so will try to get you one. You could wear it to your classes at UC and notch up a few credits with the queerkids.

I'm really writing to let you know the landlord reneged on the rent rise after I sent him a copy of the tenancy agreement stating the allowable rate of rent increases. He knows how damned hard it is to find honkies who'll live in the area and he'd sell up rather than rent to blacks—the bastard—so we have him over a barrel. Hang in there, mate. Love these Ozzie expressions! Give my love to Grove Street Gang and pass on the hot news.

Spotcha Digger (I'm not sure what it means but it's something like see ya soon I think.)

Benny.

"I've called this meeting because I'm sick of having to write my essays in this postmodern jargon that nobody else understands but the tutors. I want to know why Women's Studies is playing into this language game. It depoliticises our work." Ruth casts her eyes about the room. The entire Lesbian Studies course is here, plus several Women's Studies majors and Rita. It's Cowrie's day off, but that couldn't be helped. The issue came to a head in the Women's Studies class that morning and there was a unanimous vote to hold the meeting after the session ended.

There is an uncomfortable silence, as students inwardly debate how much they can say in front of the teachers who will be marking their essays. Then DK speaks. "I came here from driving a tractor for a local construction company. I had a scholarship at college but dropped out because of the irrelevance of the courses. I saved for two years to do Lesbian Studies at UC since it feels relevant to my life and now I find I have to play word games and study theory all the time. It's stink." DK wriggles her nose to emphasise the last point.

"It's also a class and race issue," adds Ruth. "It's about who has access to this kind of theorising and what relevance it has to effect radical change if so few women can understand its jargon."

"Well, if you don't understand the theory, maybe you shouldn't be here," suggests Tanya, always ready for a fight and always there to support the winning team.

"I came here to learn about what writers think, not what the critics say they think." Uretsete continues, "The analogy for me is having our culture infiltrated and dissipated through the eyes of Kevin Costner or Lynn Andrews. We get a skewed picture via their appropriation."

"Hang on, are you suggesting we forget theory altogether?"

"No," replies Uretsete. "Clearly we need to consider the writing or talkstory, the culture and the context. The theorists provide context for the work. But in many of our courses, we only study the theorists. The actual words of the writers about the cultures they come from get forgotten, especially with postmodern theory. It's as if the author doesn't exist. My culture lives that invisibility every day. So why should I perpetuate the silencing here in a women's studies course?"

Rita interrupts. "All right, there are valid issues raised here. But I want to see evidence that you've studied the pros and cons so I suggest that after everyone has had their say, we think further and meet again in a week to discuss the outcome. If there is an imbalance between theory and primary texts in the department, I will see that it is corrected."

"Typical," whispers Ruth to Uretsete. "Sit on the fence and hope it'll disappear."

"Don't worry, Ruth. They never got rid of the Jews and they won't get rid of us, even though we're less than three per cent of the population. We're still native to this land."

"Too right, Uretsete. And don't you forget it."

The meeting begins to disintegrate into several conversations, so Ruth suggests that those interested meet down at Michelle's Cafe on Telegraph to continue the discussions. "Students only," she adds, glaring at Rita.

Michelle's Cafe is a wild zone for the uninitiated. It's Ruth's favourite haunt, so she leads them through the stage props and opera costumes out into the garden behind. Hanging from the trees are papier maché figures of great opera and dance stars, with their own staged settings. In the middle, a pond full of vibrant fake water lilies, thrusting their purple and pink tongues at the eating guests. Purple water gushes from the Fountain of Venus, who emerges from her scallop shell naked and exquisite.

"Now, there's a decent-sized body I could go for," admits Suzanne admiringly.

DK sidles up to her, agreeing, and providing poetry to describe the shape of her Botticelli breasts. Suzanne blushes.

It's mostly the Lesbian Studies group who have come, which Ruth points out is usually the case when there are difficult issues to confront. They pull together three tables and place their orders. Uretsete returns from talking to one of the Cree waiters she knows in the cafe. "Guess what? This place was started by a local Miwok. Evidently he married an opera singer and tap dancer, Madame Michelle. She used to get into the opium and tap dance naked back-stage, much to the enjoyment of all the other singers at the San Francisco Opera. One night the curtain went up too soon and she was revealed to the City Supervisors. Harvey Milk thought it was wonderful but not all the councillors were amused. Sad to say, she never went back on stage again. That's when they got the idea of starting up a cafe. She made all the papier maché figures you see here."

"So where does she hang out now? Or did she kark

it from an opium overdose?" asks DK, always ready for the gory details and clearly into shocking Suzanne.

"That's the strange thing. Nobody knows. After she decorated the cafe, she simply disappeared. But her husband and the clients reckon they've seen her dancing around the Botticelli Venus at night in a full moon."

DK dismisses the idea. "Ah, it's all bullshit made up to attract more custom, or keep the weirdos hangin' out here."

"Don't be so sure, DK," answers Uretsete. "If she did die she could be coming back in some other form to complete unfinished business."

"Like one of your Sky People?" asks DK, afraid she might have offended Uretsete.

"Not quite—but you've got the idea right," adds Uretsete quietly.

"OK, you guys, let's get down to business," interrupts Ruth, sensing there could be some hassles if someone else questions the possibility of the spirit world still surviving after death. They debate the issues raised in the meeting for the next hour, then call it a day.

As she leaves the cafe, DK can't resist passing the Cree waiter and whispering in his ear. "Pass on my most sensuous regards to Madame Michelle next time she tap dances over your garden." She blows a kiss in the direction of Venus and exits on the arm of Suzanne.

"Thanks for the poem, Cowrie. It's very moving."

"But not yet perfect, eh?"

"Well, it's hard for me to say since I'm so close to the subject matter," Peta laughs. "But there is a tendency to move in between the energy of the magic world you create and the ordinary world, and often the feeling is broken with the transition."

"But that's deliberate. I like to immerse the reader in that magic world, but also keep them aware that life is fragmentary. Just when we think we have the dream, it dissolves, or changes into something else."

"I hadn't seen it that way. Maybe you're right."

"And maybe I could look at sustaining the magic more too," laughs Cowrie. "Hey, thanks for your feedback. I really appeciate it."

"Keep writing, kid. There's more honesty in your poem than I've read in a long while."

"You know that poem you wrote about the Sky People?"

"Sure."

"Well, I found it enthralling, but elusive where you mentioned First People. What does that mean? Is that first people as in first nations, original inhabitants, tangata whenua?"

"No. It's Chumash cosmology. My grandmother explained it to me as being like three worlds that make up the universe, all arranged in layers. I'd describe it as three compact disks, circular but flat, layered on a three-disk CD player. The middle one is the Earth, an island surrounded by ocean. The Upper World, or disk, is where supernatural beings like Sun, Moon and

Morning Star live. The Lower World writhes with dangerous creatures called nunashish. They keep those of us in the Middle World in check because they are likely to rise up and scare us any time they want." Peta makes a wicked face at Cowrie and writhes like a serpent, pinning her down on the sofa.

"Hey, you just want some ocean to douse your fire," laughs Cowrie, kissing her hand.

"Not yet, sweet Turtle. There's more to come. Now lie still and listen." She holds Cowrie's head in her lap and continues. Cowrie closes her eyes and enters into Peta's world. "My ancestors believed that many moons ago, the First People lived in the Middle World, but after a huge flood they became the plants, animals and natural forces, like Thunder and Lightning. Some flew up into the sky and became Sky People, such as Sky Coyote, the North Star, and Eagle, the Evening Star. Then the Sky People created us humans."

"I think you must be one of the Sky People, Peta. Sometimes you seem half human, half fairy. Your sensitivity, your touch, your caring, your uniqueness. And then, sometimes when we make love, I feel you sizzle in me, rushing to meet my ocean depths. You can be so fiery I actually feel a heat from deep within you, something almost supernatural, like the world of sea creatures I live in through my dreams, only with you it's hot."

"How hot, Cowrie?" Peta leans over, her hair flowing around Cowrie's face. Cowrie rises to meet her lips, feels electric to the touch, then Peta groans, lies back on the sofa, pulling Cowrie close. She parts her legs and guides Cowrie's hand between. Cowrie feels her hot, throbbing, wanting her touch. She unzips Peta's trousers, slides her fingers into the fire, knowing her ocean moistness will protect her. When Cowrie has her hand perfectly shaped, Peta slides herself across the fingers, her clitoris rising and swelling, getting hotter and hotter. Suddenly, she sinks down on Cowrie's hand, until Cowrie is deep inside her.

The sea swells within Peta, rushing to meet her fire. She throws out flames like a fire eater, but the ocean keeps surging. She wants it to enter her completely, to lose herself in the flood, be drowned by the waves, as Cowrie dives into her flame, each time moving deeper and deeper until they are both in the pit of the volcano, lava gushing over them joyously. Peta cries out as the waves of lava surge through her, over Cowrie's hand, down her arm. Gradually, the movement slows and turtle fins tenderly touch her fiery cavern, so softly it feels like fairy wings brushing the cave walls. Cowrie kisses her swollen lips, parting them to reach her moist tongue, while Peta rocks on the axis of her fingers, gently moaning, whispering in Cowrie's ear.

"I love your turtle touch. You read my fire well." She smiles, gently easing herself off and taking the fingers that fed her fire, kissing each one softly. Peta curls up around Cowrie's lap, asking her to tell about Mere's world, about Rangi, Sky Father and Papatuanuku, Earth Mother, and once again, how Hine Nui Te Po crushed Maui as he tried to enter her forcefully. During the last story, she cries. Cowrie holds her, rocking and crooning to her until she is calm again.

"My uncle raped me when I was seven and then all my other uncles, cousins and brothers thought I was easy game. I'd hide under the house to escape them. I couldn't ever fully relax before you. I'd always be waiting for the moment of betrayal. They destroyed my sacred fire and it's taken years to rekindle her again, so I could feel comfortable. They were the underworld coming to get me, and they threatened to come again if I told."

Cowrie keeps rocking Peta. She'd wondered, reading her poetry, sensing the damage, feeling her move from sweet gentleness into fiery anger at a moment's transition sometimes when they were together. Peta cries while Cowrie strokes her hair, thinking of Maata, thinking of the drunk fella urging Maui to rape beside the raging fire, thinking of how deep and long-lasting these wounds are. Gradually Peta relaxes, as Cowrie massages her shoulders. "You know, Peta, maybe we should start again, go more slowly, get you used to safe non-sexual touching before we enter into the fire. I can give you massages, and gradually you will learn to trust again."

Peta looks into her eyes. "Would you really do that for me, Cowrie? That is one of the most beautiful things anyone has ever offered. I do feel safe with you, but I still can't touch and be affectionate easily with others. I felt secure with you from the beginning, and just trusted that all along."

"Sweet Peta Owihankeshni, I would do anything for you. And this will be the greatest pleasure. Besides, I can look forward to the magic when you graduate from my school of non-sexual touching. That will keep my oceans surging forever."

"Mahalo, Cowrie." Peta touches her cheek. They remain silent for some time, each drinking in their intimacy. The small room is lit by afternoon sun, filtered through coloured birds which fly in the stained glass windows. The poppies on the table dance with the red and purple flickers. A yellow beam embraces the sweetgrass, each strand shining like gold lace. An orange glow lands on their feet, warming them.

"So, sweet Peta, now I know how Uretsete came to be named, will you tell me what magic breathed life into your flame?"

"Peta Owihankeshni means Sacred Fire. It's not

Chumash but was a name given to my mother by a visiting chief when I was born. There was a falling star that flamed out of the sky that night and my mother said she felt like one of the Sky People came to help her give birth."

"See, I knew you were part fairy, part human. You were from the Sky People, Peta, but also earth born. Maybe those men in your family were afraid of your magic, your power. Maybe they felt they needed to try to take it away, destroy it. But they never did. I feel that sacred fire in you. I know in my heart it is still there."

Tears fall from Peta's eyes, but this time tears of release, letting go.

"I have waited to hear those words. I used to try to tell myself that, but it was hard to keep believing. Now you have seen this so clearly, mirrored it to me, I will always believe it, never let those men enter my soul again."

"Kia ora! Now you just rest here in my arms. It's been a long, long day. I'll tell you some more stories if you're very good and quiet."

Peta leans into Cowrie's embrace, closes her eyes, and listens to a modern tale of how a group of Hawai'ian fisher people rebuilt a sacred heiau on land taken from them, by swimming to shore each night and carrying large boulders up to the ridge of the island, and how they never stopped until it was finished. Before the fisher people swim back to their boat, Peta is fast asleep.

Te Kotuku Marae
Hokianga
Aotearoa

Tena koe, Cowrie,

You haven't written for ages. What are you
up to? Irihapeti and I reckon you're in love
again. Is it that gorgeous Peta you
described to us in the last letter? We hope
so.

All is well at Te Kotuku. It's been a difficult
time educating some of the most resistant
to women's issues but we're making progress.
Mere always talks them around, She'd never
call herself a feminist but she's staunch. My
mother'd turn in her grave to hear such
korero! The day she adopted you from the
Rawene Orphanage was your lucky break,
Turtle. I know it's not been easy for you, and
the search for whakapapa has been complex,
but you lucked out with Mere. She sends
aroha by the way. You know she's not into
writing unless it's vital but she talks about
you often.

Irihapeti has enlarged the nursery and little
Maata helps out every day. She's managed
to interest some of the other kohanga kids
in participating. They're replanting the land
that subsided in sayer's Gully after those

British farmers lopped off all the native bush. There's rows and rows of tiny kahikatea, rimu, kauri and nikau palms in the shade house. Iri is rapt.

I'm finding the work at Te Aroha exhausting but fulfilling. Beats rubbing noses with all those Pakeha gits at the university marae. There's huge debate now over the Tainui doing a deal with the government to accept a cash settlement for land stolen from us over the past hundred and fifty years. Eva and her followers are thinking of lodging an official complaint. Seems it's the usual tale of the boys deciding to go hell for leather for the best deal for themselves but not thinking about the long-term goals for all. Like health and education. It's left to the wahine to sort that out. In the meantime, the Herald printed an article showing that our esteemed Tainui Trust Board paid megabucks for annual fees and a private box for the League Season. Hundreds of thousands of dollars. Proves their brains really do reside in their dicks, eh? Imagine what kohanga and schemes like Te Aroha could do with that kind of dosh?

Piripi has been a keen supporter of our programme. Showing he's more than just a talking head. He's worked hard with the men. He's also pioneering a scheme to reduce the

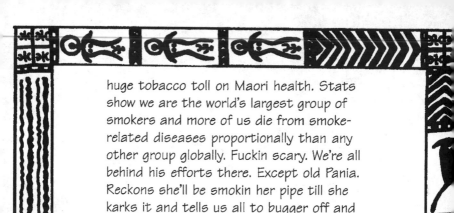

huge tobacco toll on Maori health. Stats show we are the world's largest group of smokers and more of us die from smoke-related diseases proportionally than any other group globally. Fuckin scary. We're all behind his efforts there. Except old Pania. Reckons she'll be smokin her pipe till she karks it and tells us all to bugger off and not hassle an old kuia who's done her time!

Gotta go. This is just to say hi from all of us and to let you know we're with you always. Write soon.

Arohanui

Kuini (Iri, Mere and Maata all send their aroha too) XXX.

Now that classes have settled into a routine and her relationship with Peta is relaxed, Cowrie is able to spend more time on her own research. After writing the first few chapter drafts, she decides it's useless for her to try to frame multicultural South Pacific lesbian writing inside the totally alien discourse currently in fashion. The heart and soul is taken from the work. The connections that drew these women together in the first place are lost.

The students have raised similar issues but Rita continues to delay action, telling them to document their concerns for next year. Increasingly, she wonders if she really wants to be an academic, reacting to the work produced, or a writer and editor encouraging authors at the cutting edge before they have become indoctrinated by the system.

Her eyes stray out the window of the study she shares with other doctoral students at UC and fix on the tall tower that dominates the campus, fondly known by students as the Campanile. What an appropriate symbol, and so well named. Is the rest of the world plastered with such symbols? What if all the women decided to blast them apart, all on the same day, worldwide? Like Hinekaro in *Subversive Acts*. Studies show we are all conditioned by our surroundings, that those living in natural rather than urban settings appreciate and respect life more. Would our thinking change if we altered our living environment?

She glances at the clock on the penis, admitting it does have its uses, and realises she's got minutes to get to class. She flings her books and thesis notes into her backpack and takes two stairs at a time in her rush.

Peta meets her after class as she's currently doing Friday lectures in Native American Studies. "Hi, gorgeous. Am I glad to see you! I'm pooped! I can't believe how hard it is unlearning racism with some of these little shits. Most of the class are great. Some still think we are extensions of Lynn Andrew's Fantasyland, but there are a few who resist every inch of the way. You wonder why they aren't taking physics instead."

"Let's do espresso and talk," Cowrie suggests, guiding her down toward Telegraph Avenue.

"No. I've a better idea. Let's borrow the Red Nations van and get the hell out of the city. I'd like to take you up to Yosemite, show you the place through my eyes instead of the tourist brochures, and then we can drive back down the coast via the Russian River and Bodega Bay. Neither of us has another lecture for a week and we could both do with the break."

Cowrie hesitates, thinking of all the essays she has to mark. "Only if I can bring my work too," she sighs.

"No, Cowrie, the whole point is to leave it behind, take time out, get refreshed. You'll find it'll clear your head and you'll achieve more when you return."

Cowrie admits she's spent most of the morning day-dreaming, trying to figure out how she can frame her research in an appropriate context. Maybe the landscape will provide her with new energy, new ways of seeing. "OK, Peta, you're on. Have you got camping gear?"

"That's what gave me the idea. All the gear from the last trip down to the Santa Cruz Mountains is still in the back of the van. It's loaded up and ready to go, and currently parked just over the road at the Pacific Film Archives. We can stop off at your studio and my digs *en route*."

"You mean, leave right now?"

"Why not? Or does Snapping Turtle need more time to prepare?"

Cowrie cuffs her playfully. They cross University Avenue and collect the van. As they drive away, Cowrie smiles as the Campanile fades into the distance in the side vision mirror until it disappears from view completely.

Driving over San Rafael Bridge, ocean sparkling stars beneath them, wind surfing through the open windows, Cowrie yells a whoop of joy and kisses Peta on the cheek.

"Steady on, Cowrie. We're not even out of the Bay Area yet."

"Oh, Peta. I'm so rapt you thought of doing this. I can't believe how great I feel already. I see that thesis floating away to rest on a calm beach at the back of my mind, waiting for a tsunami brainwave to catch her up and fling her into an ocean of brilliance,"

"Well, that's what I like to hear! Now, check out San Quentin Prison to your left as we leave the bridge. That's where we'll dump all the postmodernists when we're done with 'em. Round 'em up, like they did with us for the reservations, and tell 'em that they're all eligible for the best seaside view in town. San Quentin Retirement Retreat for postmods."

"Yeah—and they can build as many erect penis monuments to their dreams as they like, all over San Quentin, and hang their washing between them. Could make good carpet beaters too, or flints to sharpen knives, so long as they don't slice too close to the bone. Or it's sausage roll time!"

Peta laughs, though she hasn't a clue what sausage rolls are. Another quirky Noo Zealandism she'll learn, no doubt. Right now, she's concentrating on finding the entrance to the northern freeway. There it is.

Great. She swings the van over to the exit road and accelerates on to Route 101.

"Hey, Cowrie, we'll reach Santa Rosa about dinner time and my Mom's place is at Cotati on the way, so whad'yer say to stopping off there for the first night and we can start early the next morning for Yosemite."

"Sure. Love to meet your whanau, Peta. Who'll be there?"

"Mom works making buckskin shoes and bags for the local trading post, but she'll be home by now. My sisters Netta and Abalone are still at home, but Bean and Kelly have left. Pa scarpered years ago, once the responsibilities got too much and because, like so many other Indian men, he couldn't find work. They're not on the phone, so I just have to chance it. Unless it's bingo night, Mom will be around. Chances are, we'll get fed too."

"Did she teach you how to make cornbread?"

"Sure thing."

"Well, I'm on board. Besides, I've been dying to meet them."

"Most of my friends don't want to know. The non-Indians feel guilty that most of the Indian families live in such poverty, so they don't want to visit or actually see it for themselves."

"Yeah, that's like trying to get my varsity friends back home to visit me at Hokianga. You'd think it was like going to the end of the earth, or as dangerous as New York or Chicago. They give all sorts of excuses, but it's still obvious."

"Cotati ain't pretty, but at least there are plenty of Indians around. Still a bit of tension, but not bad these days."

Black Katz Go Gamblin, one of Cowrie's favourite Aotearoan groups, bursts from the van tape deck and she translates the lyrics for Peta as they drive and sing. "That music's really got soul energy, Cowrie. I love it." Peta hums along with the beat. After about an hour, they turn off to a small town, passing an impressive carved totem in the town square, with an Indian mural across the stage behind. Peta stops to explain the significance of the totem, then they drive to Naiya's home. Set in the dusty landscape are rows of small, squalid makeshift houses, held together with corrugated iron and wood. Flashes of Bastion Point, Aotearoa, and Aunty Meleana's place at Hilo enter Cowrie's mind.

Peta leaves the van parked on the sidewalk and they amble over to the shack. A wooden door, hanging off its hinges, is wedged open. Inside, mats over a board floor and holes for windows. An old stuffed sofa and sixties bean bags are scattered around. The house is raised off the ground to avoid flooding. Cowrie wonders if this is the house Peta hid beneath to try to avoid her uncles. An old woman jumps, shocked to see them. "Grandma. Haku. This is my friend from Aotearoa, Cowrie. Where's Mom?"

"Out in the garden. Come, give me a hug." Peta does so, just as her mother appears. They embrace. Introductions all round, then Naiya places the corn from the garden into a large pot on the gas cooker and invites them to stay for dinner. Cowrie offers fresh vegetables and fruit they've gathered at farm stalls on the way and Naiya accepts, intrigued by her accent. The evening is pleasant. Turns out Peta's sisters are up at Santa Rosa for the wild Friday night disco. "They don't often come back until the morning, but I make sure they stay with Uncle Renny."

Peta stiffens. "Mom, I don't reckon that's such a good idea. Uncle Renny was more than familiar with me as a child and I don't want him interfering with my sisters."

Naiya looks shocked. "Peta, why didn't you tell me this?"

"You had enough to worry about, Mom. Pop was out of work and I was too young to understand it all. I blamed myself at the time, thought I'd been a bad girl, like they kept telling me. I was ashamed, so the last thing I could have done was tell you. But I secretly hoped you'd notice and come and rescue me."

Naiya moves over to Peta and wraps her arms around her daughter. "I'm so, so sorry. I wish I'd known for sure. I guessed as much later, but I wasn't ready to deal with it then. Our relationship was strained enough. Please forgive me, Peta."

"Do I have a choice?"

"You can rest assured that the young ones are safe from Renny now. When the girls go to stay there, Aunty Tana keeps an eye on them. She's known Renny's ways for years, but she keeps him in check these days. The girls sleep together in the back room and Tana locks Renny's door at night and unlocks it again in the morning."

Peta grimaces. "Wish you'd done that with me. Or I wouldn't have had to run under the house."

"We didn't know then, Peta. But things are changing. The carvers donated all the funds from the totem they did for the Trade Centre in San Francisco to an abuse education programme organised by Indian healers. We women don't have to keep the secrets any longer. We're encouraged to speak out and we do."

Peta holds her mother close, cries into her breast with relief. "I can bear the past if my pain goes to heal the future," she sobs, while her mother nods in agreement, tears dropping onto Peta's shoulders.

Cowrie leaves them together and walks to the town square to look at the totem and other carvings more closely. One features a deliciously large Indian man standing astride a rock in surrender mode. His leather pouch and waistcoat are intricately carved, and so are the wings flowing out from his back. A chief in surrender, but with wings to fly. That could be hope for the future. She sighs, thinking of home, remembering the huge sea egg they'd sculpted on the beach under the guidance of Irihapeti. She hopes the vision it gave birth to is still strong at Te Kotuku o Hokianga.

Peta and Naiya stay up most of the night talking, so Cowrie drives the next day. On the road, they discuss their childhood memories and Peta laughs wickedly when she hears how Cowrie bit the hand of the man who assaulted her when she was young. He never did it again. But many years later, she met him at a tangi and she told a kuia what had happened who said she would take care of it. The man died eight months afterwards of prostate cancer that was not diagnosed in time.

Once they turn off toward Yosemite, the landscape becomes more interesting and Peta points out trees and birds unfamiliar to Cowrie. They stop for lunch under a large redwood and a cheeky bluejay hops so close to Peta's hand she can almost reach out to touch the bird. Its plumage is sky blue, topped off by a punk rock headpiece. Peta explains that many Californians consider them a nuisance, like sparrows who come to eat your crumbs. She stretches out her hand with some cornbread smeared with avocado. The bird hops near, then waits, tentatively. She throws the crumb. Next time, the bird comes closer, until finally it takes a piece from her palm. Peta is surprised it trusts her.

On the road again, they talk more about last night. The experience of finally telling her mother has lifted a huge weight from Peta's heart. She feels lighter, more able to open out and be vulnerable to others, trust them. Naiya said Renny was due to explain his actions to a tribal council meeting with all the elders, the women, and two medicine people, along with a local Miwok sex abuse worker. Peta has been invited to attend also.

At the park entrance, they show their permits and drive into Yosemite. It is mid-week and there are few people around. Peta navigates while Cowrie drives her to a grove of trees from where a track begins. "Let's stop here and take a walk. I want to show you something special."

Cowrie gets out and stretches her legs. "Do we need anything, Peta? Jacket, camera, binoculars?"

"No. Just your gorgeous self, your eyes and spirit. And some sun," Peta answers, looking up to the clouds. "Well, you might want the camera but I'd like you to see this and engrave it on your heart. You won't need the photo then."

"OK. I'll trust you on that. Let's go." Cowrie locks the doors as she's learned to do here in the States.

They stride along the track until it begins to ascend and the walking is slower. Peta points out vegetation at their feet and knows some of the medicinal herbs and roots. The small fern heads are eaten as a delicacy. Cowrie explains they are also prized in Maori herbal remedies and as a succulent treat. Gradually, they hear the roar getting closer until they are standing under a mighty waterfall. They need to crane their necks to see its full height.

They climb up the rocks at the base of the falls, so near they can dip their feet into the water. After getting comfortable on the rock ledge, Peta holds her close. The sun edges out from behind the clouds and causes a rainbow to shimmer in the spray at the foot of the falls. It expands and grows up the length of the glassy cascade, splashing brilliant colour on to the smooth rock patterned in ochre and rusty brown. As the sun brightens, the colours deepen and Peta's lips brush against Cowrie's cheek. She whispers, "They call this Bridal Veil Falls. Wanna get married?"

Cowrie is stunned, speechless. She looks into Peta's eyes, to make sure she is not joking. They are sparkling. While both are committed to each other, neither has ever wanted to be together in traditional ways. They each enjoy their time alone too much. "Are you serious, Peta?"

"Well, what kind of an answer is that?" Peta grins. "Yes, I am in a way. I know we've talked about our independence, and I know we each want to maintain it, but I also know I feel committed to you. There must be a way we can have both if we stay honest, present to each other. I guess I wanted to see what your answer would be."

Cowrie hesitates a moment, then kisses Peta gently on the cheek, moving toward her lips. She runs her tongue softly along the length of Peta's upper lip then holds back, kissing her on the cheek until Peta's soft moans urge her on, until she feels the moist closeness of Peta's tongue enter her. Like flames in a breeze, the tips of their tongues flicker against each other, tap dancing to the rhythm of the sparkling spray.

They enter deeply, their tongues drinking in the rainbow-painted drops, until they are lost within the cavern whose walls are etched with ancient stories, lit up by the glow of their lust. Outside, the water roars down the vertical cliff; inside, stalactites reach down sensuously from the roof of the cavern, dripping their sweet moisture on waiting tongues, sliding coloured sky tears over their naked bodies to fall on to the thirsty ochre earth below. They glide deeper and deeper into the cavern, floating on glassy black water. Above them, glow-worms lighting their way, round them, a hushed silence, holy. Ahead, a small glimmer of light in the distance. Embracing, they fly toward the sun, moisture still dripping on them until they are showered with sprinkles of colour and the light causes their bodies to act as a prism, twisting and turning and sprinkling painted raindrops on to the cavern walls. They have flown into the heart of a rainbow and remain suspended in mid-air, reflecting the vibrant colours that paint parrot-feather wings on to their souls, all over their naked bodies.

After a long time, Cowrie feels Peta begin to withdraw her tongue and they slowly descend to earth, to the rocks below. She strokes Peta's cheek with her fingertip, not wanting her tongue to leave Peta's body, not wanting Peta's tongue to leave hers, ever. She has only felt this way before in her ocean dreams. She wonders if Peta feels the same. One look into Peta's eyes tells her all she needs to know.

Peta smiles, holding her close. "So, how are you, my sweet Turtle?"

"I think I have just swum through a rainbow waterfall and out the other side."

"Well, maybe you did."

"Did you?"

"Yes."

"Me too."

They remain snuggled together for ages, not wanting the feeling to leave them, drinking in the roar of the falls, the sweet wet spray, the birds that flitter in and out of the bush below them, glancing shyly at their closeness and retreating again to give them privacy. Some time later, Peta suggests they return to the van since they'll only just make the camp by dusk and they want to set up their tent before it gets too dark.

When they reach their camp ground, in an isolated part of Yosemite, they are exhausted. They pitch the small round tent, drag out the sleeping bags and curl up close. Cowrie notices that something has changed in Peta. Her eyes are clear, vulnerable, less defensive. Over the past few months they have been practising non-sexual touching, building the trust again gradually. Today they entered new territory again. She knows it will be much easier now. They lie together and tell each other stories of Morning Star and Sky Coyote, Hine-titama and Papatuanuku, until they are so sleepy they drift off in each other's arms, cheeks touching. Gradually, their breath falls into the same rhythm and they sing their unique dreams in unison, as if one soul creature.

They tramp the ridges, through the forests and camp beside the lakes of Yosemite, breathing in her ancient stories and discovering her secrets hidden under mossy glades, in the inviting slits of rock crevices and caves, within her watery oceans. At night, they light a fire to cook their food and warm their souls, and tell stories, dreams, discuss the possibilities of their commitment and how they can retain their own individuality and identity also, keep their freshness for each other. They know that to live together will make this difficult and decide to strengthen their commitment, but remain living apart, just spending time together when they feel like it.

"Maybe that's just selfish. We need to be there for the rough times as well as the celebratory, Peta."

"Sure, but our work takes us in different directions and we must maintain our independence too. We both want that."

"I miss not having you there in the mornings when I wake, but then again, I also like waking to the freshness of dawn, rising out of sleep to write a poem."

"Exactly. We need to have both, and we do have both. It's just that we've formalised our commitment a little more, allowed ourselves to enter deeper."

"So you don't really wanna get married?"

"Well, yeah, I do. But not in the traditional ways. I want us to figure how it will work for us because we both need such a lot of space and time for ourselves. If we lived together, unless we had separate quarters, we'd suffocate."

"True. Even in the best relationships, I nearly go mad after the first flush. At varsity I lived with a lover in a flat and I thought I'd die of suburban neurosis after the first six months. Not that I didn't love her. It had nothing to do with that. I did. More that I needed to sleep alone at least half the week, be in my own dreamspace, come home to an empty house and rejoice in the freedom of quietness or the music I wanted at that particular moment."

"Yeah, know that so well. It's been the point of other relationships ending when the lover felt rejected because I actually dared to speak the truth," The flames have now died down and the embers of the fire are perfect for roasting marshmallows. Peta reaches into her pack and takes out a bag of the largest marshmallows Cowrie has ever seen. "Now, sweet Turtle, take this twig and spike half a dozen mallows. See, like this. Then you need to hold it just above the embers, far enough away that they brown and melt inside, but do not burn."

Cowrie watches her expertly roast the first batch. Peta eases a smoking treat from the twig and it sizzles as it meets the moist wetness of her lover's waiting tongue. Cowrie burns her first treats but finally manages to get a batch right. Peta rewards her with a sticky kiss. After a while, Cowrie broaches the subject she has been trying to avoid all week. "So, Peta, if we're now 'engaged', you'd better not bugger off to that research position at Kahnawake Reservation, or I'll dig out the divorce papers and wave them in your face!"

"It's still up for grabs, but I want to go back there to see how the land struggle is progressing and to spend time with Nanduye, my best friend from college days. She was on a scholarship at UC with me, and we became life-long friends. She returned to the reservation when they needed a lawyer to represent them. She's still there."

"How come you've never mentioned her before?"

"Now, now, Snapping Turtle, no need to get jealous. She's my deepest soul mate and we'll always be spiritually linked."

"That's what you said to me when we first made love."

"Yeah, but you are different. And you are likely to return to Aotearoa, so I need to have a soul mate here as well."

"True. But I hope you might visit Aotearoa with me too."

"Sure. I will. But not to live. I've got my work cut out here."

There is silence between them. A rift they've never acknowledged, a truth that edges into their dreams.

"C'mon, Cowrie. Would you ever live outside Aotearoa, or Hawai'i? You're called by the land, your spirit resides there. Could you ever be here permanently?"

Cowrie knows Peta speaks the truth, does not want to admit it.

"I'm not sure yet. I'll keep an open mind. But I do feel that pull back home. You're right, Peta."

"Now come here, Cowrie. Let's not ruin what we have. Let's enjoy our current commitment and see what happens." Peta draws her close. But deep inside, Cowrie fears she will return home, wonders what the commitment they've just uttered is to, unless to make the most of the deep joy they share for the time they do have together.

Peta curses the subject of Kahnawake has been raised. She knows that the pull to work with Nanduye is strong, that she is dissatisfied with the dominance of the men in the work she does in Oakland. If it were not for the women's sector, she'd have moved ages ago. But she also feels the lure of Cowrie, her imagination, her honesty, her ability to stay through the tough times. They hug, each knowing that there will be a time of truth to come, even in the midst of their closeness. Neither of them allowed themselves to face it before. But coming away, experiencing renewal and togetherness, has ironically heightened the sharp reality they will endure. While Great Turtle Island is connected to Aotearoa beneath the water, over the ocean they now seem such a long, long way apart.

Towering rock faces, vertical grey cliffs diving down into lakes, impenetrable country which would set a gleam in the eye of any Thelma and Louise. Sometimes they fantasise driving off the edge, flying out over the cliff, suspended in the warm air. But always, deep within, the doubt that now pulls their reality, tucks at the edges of their dreams, makes them want to relish every second together, lest it be the last. The final night, they drive toward a lake at the far end of the park near the Sierra Nevadas. Peta has timed it for sunset and they crawl towards the lakeside through mountains embraced by snow, even in the summer heat. Alpine cabins begin to appear and signs of civilisation are dotted about the lower slopes, speaking tales of winter madness. They arrive at the lake as the sun begins to lower and the road winds around to a salty wasteland. In the distance, small islands near the shore. Peta stops the van at a rocky outcrop and gestures Cowrie to follow her. "You can bring your camera this time, Turtle."

Cowrie is secretly disappointed, wanting to remember the lake as Peta taught her to never forget the rainbow-tinted waterfall. She reaches for her lenses and slings the pack with their kai for dinner over her back, in case the trek is a long one. They head in the direction of the lake, past bulbous rocks that bubble in the heat. Moving closer, the islands are like stalagmites rising mystically out of the lake. They reflect in the glassy water and take on the colours of the setting sun at each subtly changing movement. There are clumps of island rocks that resemble a family in flight, a dragon puffing smoke into the eyes of a large lizard flying into a rock cloud.

They turn a bend and a whole vista of imaginative shapes rise out of the water. Cowrie can hardly believe her eyes. Peta explains they are tufa rocks and goes into lengthy detail on the sulphuric properties that cause them to form. But all Cowrie can see are the alluring sea creatures of her childhood come to life, struck in stone, in the middle of a lake that resembles an azure mirror which reflects each image to double the impact.

Sea horses link tails and dance in the middle of a wild storm, tuatara with wings loop through the night sky, a mother seal touches the tail of her pup tenderly, just as it enters the glassy ocean. A family of turtles float past, and behind them, whales raise large flukes to break the calm surface, while a kahawai flies out of the water, sculpted in stone, hanging on to a rock edge forever. Salmon swim upstream, trying to avoid the paws of large white bears, bending down to scoop them from the water in mid-flight. Dolphins nose their way up tufa faces, swimming toward the setting sun.

Peta stops talking. She is looking into the sunset reflected in Cowrie's eyes, tears welling at the edges. "Hey, partner, this is supposed to be a joyous treat."

"It is. I just feel overwhelmed. To see these magnificent creatures cast in rock at sunset is really something."

"Magic, huh?"

"Sure is."

They find a ledge near the water and sit in silence, contemplating the shapes, allowing their imaginations to fly, until the orange glow lifts off the rocks and darkness begins to lower around them, bringing the cold snow air down from the towering peaks surrounding Lake Mono.

Cowrie reaches into her pack for a jacket and remembers the mangoes she'd included for dinner. She brings them out and hands one to Peta.

"Got a knife, Cowrie?"

"No need." Cowrie carefully slices the mango with her fingernail, right around her fleshy rim. She then peels back the dappled red skin as if it is a hide, all in one piece, sucking it on the inside to make sure she has not wasted any juice. Then she holds the mango to Peta's mouth, its dazzling orange and gold flesh inviting her seductively. The juices rise in Peta and she moves her lips toward the fruit. Cowrie does the same. Together, they eat mango Pacific style, and do not return to the van until very late that night.

On the way home, Cowrie and Peta spend a delicious day with friends of Peta who live in a small cottage surrounded by giant redwoods in the picturesque village of Villa Grande looking out over the beautiful Russian River. They take a picnic lunch in the canoes and explore the river, seeing blue herons preening themselves while balancing on a tree root, seals at the mouth of the river, and even a small turtle sunning itself on a rock. At night, they smoke salmon over an open fire and tell their coming out stories with outrageous laughter. Sadly, they say farewell on the last day of their journey and drive down the coast toward home.

"I can't believe how coming out stories still bind us together as lesbians. It's like an ancient ritual and crosses borders of age, class, culture, eh Peta?"

"Sure. It's interesting. But it also differs depending on the audience. Like, I don't usually share that stuff in my own culture because it's not appropriate, even amongst us women."

"Yeah, same with me at home, but we exist on several levels at once, within our mixed-blood cultures, within our own gender and also as lesbians. I like it that lesbian culture has developed rituals that bond us. It's a part of our identity, so long as it is never seen as fixed. It can't be by those of us who live in multiple worlds of identity, each with our own language and customs."

"Well, I disagree. I don't think the issues are that simple. But I do see what you're getting at, Cowrie."

They drive, mulling over the discussion in their heads.

"Hey, have you ever seen a Miwok village, Cowrie?"

"No. Can't say I have."

"Well, Tayo, an old family friend, is curator of a Miwok village recreated by the local tribes as a part of a project to try to get people to understand more about Miwok life and the coast tribal traditions. He lives with some fishermen at Tomales Bay. Most of the tribe now work for the oyster farmers there, and they're saving to run their own oyster farm to employ younger Miwoks. Anyway, the village itself is a bit plastic because it lacks people but it's the best you'll experience and you can use your imagination from there."

"I'd love to see it, Peta."

"Good, then we'll swing by Tayo's for a few raw oysters and see if he'll take us out to the village. It's closed to tourists mid-week, so we'll at least explore it in its natural state."

At Tomales Bay, they turn off on a bumpy farm road and come to a cluster of driftwood, tin and eucalyptus shacks where the oyster fishers live. A large stack of empty oyster shells lies to the left and next to it, ground up husks which go back into the land to feed the crops. Two men are slicing open shells and flicking the flesh into bowls. Cowrie's juices run wild.

"Hi, Clem. Yer seen Tayo?" Peta asks.

"Havin' a smoke," answers Clem. "Haven't seen you for a while, Peta."

"Na. Been too busy in San Fran."

"Still stirring up the dust, huh? You radicals never learn," Clem laughs.

"Without our funding skills, you wouldn't be

building an oyster farm, Clem, so button it." Peta is half serious, half amused.

Clem smiles to himself, continuing to shell the oysters.

"This is my friend from Aotearoa, Noo Zealand, Cowrie. She's also from Great Turtle Island, Hawai'ian turtle, that is."

"Yeah, Pacific rather than US turtle," Cowrie grins.

"Yer lost me there," replies Clem. "Wanna oyster?" He doesn't wait for an answer, but offers Cowrie a large, fleshy raw oyster, about the size of Bluff beauties back home, not the small, sweet rock oysters from the rocks near the marae.

"Love to," replies Cowrie, leaning forward to suck the fleshy treat from inside the half shell. As it moves around her tongue, slides down her throat, she is transported back into Aotearoan summers, collecting kina in kete, oysters off the rocks, and roasting pipis over beach fires. The good old days, before immigrants stripped the coast of kai moana in their greed to have free food, not thinking about the native traditions that always ensure sustainable growth, taking just what is needed for a fresh feed.

"Ka pai. Delicious. And that's coming from an oyster connoisseur."

Clem hands her another. They stop for a break when Tayo arrives, sampling some of the new oyster varieties spawned from Canadian stock. Cowrie asks if they've ever tried oysters from her home. Tayo did, once, when the Miwok elders were invited to Te Maori exhibition by the New Zealand Consulate in San Francisco. Evidently, the food was superb, and they sampled Bluff oysters and green-lipped mussels. Heron's Flight wine wasn't so bad either. Cowrie laughs, telling them it's from a vineyard in Matakana which was started by a local woman and a fella from

Great Turtle Island. They joke about what a small world it is.

"Tayo, would you take Cowrie up to the village? I'd like to hang out here for a bit and go see Aunty Iyatiku. D'yer mind, Cowrie?"

"Not at all, if Tayo's OK with it."

"Sure. I love it up there. Gives me a chance to be nostalgic for the old ways," replies Tayo.

"More like bore the shit out of visitors with yer stories," Clem adds.

Tayo cuffs him, standing up to go. "Can you drive that thing?" He points at the van.

"Yep."

"Then hop in and I'll tell yer where to go."

The village is isolated, stark. But Tayo says it's as authentic as they could make it. The houses are created from willow poles dug into the earth in a circle and bending in toward the centre to form a dome which is lashed together at the top. Smaller saplings are tied horizontally in a lattice structure. The arched doorways used to be made from whale rib bones, Tayo explains, but this one is of bent willow.

He takes Cowrie to the next dwelling. "Bulrushes, or tule reeds, are used to thatch the houses."

"How do the bundles of bulrush stay on, Tayo?"

Tayo bends down to the earth. "See, you begin here and layer one on top of the other, like shingles." He indicates the actions of layering. "Keeps the rain and wind out. Then we make a hole at the top to breathe, but with a deerskin covering to stop the rain."

"It's amazing, Tayo. You've given me some good ideas for housing back home on the marae."

Tayo smiles. "Looks easy, Cowrie. Not so simple to learn."

"Yeah, I bet. But d'ya mind if I sketch it so I can take it home with me?"

112

"No. Not at all. I'll just go over and rustle up some friends. Come over to the big bay tree, see that one, when you've finished."

Cowrie wonders where his friends might come from, out here in the wilderness, but takes out her sketch book and draws the design of the willow poles and the reed thatching. Inside the dwelling is the remains of a fire. Tayo already explained it was only for bad weather use, that normally they'd light a fire outside. That'll also explain the ventilation hole, she thinks.

Tayo returns to show her round the whole village, taking her into the sweat lodge usually reserved for the men. It is an underground pit, with shards of light coming down through the patterned willow over a hole in the roof. Cowrie imagines smoke from the sacred pipes swirling around her, drawing up to the sky through the slits in the roof as Tayo speaks. She is honoured that he is willing to share this ritual place with her.

When they emerge, the light seems stronger, sharper. Cowrie squints to adjust. Tayo takes her over to a giant tree.

"Here, let's sit on this bench under the pine nut tree." He bends to pick up a fallen nut, still encased in its shell, and holds it to the light.

"What do you see, Cowrie?"

Cowrie looks closely. "Oh, yeah, a nose going down the middle, with two sad-looking eyes and a downturned mouth."

"Wanna know why she's so sad?"

"Sure."

"In my tribe, it is a Miwok tradition that each elder gives birth to a child to be the next elder and she has to spend a year under the blanket. That is part of her training. She cannot speak or dance or sing or respond.

She has to learn to listen, for listening well is true wisdom."

Cowrie blushes, thinking of how hard she has tried to listen in her life, how many boundaries she has broken by not listening well enough.

"One day the girl in training to be an elder, just like my mother and her mother before, is lying under the blanket when a group of little girls come to play. Every other day for eleven months she's resisted them. She only has one month to go. But this day, her mother is washing clothes down at the river, and the girls get her to dance and sing with them. She remembers not to talk, but forgets that dancing and singing are not listening."

Cowrie smiles to herself, knowing how difficult this training would be. No dancing or singing would destroy her soul. She identifies with the little girl strongly.

"Once she realises she has broken the sacred bond, she runs with the other girls over the fields to a large pine nut tree, just like this one. They climb the branches, the little girl wanting to reach the top first. Then a wild wind rages, and the other girls scramble off the lower limbs, leaving the child swinging high in the upper branches, afraid for her life. She screams."

Cowrie's heart flies to the top of the tree.

"Down at the river, her mother hears her cry and is angry because she knows eleven months of training are lost, her daughter will not be an elder. But she naturally rushes to rescue her child. Once she reaches the tree and sees her daughter clinging to the weak upper branches, she scales its trunk. The wind is raging through the branches and it is a very difficult climb. Just as she reaches out to grab her daughter, the child turns into a pine nut."

Cowrie's heart shrinks. She remembers her dream

of turning into a nut as Mere reached for her the night before the marae opening.

"And here she is. Look at her sad little face, forever inscribed on every nut." Tayo turns the pine nut so the sun glowers off its shell. The face is so sad, so full of longing. Cowrie holds back the tears. Tayo places the pine nut into the palm of her hand, folding her fingers around its shell. "You keep this, Cowrie. It is for you."

Tayo rises and picks a leaf off the bay tree. He shapes it in his fingers and puts it to his mouth, whistling bird calls. Within minutes, several bluejays scamper out of the bush, looking for their mates. They stare, entranced. Cowrie unfolds her hand, looking at the sad little face, ashamed she did not follow her listening instinct earlier in responding to Peta's abuse when she first intuited it. She knows the gift will help her to be strong enough to do so in future, to listen carefully and have the courage to act on her inner knowledge.

Tayo and Iyatiku insist the women stay for dinner. Cowrie and Peta offer what food they have, corn from a roadside stall and smoked salmon from their Russian River feast. They sit outside around the fire, eating oysters and pawpaw, followed by hot smoked salmon, corn and fresh zucchini from the garden, sliced down the middle and roasted with pine nuts on top. Afterwards, they tell stories, laugh and Iyatiku teaches Cowrie a Miwok fishing song. In return, she sings them waiata to make sure there is a benevolent oyster crop and to protect their new farm. Too tired to drive home, they pitch their tent near the fire and plan to leave in the morning.

Dawn rises over the Tomales Bay hills and shines through the sides of their tent. It casts a warm glow on their faces as they lie, cheek to cheek, wrapped around each other.

Suddenly, the splutter of a tractor engine and a voice yelling out. "Be careful pickin' up them shells, Jake. There's a tent fulla gals behind." Jake stops the engine and peers over the pile of shells. "Well, I'll be darned, so there is. Time for a mornin' coffee then. I've bin up since sparrow's fart. These gals any good at cookin'? Could do with a feed too."

Peta flings off the sleeping bag covering them and pokes her head out the tent opening.

"Well, get off yer butt and make us coffee and eggs, Jake!"

Jake peers at the face protruding from the tent. "Why, if it ain't young Peta Owihankeshni. Whad'yer doin' up this way, gal? Good to see yer."

116

Peta wraps Cowrie's lavalava around her body and crawls out of the tent to hug him.

They eat a scrumptious breakfast cooked by Jake while Cowrie sleeps in. Later, on the drive home, Peta explains that Jake is in charge of training the young Miwok volunteers for the new tribally owned oyster farm. Men and women are involved in all parts of the operation and they have established community organic gardens to feed all the workers, enriched by the broken oyster shells mixed with seaweed compost. Some of the group have started up a nursery to grow seedlings for the gardens and also to replant Tomales Bay, bereft of trees after generations of cattle farming.

Cowrie suggests that it'd be good for Irihapeti and the nursery workers at Te Kotuku Marae to make contact with the nursery here at Tomales. "Maybe they could swap information. Even though the vegetation is different, the climate is very similar—and I'm sure pohutukawa trees would not only beautify the bay but grow superbly here. I bet there's Californian trees that'd do well at home too."

Peta is enthusiastic about the idea, and agrees they should swap addresses and make sure it happens. "Home, eh, Cowrie? You missing it, huh?"

"Yeah, especially on this trip, Peta. I can handle it in Berkeley. Not so many memories—but up here, the land and people speak to my soul, remind me of home."

"Why don'tcha go back during the summer vacation? You'll have several weeks and you need to see your family and friends."

"Will you come too, Peta?"

"Next time. When I can raise the funds. But I'd like to go back to Kahnawake, check out this job and see my friend."

"So you are still seriously thinking about working there?"

"If it weren't for you, sweet Turtle, I'd be there now."

Cowrie is silent. They've come back to this place. They'll continue to do so. This is the reality of international relationships. She is mourning the time apart already. Then she remembers that if you really, really want something so much, let it go, and it'll come back if it is right for you.

"OK, Peta. I will go home for the summer. It's covered by my scholarship. Besides, I know I can work on my thesis better on the marae, surrounded by all that aroha. Maybe it'll give me inspiration for a new way in to the work."

"And what about me going to Kahnawake?"

"I want you to go. If not, I'll always be thinking you might take off there. I'd rather you saw your friend again, checked out the job. Besides, Canada isn't that far away when I'm in Berkeley. Not as far as Aotearoa. So we'd still be in close contact, eh?"

Peta gives a whoop of delight. "Thanks, Cowrie. I've been waiting so long to hear you say that. I would've eventually gone anyway if I felt it the right thing to do, but I really wanted you to come to that decision yourself, and feel OK about it."

Now they have broached the subject of their fears openly and begun to discuss the possibilities, the anxiety disappears and soon they are figuring ways to remain in touch even at the distance of Aotearoa.

"I'll do tapes from Te Kotuku. That way you'll get to hear the voices of Irihapeti, Mere, Aunty Rawinia and Kuini when she's up."

"Yeah, I'll reply with the same, and Uretsete can fill you in on the progress of the students in your storytelling group. I hear they've decided to stay together over the summer vacation. You've really started something there, Turtle."

Cowrie beams. She's also really pleased with the group. Suddenly, the world seems full of possibility again. Ideas of how it can all work race through her mind.

"Hey Peta."

"Yep?"

"What do you think UC Berkeley and the Fulbright Foundation would say if I stated that their current academic system does not provide the means to successfully communicate Pacific and oral literature within the scope of a doctorate. That I request permission to devise a doctorate that allows for oral interviews, to show the true nature of talkstory, which can never be fully conveyed on the page?"

"Right on Cowrie. Now you're talkin' sweet! Tell them it's the job of the cross-cultural scholar to find appropriate ways to communicate this research material—and either they're open to this, or you'll ditch the doctorate and work on the material for a feminist press to publish."

"Hang on, Peta, there's still heaps of work to come yet. I've got to convince them that it's viable, academic, rigorous and acceptable."

"Yeah, and it will bring them glory. Don't forget how the old academic wheels turn."

Cowrie grins. There's a vast job ahead, but it's a possibility at last. She can't continue trying to describe Pacific indigenous traditions in postmodernist language. It's insulting. It's like telling Maoris to learn Latin to train their minds, as happened when she was at school, while refusing to accept the language of the tangata whenua.

"So, Cowrie. Are we still married? Bridal Veil Falls and all that?"

"As soul mates and lovers, yes. As committed

friends, yes. As in me cooking while you put out the garbage, no!"

"Bored already? But we've only been together in this new way for a few days. Fancy some SM to liven things up?"

"Peta Owihankeshni, the day you or I get into that is the day of our solemn divorce, I can tell you now. Haven't we had enough abuse, heard enough from others, to last a lifetime?"

Peta laughs. "Glad to hear that, Snapping Turtle. You know, you really are very attractive when you get on your high seas about issues. The moon dazzles in your eyes and passion fumes from your flared nostrils. Why, I might even stay over at your studio a few days while you work on your thesis plan so I can have input if it fires you up this much. Purely professional of course. No kissing while we work." Cowrie reaches over and squeezes Peta's thigh as she drives. "Then again, I might never make it home."

Peta stops the van beside the beach before the San Rafael bridge and kisses Cowrie softly, passionately. They fly through the rainbow waterfall, into the cavern, in seconds. This time, there are others waiting for them. Miwok, Chumash, Nga Puhi, Kanaka Maoli and Pakeha voices. Voices of the women they work with, voices of the tribes they come from, urging them on in their work, their relationship. Urging them to break boundaries and cross oceans as their ancestors did, to give birth to new lives, dare to dream a future for themselves and their daughters. Together, we have strength, we are part of a new creature emerging, one that will refuse to be abused or made extinct. One that honours the birth-givers, creators, artists and activists. Boundary-breakers of the present who give birth to the future.

For the next few weeks Cowrie works hard on her thesis and prepares to go home for the summer vacation. Benny makes a whirlwind visit *en route* to the Queer Conference in LA, dropping off the pink satin tie featuring Lady Di as soft butch. They manage a dinner together with Lori and Squish, and both of them decide to attend the conference also. Lori is working on an exhibition featuring butch-femme wearable art and hopes it isn't too late to enter her work in the Bring Your Own Art Exhibition.

In the yard, Benny adds the final touches to her revamped BMW before leaving. Lori is painting a version of the soft butch lady Di on the gas tank.

"Reckon you're after impressing one of those cool British dykes with this, Benny?"

Benny blushes. "Lori—art does not have to be for a reason. I just happen to like the image."

"Yeah, but as an artist, I know that images always have meaning. So whad'yer up to?"

"Queer culture is international. I want to move away from American images only."

"But what's so new about exchanging Madonna or Hillary in drag for Lady Di? Ain't it the same idea dressed up in the Union Jack instead of Stars and Stripes?"

"Yeah, in a way. But surely that proves we go beyond patriarchal geographical boundaries."

Cowrie hears the last few sentences as she extracts the OJ jug from the fridge near them. She laughs. "I reckon you two are fooling yourselves. Stretching across borders goes deeper than images. You need to know the the roots of the cultures to play successfully with subverting the imagery."

"Spoilsport," replies Benny. "Now that's just typical coming from an academic. Why can't we play with the images anyhow?"

"You can. Just be aware of what you're doing."

The phone rings, sending Cowrie scampering back into the apartment.

"She's real resistant to queer culture, huh?"

"Give her time," smiles Benny. "You should see how cute she looks in that pink satin tie."

"You fancy her, Benny?"

"Na. Too PC for me. But I do reckon she's much more wild underneath that exterior. We've had some excellent laughs together. And she's taking some risks at UC challenging Rita and the PhD system. That shows guts."

"Yeah. She's OK. I like teasing her. Takes the bait every time. Especially with the SM routine."

"But you're seriously into SM. I mean, it's not just a facade is it?"

"Come on up and check me out," grins Lori.

Benny smiles. "I'll take your word. Now, d'yer reckon we should have butch Di in a purple satin suit with a pink triangle on her lapel or shall we power dress her?"

"Combination of both. Leave it to me."

They huddle together like kids, plotting the exact requirements for the image which will be Benny's status symbol for the next few months, while Cowrie tells Peta over the phone about her surprise trip to Hawai'i *en route* home to Aotearoa.

"Turtle, promise you'll write me from Te Kotuku? I'll be sure to reply and keep sending you sweetgrass to burn so I'm always with you." Peta kisses her cheek tenderly, folding her arms around Cowrie.

"I'll send you letters with shells from the beach—paua, tuatua, mussels and feathers dropped by tui, matuku moana and kereru. You'll have a gallery of oceanic art in your hut at Kahnawake so you won't forget me."

"Not much chance of that, my sweet." Peta hugs her close. In the background, the haunting sound of Keo playing his conch shell from a tape sent by Koana fills the room, enters their bodies.

"I can't wait to see Koana's face when I arrive. Keo and Paneke know I'm coming but they promised not to tell Ko and Ela. I especially want it to be a surprise for Pene and Neli."

"What if they're in the middle of a domestic row when you emerge suddenly on their doorstep?"

"Then I'll walk the beach and wait some time before I enter. Besides, both of them have been through so many disputes in their past relationships, they've been working closely on clearer communication, for the sake of the kids too."

"They're not lovers are they?"

Cowrie changes the tape over. "I don't think so. Ela spends time with a bro she likes but I reckon Ko would be ready for it. She's changed heaps from my time on the Big Island and her work with the Kanaka

Maoli Land Movement has strengthened her sense of self. She's met some Hawai'ian dykes and likes the way they've challenged the status quo. She called last week and we had a great korero."

"Glad to hear it. You're still really fond of her, Cowrie. It's an important relationship and you should put time into it."

"Mahalo, Peta. I guess I should say that of your relationship with Nanduye also. I'm sorry I got so threatened earlier. It's just that we can never have guarantees when it comes to movement and change and so I wanted you to commit to me before going to Kahnawake." She pushes the play button and turns to face Peta.

"Turtle, I'm as committed to you as I'll ever be to anyone. Beyond that, I can't say what the future will bring. Just feel secure in the depth of my love and trust me. We've talked about how dedicated we are to our indigenous work and so we'll always be called back to our own shores to fulfil those goals. But that doesn't have to threaten our relationship. We just need to pioneer new ways of being together and staying true to our life's work." Peta reaches over to pour more coffee from the filter as Cowrie sits down next to her.

"Yeah. I know exactly what you mean. I do trust you Peta." She takes Peta's hand, squeezing it.

"Thanks, Cowrie. After all, I could get uptight about your love for Koana and you visiting her again. Maybe you'll both fall in love if she is now ready for that. Who knows?"

"I do, Peta. Had you and I not met, then maybe that'd be a possibility. We'd have worked through the 'ohana issues. But not now. I want our love to be as family, like sisters. I've never had a sister and Ko is as close as I'll ever get."

They spend the rest of the afternoon in bed, making love, reading poetry to each other and taking turns to climb down the ladder to get food or tea. They laugh through a collection of dyke cartoons and decide to stay in for their final night instead of going to Sala Thai. Peta agrees to take Cowrie to the airport the next night and they make last-minute plans to dine out at Plantation Pizzeria *en route*.

Two days later, Koana and Ela are sipping tea in their garden at Na'alehu, Hawai'i, when a large, handsome woman brushes softly past the banana palms at the side of the house and looks keenly into the taro. She is carrying a woven kete of gifts, wrapped in bright coloured shell paper, wears a head lei made from ti leaves and is festooned with plumeria flowers hanging from every available part of her body.

"Aloha, sisters," she calls and sets down her kete.

"Cowrie!" cries Koana. "How did you get here? I thought you were studying in San Francisco?"

"I still am, but I've got two months between semesters and I'm *en route* home to Aotearoa to work on my thesis and see whanau, so I thought I'd drop by."

"So how long are you here on the Big Island?"

"As long as you'll have me, cousin. Actually, just a couple of days. I hoped you'd be home. It was a free stopover." Cowrie grins.

Koana hugs her and Ela invites her to sit with them. "The twins still have your hammock strung up on the back porch, Cowrie. You're welcome to stay just as long as you like."

The bright Navajo hammock she'd bought on her first trip to the States still hangs where she'd left it. "Mahalo, Koana. It'll just be a few days but I'm dying to hear all the news. I gather from your letters that your living together has worked out well and that Chad has returned to Texas—where he belongs, I might add."

They all laugh. But beneath the laughter Ela looks grim. "So long as he stays there, Cowrie, we're safe. But he really resents the support 'ohana have given me here and my new independence. He never took much interest in our children when we were married, but now he's contesting guardianship just to have power over me. They like the wealth and toys they get in Texas, but really want to live here with Nele and Peni. We're trying not to let it destroy us."

"I've know just the right lawyer to handle your case, Ela. A friend of Peta's. This woman was part of a team that helped win back a white boys' golf course set inside the Kahnawake Reservation. She's hot stuff, so Peta reckons, and is trained in both Canadian and US law. She's got the support networks established and when she was practising in Berkeley she specialised in domestic violence and guardianship cases."

"I'm willing to try anything to keep my children. Let's call her tomorrow."

The three women spend the afternoon catching up on news. Paneke is now taking lomilomi classes to help train young Hawai'ian women in the ancient art of traditional massage and healing, using her steambath rooms and the open-air massage space as the workshop area. The University of Hilo continuing education unit has helped sponsor and run the courses and she also teaches privately. Cowrie's cousin Keo is now head of the sugar-cane workers' union and they are fighting battles against the industry over the controversial practice of burning the cane stubble, which has resulted in several workers going partially blind. There is no compensation offered and no moves to stop the practice. The company refuses to believe the problem exists. They figure that the low-paid Hawai'ian, immigrant and poor haole workers are unlikely to cause much controversy. But evidently, Keo has got the other sugar-cane workers together and they are fighting this through the Kanaka Maoli movement to take back Hawai'i from mainland control, return it to its Pacific identity. According to Koana, it's becoming very big now, with more and more support, even from some of the church groups.

Cowrie fills them in on her work at UC Berkeley and on progress at the marae, from Mere and Irihapeti's letters, since she'd left Aotearoa. Ela and Koana are very interested in the women writers' hui and tell her about the Waianae Women Writers Group on Oahu, how some local women also want to write as well as do talkstory, so that more people get to hear of their experiences. The afternoon passes quickly as they share their news and gain hope from the work that is being done rather than depressing themselves with contemplating the vastness of what still needs to be accomplished.

Koana's twins, Nele and Peni, arrive home from school, struggling to be the first to hug Cowrie. "See, Peni, I told you if we left her hammock up she'd come back," cries Nele, excited to see her aunty again.

"Yeah, but it was me who fixed the busted rope at the end. Otherwise it wouldn't be there," retorts Peni.

"Why don't you all catch up while Ela and I prepare dinner?" suggests Koana. "Shall I invite Keo and Paneke down, Cowrie? Keo now has use of the sugarcane truck, so they can come after he finishes work."

"Kamaha'o! I'd love that. Mahalo, Koana."

Ela and Koana gather up the afternoon tea gadgets and move toward the house. Cowrie notices how Koana puts her arm around Ela, guides her up the porch stairs, like a partner. Nele and Peni waste no time telling Cowrie about how wonderful it is to have

Ela's children living here. She'll meet them tonight after they have finished their Hawai'ian language class. They lost so much of their language while living in Texas, but now it is coming back to them gradually. The classes are held all over the island now. They ask Cowrie all about the marae they'd heard about in the letters, what the kids do there and when she will take them to Aotearoa.

Cowrie grins, telling them they've grown too tall to sneak into her pack but if they work hard, they might get to the next Indigenous Pacific Conference with Koana, and Cowrie will be there. It'll be held in Aotearoa in two years and Koana has told her in letters she is saving to bring them all. The twins get wound up over the possibilities of visiting the South Pacific, confusing all the island animals as one, but both agree they want to see a live wombat.

The dinner is a feast, with Paneke bringing down a huge carved-out watermelon filled with fruit. They've also brought a half coconut shell which they offer to her, wrapped in ti leaves, as a taonga. Turtle Woman surfs the waves, jubilant and powerful, etched on to the inner husk of the coconut. This is the image from her dreams that took her to Hawai'i in search of her grandfather's family, that lead her to Keo, Paneke and Koana, that they now return for her to take home to Aotearoa. This is a sign of their acceptance of her as 'ohana, as family. The symbol that taught her to follow her dreams, to listen to them and learn from them. She holds the half coconut up to the candle light, and Turtle Woman, Laukiamanuikahiki, smiles at her through the shell.

Koana arranges to spend the next day with Cowrie so they can catch up on more intimate news. It turns out that she and Ela are not lovers but have established a very warm and close relationship and since it works so well for their kids they've decided to stay together. Ela sees a guy from Hilo every week at her language class and she stays with him overnight.

"Does that bother you, Koana? I sense you are really fond of Ela."

"Yes. I'm attracted to her, Cowrie. But she's 'ohana, like you, and it'd bring the same problems. Also, Ela is sure she's heterosexual and about as frightened of considering otherwise as I was when you were here."

"But you did make love to me, in your own way, with your lomilomi hands, Koana. And I've never forgotten that."

Koana blushes. "Sorry I couldn't give you more, Cowrie. It wasn't just the kapu of being 'ohana. I was confused by my feelings. And while I really love your energy as a friend, I think it'd swallow me up as a lover, even if we'd decided to go that way."

Cowrie sighs. The same old issues. Breaking boundaries, crossing borders, being too large, too loud, too much energy, too much life. Koana notices her going quiet. She is not sure what to say. She touches her hand. "Cowrie, it's not just you. I saw my mother lose herself in my father and I never ever want that to happen to me. That's why I chose Aka. He kept to himself a lot, allowed me the freedom I need. I had lots of emotional space. I have that with Ela too. But with you, I'd feel like I was living with Pele every day, and I'm not sure I could handle that."

"Well, I can't think of anyone I'd rather live with. I wish Pele would assume human form and take me away forever," sulks Cowrie.

"But what about Peta? She sounds fantastic. I must admit, I felt a little jealous when you first wrote and told me about her."

"Did you? You never said."

"That's because I knew you'd get on the big bird and fly over from the mainland if you thought I'd changed my mind."

Cowrie grins. "Well, yes, before I got involved with Peta, I might well have done so. You're right Ko, as usual. I've just had this message about being too everything for too long and sometimes it really gets to me. I long to be around people who just love and accept me for who I am."

Koana squeezes her hand. "I do love you for who you are, Cowrie. It's just that we have different energy levels and I think we should accept this and just enjoy our special friendship, which is deeper for what we have been through together. I'll never forget your support when I needed you after Aka's death. And I have really missed you."

"Yeah. I could tell by your letters. They were very special and so are you Ko. Look, I'm just feeling a bit insecure because Peta has moved in with her best friend from college days at Kahnawake and I keep having these dreams that they'll become lovers, that I'll be abandoned again, like I was as a baby at the orphanage. It's my stuff to deal with."

"Well, if that happens, you just have to let go, Cowrie. You can't fight people's emotions. If Peta is right for you, she'll come back. If not, you have to heal and know that Pele is still here for you no matter what. And so am I—as your cousin and your friend."

"Mahalo, Ko. And I'm rapt things have worked out so well for you and Ela. It's all for the best, eh?"

"'Ae, Cowrie. But you don't always need to hide your hurt. You can let it out to a friend, you know. You don't have to be Pele and in control all of the time!"

"Let's visit her, Ko. I feel in need of some of her fiery energy right now. Hey, d'ya know what Peta's name means? Sacred Fire! How about that?"

"Maybe you have met your Pele, Cowrie. She sounds pretty fiery as well as being thoughtful and sensitive, from your letters."

"I've got some sweetgrass from Peta. Let's make an offering to Pele and see what she says about it."

"Kamaha'o. I know just the place to do this, and you'll love it. Honu is parked over at the post office so you can drive me there, like old times, eh?" Koana jumps up from the grass where they have been lying and pulls Cowrie to her feet. "This will be an experience you can tell Peta, for sure."

An hour later, Honu is spluttering her way into Volcano National Park and Koana directs Cowrie to drive from Kiluaea toward the sea. They are surrounded by shiny black pitted rock from the recent lava flows and in the distance, Pele is smouldering her way towards the ocean. As they get nearer, the heat increases and they park next to a sign advising people it is dangerous to go further. They climb down from the truck and Koana leads her onto a path behind the ocean, where a few kiawe trees have escaped the latest flows. Then they head out over the hardened magma towards the waves.

"Hell, Ko. Isn't this a bit risky?"

"So, who's afraid of fire now?"

Cowrie follows her steps, remembering her journey through Pele's crater with Paneke, and how important it is to respect local knowledge. Koana explains that the park ranger, Kehaulani, took her out here one night and showed her this exact path, marked by small boulders. They reach a bay and, after lighting the sweetgrass in a ritual offering for Pele, enter the ocean. Koana leads, stroking out to a small island of rock. There is a roaring sound and the water is becoming rapidly warmer. As they emerge on the other side, the sky is lit up by an orange glow as Pele rages down the slopes of Kiluaea and into the water, sizzling as her flames explode into the waves. Cowrie feels a rush of excitement at being so close to the fiery lava. She and Koana float on the surface, exulting in the energy as Pele surges toward them, each flow reaching another foot out to sea.

"So this is what it'd be like living with me, Ko," Cowrie whispers into her ear.

Koana smiles widely. "That's right, Cowrie."

"Now I feel OK about it. She's magnificent."

"Knew you'd enjoy her. Only locals come here. But we know how to respect Pele."

"I'm glad we gave her that sweetgrass offering before diving into the water."

"'Ae, she'll appreciate that."

"Ko, I'm dying to swim closer. There's a magnetic energy pulling me to her."

"Yes. We know that too, Cowrie. But don't. Pele will eat you up."

Cowrie lets herself float just a few feet nearer. Koana swims close, eases her back. "Be careful Cowrie. Look. Watch this." She plucks a floating twig from the water and throws it about twelve feet in front of them. It dips, then sizzles, disappearing from sight.

"Wow! That's awesome! Thanks, Ko. For bringing me here, for being so honest with me."

Koana smiles, looking past her to the mountain slopes behind, remembering the vivid red glow when she and Kehaulani swam here the first time, how elated but frightened she was, how she wished Cowrie were here too. The sea was pitch black around them, the land darkened but for rivers of molten gold flowing like treacle over the rock layers, deep yellow at their core, blood red at their smouldering edges. The sparks of the flow sizzled into the ocean, bleeding into the waves lashing around them. The water was on fire.

Waves lap around her ears as she floats in the warm sea, watching Pele's lava flame red hot, sending steam from the ocean as it crackles and sizzles into the water, seething over the newly formed reef. Koana floats near, touches her fin then glides away.

"Pork or fish, ma'am?" The United Airlines hostess wakes her abruptly.

"Neither, thanks, I'll just sleep."

Cowrie loves this feeling of being suspended between heaven and earth, in the zone between waking and sleeping. She pulls the blanket over her head and swims back into her mind, reliving the past two days and her former visit to Hawai'i in vivid detail. The journey through the Kiluaea Crater and the fire sizzling up her arm, around her head. Was it Pele or Peta? Standing naked astride a steam vent at midnight on her final day with Koana, letting Pele enter them, become one with them, inspire them. Looking down into the deep slit in the lava, wanting to dive in and be embraced by the warmth of Pele's fire, but knowing it'd be a journey of no return.

Now she is crossing a bridge with Peta and other refugees, all carrying bundles of clothes and sweetgrass. They are surrounded by lights, red, orange, yellow, green, blue, indigo, violet. They look down to see colours layered like a rainbow. Peta leans over, her hand slips from Cowrie's and she is falling towards the ocean below. She braces herself for impact, making her body sleek, and dives through the water, deeper and deeper. Jade green turns to deep indigo, black. She gasps for breath, feeling water race out her gills. She rises, surging toward the surface and dives out of the waves, her back arched, her fins erect. From the Rainbow Bridge, the moving throng sees a dolphin emerge from the ocean where their companion fell, thrusting her body from the water in joy, and they know they will all be safe. It is a sign. Cowrie is distraught, wanting to dive down and join her friend.

A nasty smell enters her nostrils. "It's fine ma'am. Just spraying for the Noo Zealand Department of Agriculture and Fisheries. It's standard practice to keep the country safe from disease," the steward intones, holding cans out either side of him. Cowrie retreats back under her blanket, trying to re-enter her dream, find out what happens next, but she is too awake. The plane begins its descent.

She walks through customs, declaring nothing but Kona coffee and macadamia nuts, and is met outside by Mere, Irihapeti, Kuini, Aunty Rawinia and some of the women from the writers' hui. They chant a powhiri in welcome and are holding toetoe branches, their feathers moving as they sing. A lei of pohutukawa blossom is placed on her head and they gather round to hongi, tears in their eyes.

Cowrie didn't expect such a welcome. Mere said she'd come with Irihapeti, but to see them all is overwhelming. They walk her out to the carpark and lead her toward a brightly painted mini-bus. On the side, a white heron in flight over Te Kotuku o Hokianga, and at the back Te Kotuku Nurseries, Hokianga. She bursts into tears of joy. Irihapeti hugs her. "Yep. Our funding worked, girl. We wanted it to be a surprise for you. The iwi trust and internal affairs covered the cost and it's used for kohanga reo, school trips, the nursery, and Te Aroha."

"What's Te Aroha?"

"That's the name of our women's group to support abuse victims and bring abusers to justice on the marae. It's only love that can heal this abuse, hence the name," Mere explains.

Cowrie holds her close, thinking of Maata, of Peta, of her own childhood. "Kia ora, Mum. You're right. It's happening on Great Turtle Island too, the women coming together to address this in ways that make sense to us, that can make us whole again. Throwing the offenders in prison does no good. They just learn new ways to reoffend."

"With Piripi's help, we've got the men working on rehabilitation too. They need to do that work. It's not our job. It's their problem to fix. We just act as advisors. They have to put in the hard work to be accepted by the iwi again, and it may take a lifetime for that to happen."

"Abuse stays with us for a lifetime, so it's only just," adds Kuini. "Besides, some of the men are teaching their sons better. Now they know what we will and won't accept. They need to find their own mana, learn to become warriors in a different kind of way."

The journey to the marae is full of news about the nursery, kohanga, the establishment of a craft trust to employ the young people in bone carving, tukutuku weaving, pounamu sculpting, the creation of new kete designs. The van is bursting with the energy of their dreams come alive, given wings since te kotuku flew over the marae, gracing it with her presence.

They are driving up the West Coast through the Waipoua Kauri Forest. On either side, giant kauri tower over them, their girths as wide as the van, their roots stretching deep into Papatuanuku, their trunks leading the eye up high into the heavens where Ranginui holds up the sky. They stop mid-way to pay homage to Tane Mahuta, God of the Kauri Forest, and walk to the shrine at the foot of the tree. Every time, it is awesome to be dwarfed by such magnificence, such ancient wisdom held within the silent branches. They offer karakia and as the prayers are uttered, Cowrie notices a large kereru nesting in the upper branches, brown feathers splashed with green, white chest shining in the sun. Maui often transformed himself into a kereru. Maybe it's a sign that men can change, that the efforts of these brave wahine toa are not in vain.

Cowrie wakes to memories of last night. Te Marama, the women writers' group, made her a feast of kai moana and fresh organic vegetables from the nursery. They celebrated until dark, then Irihapeti led them to the beach where they enacted a ritual for her return home. This time they sculpted a large egg from the sand, cracked at the top where a turtle was hatching out. Kuini painted three signs which she strung off the toetoe branches poking out from the egg: Aotearoa, Hawai'i, Great Turtle Island: Te Kotahitanga. Other women added the Pacific Islands they came from. Soon the egg was festooned with toetoe flags, like kina spikes, their feathers flying in the wind, conveying their messages back out to sea. They sang waiata and offered karakia for the safe passage of the newborn turtle, symbolising all their journeys, from the sand dunes to the ocean.

"Kia ora, tamahine. Here's a hot cuppa." Mere places the tea on the mat beside her bed and takes Cowrie's hand in hers, stroking it gently. "I'm so pleased to see you home, even for a short time. We are proud of your work, Cowrie."

Cowrie thinks of DK, the students, the SM debates, her challenging of the university system, and sighs.

"Are you happy there, Turtle?"

"Yeah. But it's not all easy. Remember the recurring dream I had as a child? Sometimes I feel I am back inside that wave, about to be crashed like a coconut, smashed on to the rocks below, my belly oozing thick white milk." Mere strokes her forehead as Cowrie always loved her doing when she was a child. So gentle, so soothing. Enough for her troubles to swim back out to sea.

"So what prevents you from entering back into that wave which tries to destroy you?"

"My studies, Mere. It's not that I can't do the work. Just that I can't fit it into their system. When I'm analysing contemporary women's fiction, it's fine, but as soon as I try to place our Pacific writing and storytelling into that tradition, it doesn't work. Our tradition needs a context of its own. I need to discover a way to present it with impact, so that others are challenged to come into our reality, instead of us always fitting theirs. It doesn't feel ethical to continue to reduce our lives to a foreign pattern of thinking. D'you know what I mean?"

"Only too well, Cowrie. Remember, my generation were beaten at school for speaking our own language. I spoke Maori at home because neither of my parents knew English, then I had to learn to speak English at school. It was like living in two worlds, but never fully belonging to either."

"I know what that's like. But I'm still not sure quite how I can pull it all together, find a legitimate and fair way to present my research which does not deny our Pacific heritage."

"Cowrie, you must follow your heart, listen to your dreams. They will tell you where to go, how to do it. This is all I know. It worked for my mother and her mother. It's the best I can offer."

"I do listen to my dreams, take note of them. But right now, they are telling me my best friend might be transforming into a dolphin, and swimming away from me, not how to complete my research."

"That reminds me. There's a pile of letters for you, including some from your friend Peta. I'll get them in a minute. Have patience Cowrie. Know that I have faith in you. You will always be a boundary-breaker. It is not an easy task. But it is your role, has been from your birth. You will pioneer new ways of thinking and others will follow. But it is never easy to be first to do this."

"I can handle that role, enjoy it, but I'm also worried about breaking boundaries. While it's important to challenge systems when they do not meet our needs, take risks, make our dreams come true, there's also a down side. Sometimes I find myself pushing at the boundaries of others, inevitably more private people than me, and I hurt them without even realising, just by being myself."

"You need to learn the difference between breaking boundaries to achieve freedom in your work and breaking boundaries that infringe on others. I watched you, as a child, in such pain when others rejected you, not because they didn't love you, but because you just surged through their defences like a tidal wave. You need to learn to take things more slowly in personal relationships, learn to respect the boundaries of another because they are there for a purpose." Mere holds Cowrie's hand in hers to make sure she feels loved, not offended.

"I learned a strong lesson about listening and boundaries from a Miwok elder on Great Turtle Island. It frightened me because it was about a mother and daughter and I thought how devastated I'd be if I ever lost you, Mere." Cowrie tells her Tayo's story.

Mere listens intently to the end. "There are many Pacific equivalents of this story, Cowrie. It is a good lesson to learn for developing inner wisdom, listening to others, especially in personal relationships. But don't let it stop you being a pioneer, thinking for yourself, acting creatively. Who knows, that little girl who was transformed into a pine nut could have turned out to be Hine Nui Te Po, possessing the power to reject exploitation as a woman. You need to be able to listen carefully, but also act when necessary. That will come with practice. You have all those qualities within you now."

Cowrie squeezes Mere's hand. Tears edge their way into the corners of her eyes. "Tena koe, Mere. I needed to be reminded of that."

"Kia ora. I'll get your mail. I'm sure that your friend would not write so often in so few days if she did not value you deeply."

Cowrie sips her tea, glad she is home, knowing she will find a way to challenge the university, come up with a creative alternative, somehow. A bundle of letters and a parcel are in Mere's kete when she returns.

"I'll leave you to read these, Cowrie. I'm due at kohanga reo now. Don't forget my words."

Cowrie thanks her, takes out the letters and examines them. Most are from Peta. She opens the parcel first. Stalks of sweetgrass tied with flax. Hanging from the end, a small abalone shell, like the one Peta gave her when they first met and a message: "Haku, sweet Turtle. I miss you. Every night I dream you are here, your sea creatures swimming over my pillow. I send you kisses for every moon we have missed together. Peta." She sighs with longing, remembering their kiss beside the waterfall at Yosemite, the way Peta looked into her eyes at San Francisco airport when she left.

Cowrie relishes a morning of Peta and settles back into bed to read her mail, hoping by now Peta has received the turtle dream-catcher she sent over from the Big Island to embrace her sweetest dreams, letting them drip down on her sleeping head, catching the nightmares in its net.

Peta's reunion with Nanduye and her family had been all she expected. Cowrie spoke with them briefly on the phone from Hawai'i when asking Nanduye to represent Ela in the Texas Law Court. Nanduye agreed and sounded as friendly as Peta painted her to be. The job offers good wages and is right up Peta's alley, working with activists examining land and treaty rights, and she is tempted to take it on fulltime. Cowrie's heart pounds as she searches the page for confirmation Peta will be returning to Oakland. She's decided to take a six-month contract and leave it open for review. "I want us to discuss this, Cowrie. It's a decision we must both make." Then, further down the page "After all, sweet Turtle, we did get married at Yosemite. Divorce ain't that easy now. Not that I'd take out the rubbish anyway!" Cowrie smiles, remembering their conversation.

The other letters are poems, deep and heartfelt, charting Peta's love. Cowrie sent her a poem from Hawai'i, after she and Koana swam near Pele's sizzling lava. She now realises Peta was as nervous of her reunion with Koana as Cowrie was of hers with Nanduye. Cowrie knows if she didn't have a lover, then she would still feel attracted to Koana. But now there is such a bond between her and Peta, and seeing Koana so happy with Ela, she is able to enjoy their contact without the longing that used to be there constantly. The final poem suggests there is a strong and deep spirit bond between Peta and Nanduye, one which Peta feels she must honour and explore further. Cowrie takes a deep breath. Remembers that she must honour this bond they share, and protect herself also, not let herself be crushed on the rocks.

Among the letters is a postcard from DK, who notes at the top she got her address from Uretsete. "Hi there, prof. How's it back in the islands? Basking in the sun reading our essays no doubt! Hope you like mine on SM! Just thought I'd let you know Suzanne and I are lovers. You were right. She's gorgeous. No need for whips these days. She rides me into the night oceans and she's even got me taking walks beside the sea and all that romantic crap. She says hi and to thank you. See yer next term. DK."

Cowrie cannot believe DK has dared to write this on an open postcard. The corner store which receives the mail is so slow they read everything. It's the main gossip network. She imagines Yolanda at the dairy, with her pink hair-do, fake red nails and whimpering voice which is always submissive around men, reading DK's postcard, and suddenly she laughs wildly. Who cares now? This is her life, and she is proud of her work, even though some back here might not appreciate it.

An aerogramme from Uretsete updates her on the progress of the storytelling group. She has drawn in her Chumash elders to take some sessions, and Ruth invited her Yiddish grandmother. They enjoy the group better than their UC classes and wonder if Cowrie can get it into the official programme for next semester.

Great idea! Why not? This could help pave the way for changes to the doctorate. Cowrie puts the letters aside and sits up in bed writing a proposal. She works all day, linking the storytelling sessions with her doctoral thesis, noting ways to record the progress as women from the different cultures hear each other's stories, listen carefully, as on the marae, without any interruption, so that the full impact and power of the storytelling comes across. So they feel it in their hearts as well as hear it in their heads. That's what's missing. It's the ritual, the sense of presence, the atmosphere that's so hard to create on the page. This is what she must find a way to convey. Analysis breaks it apart, cracks the egg and destroys its life, rather than giving birth to new energy. She needs to piece it all together again, just as the storytelling class created such close bonds among such different students.

How can I convey the pure beauty, the power of women, the traditions of the largely matriarchal indigenous Pacific alongside the devastation of our islands being targets for US and French nuclear experiments? How can a doctorate ever frame the horror of a living holocaust that most of the world turns a blind eye to? Cowrie knows she needs to engage mind, emotions, soul to get her message across, let the stories speak for themselves, reach the hearts of people.

The next few weeks, nothing can prise Cowrie from her desk except for kai, kohanga reo classes and attending Te Aroha meetings, which fill her with more passion and urgency for her work. At the end, she has two proposals for Rita, one for the storytelling class for the next semester and one for her PhD. She places them inside envelopes, ready to send, then walks over the dunes to the beach, already feeling the heavy burden lifting from her heart.

Cowrie passes the driftwood log in the shape of a whale where the women hung their jackets before the ritual of the hatching turtle. She hitches her lavalava over a branch and enters the ocean, diving into an approaching wave, its belly lit by moonlight. She swims through the breakers, lies floating in the safe sea beyond for some time. Then she thrusts out her fins to surf in on a wave, jubilant and ecstatic in her joy.

Refreshed, relieved, she returns over the dunes and creeps into bed, not wanting to disturb Mere. Soon she drifts into a deep, deep sleep. She is surfing in to shore, toward a slit in the cliff face. Waves lift her on their backs, delivering her into the heart of a cave. Around the walls, ancient symbols she recognises, unihipili from Hawai'i, rock drawings from Aotearoa, and in the distance, a flickering light. She enters deeper into the cavern. Women sit naked, chanting around a fire, their faces painted ochre, white and yellow. Through the flames, Peta gestures her to join them. She bends as two women part like waves to make way for her. She smells sweetgrass burning, hears the surge of waves following her up the cavern and ebb out again. But the next wave nearly reaches the flames. The women chant, as if urging it closer. She is spellbound by the ritual. A huge wave washes over them, nearly pulling them out with its flow. The flame diminishes, flickers slowly as they link arms, holding each other against the pull of the ocean. As the wave recedes, a breath of air rescues the flame and sparks it into life, catching the dry tinder at the upper edges of the cave, warming them, lighting up the images they have painted on the walls.

In the glow, whales rise up rock ledges, sea horses hang from seaweed homes, dolphins swim with their young, birdwomen with huge wingspans fly over the cave walls. A mother turtle lays scores of eggs and further down a slit in the cavern, the turtles hatch, each one heading for the ocean. A hawk hovers above, waiting for a feed. But the turtles have formed circles around those crawling toward the ocean, protecting them. Finally, they enter the sea, free at last.

Across the flames, Cowrie catches Peta's eye before

she disappears. Flames roar around her, inside her, warming every part of her body, licking her like tongues from within. She is wet to their touch, feeling fire rise in her loins, up through her belly, entering every cell, warming her throughout, touching her with tenderness. Peta.

There are voices in the distance, wahine singing, holding toetoe branches high over their heads, their waiata turning into a wild chanting that issues from the mouth of the cavern and hovers over the waves, the wind carrying the voices far out to sea where the wings of a strange but elegant flying creature, half fish, half bird, rises from the ocean. Hokioi, the dream bird, is sung into life by women and released into the welcoming night sky.

Peta and Cowrie are walking the Rainbow Bridge from their island to the mainland. Peta leans over to see the ocean. Her hand slips from Cowrie's and she plunges into the black water below. Within seconds, a sleek dolphin surfaces where Peta fell. It lets out a haunting cry, as if in farewell. A mate swims toward the dolphin. They dive out of the water in unison and disappear into the dark ocean beyond.

Cowrie wakes sweating. She throws the duvet aside. The night is hot and sticky. The surf pounds in the distance. Taking the half coconut shell Paneke and Keo gave her in Hawai'i, she scoops water from the bowl next to her bed and pours it over her head, letting it trickle down her body and on to the sheets below.

Moonlight slants across the room, hovering over a picture of Peta and Nanduye standing victorious on the golf course they helped win back for the Kahnawake Reservation Committee, the Mohawk flag dancing in the breeze behind them. She picks up the picture, kisses Peta, then lights her sweetgrass. Smoke rises, obscuring Nanduye from the photo for a moment. Gradually, the sweetgrass burns back toward the abalone shell which is tied to its end. The shell is tinged before Cowrie can save it. As if hypnotised, she watches it blacken at the edges. The tie that holds the shell to the remainder of the sweetgrass burns and the small abalone drops to the floor.

"Cowrie, what's that smell? You burning sweetgrass again, or is the cottage on fire?" yells Mere from the next room.

"It's OK, whaene. Just some sweetgrass. Woke from a nightmare. Go back to sleep. I'm fine."

"You sure?"

"'Ae."

"Ka pai."

Cowrie picks the delicate abalone from the floor. She turns it over in her hand, the moonlight catching the soft pink, blue and pounamu shades, then raises the shell to her lips, using her tongue to lick away the surface burning until it shines. She takes her hei matau from her neck and threads the abalone onto the leather, so the shell sits next to her coconut turtle and carved bone fish-hook. Now Peta's gift lies on her naked skin, she feels calmer. The wild surf rides the beach beyond, jubilant to be crashing on to the sand in the embrace of a full moon, her spring tide licking the feet of the dunes.

Irihapeti stands over little Maata, helping her make holes in the soil tray for puriri seeds. Maata's face is lined with concentration. She pokes her fingers into the black earth and carefully places one seed, then another, until the entire tray is full. Gently, she sprinkles water over the soil and beams up at Irihapeti joyously. Irihapeti smiles back and thanks her for her work. Maata sees Cowrie entering the nursery and beckons her over.

"Tena koe, Maata. You gonna fill all these?" asks Cowrie, indicating the dozens of trays waiting for their seed.

"'Ae," beams Maata, reaching out for the second tray diligently.

"Ka pai! You'll probably be running this nursery when I return to Te Kotuku."

"Hang on there, mate. I'm not ready to retire yet," grins Irihapeti. "Maata, would you like to keep planting puriri while I show Cowrie the seeds we've selected for her to take back to the Tomales Bay Nursery?"

Maata nods her head, too intent on the planting to answer. Cowrie is delighted to see her so involved. Irihapeti leads Cowrie from the workroom to the shade house. "She still has nightmares but she's so much better now. Every day she comes to the nursery after kohanga ends and stays here until dinner time. Doesn't want to leave."

"That's great, Iri. I can hardly believe the change

in her. Has that bastard father ever fronted up at Te Aroha meetings?"

"Yep. He had to face a committee from his marae and representatives from his own iwi. His mother was in tears and his father looked as if he'd kill the fella. Reckon that's where the harm started. His old man beat him as a kid, and his mother. He went on to do the same."

"Was Maata beaten by him?"

"Not that we know. But there's some evidence that she was sexually interfered with."

"I thought as much, from the nature of her disturbance and some of the pictures she was drawing at kohanga reo before I left. Shit! So what was the outcome of the meeting?"

"He and his old man had to agree to attend rehabilitation workshops with other abusers from his iwi, and Maata's grandmother is also going to a support group run by her local marae and Rape Crisis. Since she refused to leave him, it was decided that Maata was best here, where she's known, rather than living with her grandparents at Tolaga Bay. Especially while her grandfather is still in rehab."

"Thank Pele for that! Sounds like the case had the best results possible under the circumstances."

"Well, yes, but it's still gonna take generations to change anything. I got the feeling that neither of the fellas would be in rehab but for it being marae justice and the only alternative to a prison term."

"Yeah, but imagine how useful prison would be. Just cement the old habits and provide a few more. At least this way there's a chance the patterns can be broken, new ways learned."

"You're right. I just get frustrated with the time it takes. Now, d'ya wanna see what goodies we've prepared for your friends at Tomales Bay?"

"Sure."

"You sound like a bloody Yank when you say that Cowrie!"

"Sorry. Got used to it over there. C'mon, then, gi's a squizzie at ya seeds!"

Irihapeti laughs. "Jeez, sis, you're one extreme or the other! No in between."

"Yeah, well I have been told that before. So what's new?"

"These," Irihapeti replies, pointing to a row of young pohutukawa with yellow spikes exploding from their fingertips. They look just like the Hawai'ian lehua from the o'hia tree. Irihapeti notices her surprise. "Yep, they're from those seeds you brought back to Mere from Paneke. I've checked the temperatures with Clem at Tomales Bay and we reckon they'll grow well there, if they do OK here. It's a bit colder but they like the raw coastal climate."

Cowrie bends to examine the lehua more closely. The yellow blossom is startling, darker than in Hawai'i, possibly because of the shade house. Beside the o'hia trees are native pohutukawa, their red spikes erect, as if issuing a blood challenge. She remembers Paneke crying out to her when she broke off the lehua before entering into Pele's crater, the scarlet explosion ringing in her ears afterwards. The heat enters her bone carving, scorching it into her skin. Flames sizzle up her arm, around her head. She feels dizzy.

Irihapeti turns to see Cowrie sway backward, then stumble into the bags of compost behind. She reaches down and notices Cowrie's eyes are dazed, as if she is in another place. Gradually, she comes around.

"What happened?"

"You just smelled the blossom and went troppo, sis!"

"Yeah. I need to get outa here. The heat's too much."

"C'mon, Cowrie, let's have a juice. You can check out the rest of the plants and seeds later tonight when it's cooler." Irihapeti leads Cowrie back to Mere's cottage where they drink fresh orange and mango juice. Cowrie wonders why Pele is returning now, what lessons are in store for her from the Goddess of the Volcano. She decides not to mention it to Irihapeti until she's figured it out for herself.

After kohanga, Cowrie takes Maata across the dunes to dig tuatua for dinner. Between them, Mere's handwoven kete, still wet from last night's feed. They walk the beach until they reach the driftwood log where Kuini, Irihapeti, Cowrie and the women writers' group had hung their clothes before entering the sea to celebrate their sculpting of a giant sandcastle in the shape of a sea egg. Cowrie tells Maata the story as they strip off their outer layers, ready to get wet and sandy. Maata asks many questions.

"So what happened to the egg? Did the tide wash it away?"

"Yes, eventually, but as the water came up around the moat, we sang waiata and did a ritual to celebrate all our journeys."

"What did you sing?"

"Wahine ma."

Maata bursts into song: *"Wahine ma, wahine ma, maranga mai, maranga mai, kia kaha!"*

She knows the waiata by heart. "Did you learn that at kohanga, Maata?"

"'Ae. And we did actions to go with it." Maata demonstrates, grabbing a broken toetoe branch lying half buried in the sand and using it to emphasise her point in the final *kia kaha*. "It's urging women to gather round and help each other be strong. Us girls sing it skipping too. See." Maata skips in rhythm to the beat. Cowrie laughs. This young child seems to incorporate her mixed heritage, be aware of her strength as a wahine toa, even at this age. She wishes she'd had the benefit of the kohanga when she was growing up but knows that living with Mere was the next best thing.

"C'mon, Cowrie. Let's dig tuatua now!" Maata pulls at her arm and then rushes off with the kete, down to the water's edge. The tide isn't quite low enough and they need to plough knee deep into the water to reach the best tuatua beds. Maata's arms are too short to reach the shellfish and still keep her head above the water. She panics when a large wave washes over her.

"Hey Maata. Do it this way."

Cowrie takes her by the hand and shows her how to use the tips of her toes to dig down to explore for live tuatua. Maata likes this method and soon she is dancing about, her tiny toes and then whole foot burrowing into the moving sand, her voice screaming every time her toes touch a tuatua. She picks up a shellfish still feeding, its long tongue spitting out juice as it retracts into the safety of its shell.

"Look, Cowrie! It's alive. It's spitting at me!" She turns the elongated end of the shellfish toward her nose and nearly goes cross-eyed watching the long tongue disappear back inside the shell.

"It sure is, Maata, but make sure you don't let go of the kete or we'll all be without a feed tonight."

The basket is not yet full enough to stand its ground against the waves, and begins to float away as Cowrie speaks. Maata lunges toward it, tripping over as a large wave catches her by surprise. Before Cowrie can reach her, the wave draws her into its undertow and the heavy swell pulls her out to sea. Cowrie drops her handful of tuatua and dives into the next wave, lashing out wildly, as strongly as she can. She knows the dangers of this beach so well and curses herself for ever letting Maata enter the water. She should have waited until the tide was lower and they could have dug for tuatua in safety. The last thing Maata needs is to endure another scary experience right now.

She can hear Maata's voice, high pitched in her panic. The child is floating so she moves out slower than Cowrie, who dives beneath and beyond each wave. But the swell has taken her small body beyond the breakers and out to sea. Cowrie must make sure she doesn't get herself caught in a rip tide or they will both be history. She prays to Pele to give her the strength to reach Maata in time to get them back to shore.

The surf pounds in her ears, her heart lunging at each new wave, her arms tearing at the water. She can no longer see Maata but hears her voice in the distance. The wind lashes the surf at her face. She takes a huge breath and dives beneath the waves, swimming under them so she is not pulled back by their power. Her body expands to hold the intake of air and her fins scoop the water skilfully, her shell balancing her as she skims beneath the waves rapidly, effortlessly, until she reaches Maata. Her nose surfaces first, bumping against Maata's shoulders. The child floats on the water, still, lifeless. Cowrie swims under her, lifting her small body onto her back, coaxing her arms around her neck, holding her hands gently between her teeth so the child does not slip off, then eyes the approaching surf, searching for a wave that will coast them towards the shore.

Back on the beach, she applies the kiss of life to Maata until gradually the small child starts to cough up sea water. Relieved, Cowrie rolls her over to let out the salty remains, then wraps Maata in her towel, crooning to her, holding her close to warm her frail little body. Gradually, the child's eyes open, as she reenters life. Tears of relief drop onto Maata's face and she wipes them away with the edge of her lavalava, kissing her cheeks. "Maata, sweet child, I'm so glad you came back."

Maata shivers. She smiles weakly. Cowrie holds her close, rocks her body, singing to her softly, knowing how well Maata responded to this in her grief at the kohanga. Soon, her body warms up and her eyes begin to sparkle again. Cowrie knows she must now get her home, pour some hot liquid into her body and get her to the warmth of a soft bed.

She lifts Maata, gathers their clothes, and carries her back up the beach toward the cottage. As they disappear into the dunes, the surf sweeps up over their kete, still lying on its side in the water, and releases the remaining tuatua into the sea. They quickly dive under the sand, burrowing their way back to freedom with the power of their tongues.

Cowrie bathes Maata in a tub, adding boiling water from the stove fire to the rainwater already gathered in the tank. Maata sits still as Cowrie pours jug after jug of warm water over her body. Like Cowrie, she loves the feel of the liquid on her skin, the soothing touch as it trickles down her belly. But her eyes are still haunted. Cowrie worries that this experience may damage Maata's recovery from abuse, cause old memories to resurface. The child has hardly spoken. But gradually, as the water warms her body, she regains her voice.

"Kia ora, Cowrie," she whispers into her ear.

"Why are you thanking me, Maata? I nearly got you drowned."

Maata looks into her face and reaches a finger to touch Cowrie's cheek. She murmurs, "'Cos you saved me. I was really scared when I cried out to you, but I knew if I just lay there and floated you'd come and rescue me."

"How did you know I'd make it against all those waves and the undertow?"

"'Cos you belong to turtle iwi. Remember that story about the Turtle Woman you told me and how it was possible to swim back into the wave that nearly destroyed you? Well, I remembered it when I was ·frightened and I knew you'd reach me and carry me back. So then I relaxed and just floated on the water."

"Thank Pele for that. It probably saved your life, Maata."

Mere enters the room with some hot milk. "Thank Laukiamanuikahiki, Cowrie. She sounds like the rescuer."

"'Ae. True enough."

"But why on earth you let little Maata dig tuatua in those waves is beyond me, Cowrie. You should know better."

"Yeah, I should, and I feel ashamed too."

Maata looks at them, nodding her head from side to side as she's seen grown-ups do. "You shouldn't blame Cowrie, Aunty Mere. Without her talkstory, I might not be here now. I got rescued by Turtle Woman and that makes me special, like Cowrie."

Mere looks at Maata, then at her daughter. "Well, young Maata, you just might be right there. She is special, even though she misbehaved, and you've learned the lesson of the waves. You know how to rescue yourself now. That means you're a grown-up and to celebrate, I think I'll make you some pikelets for tea."

"With real blackberry jam and lots of whipped cream?"

"We made jam this summer, but the marae cats finished off today's cream. You'll have to wait till Eruera comes after the cows are milked tonight."

"No. Want pikelets and jam now," stresses Maata, slipping back into her childhood needs.

Mere chuckles, disappearing into the kitchen. Cowrie lifts Maata from the tub, dries her and wraps warm pyjamas around her, tucking her up in bed. "How about a hottie, Maata? I know it's summer but you must stay warm. You're probably still in shock."

"Want the hottie Aunty Mere always gives me when I stay over. With the teddy bear head and the knitted coat."

Cowrie remembers it well, since she loved it as a

child also. She reaches the hot water bottle from the nail behind the door and takes it into the kitchen to fill with boiling water. Mere is mixing the flour and eggs for pikelets. The kettle is already steaming on the fire. Cowrie pours the water, filling the teddy shape, thinking about how much she loved this ritual as a child.

Mere nods, gesturing with her head toward the hottie. "Brings back more than a few memories, eh Cowrie?"

"Yep. And good ones too." She hugs Mere with one arm, while holding the hottie out with the other. Then she reaches for the bear cap and screws it tight.

Maata looks so peaceful when she returns, cuddled up in her bed, only the top of her head above the sheets. Cowrie slips the hottie under the covers. Maata reaches out. "I like it here, on my tummy," she says. Cowrie smiles to herself, knowing that is her comfort zone. At least Maata can ask for what she needs. She bends over to kiss the child good night and Maata's little fingers reach up to touch the small abalone at her neck. "This one's new. Whered'ya get it?" she says, fingering the soft edges of the shell with its pink and blue interior.

"My friend Peta sent it out from Great Turtle Island." Maata looks perplexed. "You know—she's the one who took me to the Tomales Bay Nursery and that's the place Irihapeti is preparing the seeds and plants for."

"D'you love her more than you love me?" Maata asks seriously.

Cowrie has to think a minute. Maata's directness has taken her by surprise.

"Well, it's a different kind of loving, Maata. But no less powerful for that. I love Peta and I love you and I love Mere and Irihapeti and Kuini. And these are all deep loves. People who are very important to me. But each love has different qualities. Each one is special."

"You sure?"

"More sure than I am about anything else on earth, Maata."

"So I'm one of the five best?"

Cowrie laughs. "Reckon so, kid. And only the very, very best get to meet Willemina."

"Who's Willemina?"

Cowrie walks over to the old carved chest in the corner of the room. She heaves it open and takes out a rather bedraggled looking stuffed pet with straggly fur and piercing eyes. She returns and places it on Maata's chest. "Meet Willemina Wombat. She was given to me by a very special friend when I was at school, an Aboriginal girl from Wagga Wagga. She and I played together at school and told stories on the beach at night. Most of the other kids left us alone. But we had each other."

"Where is she now?"

Cowrie looks sad. "I don't know. She was adopted and one day her mother came to school and just took her away. All I had left was the wombat she gave me. I've treasured it ever since. I still hope I'll meet up with her again one day."

"Can I keep her after tonight?"

Cowrie hesitates a moment, then says "Kia ora. You can look after her until I get back to Te Kotuku. You need to treat her with care and make sure you give her lots of loving—and she will love you back. And any time you miss me, or get frightened or angry, you can tell her and she will understand. Wombats are good at that."

"Does she talk?"

"Only if you know how to listen. Now, it's sleep time for you, Maata."

"Not before my pikelets."

"I'd nearly forgotten. Mere, how's the cooking going?"

Mere appears with a tray of pikelets and Maata manages three before she is fast asleep in Cowrie's arms, her hottie over her legs and Willemina Wombat clutched to her chest. Cowrie slides her under the covers and slips out of the room.

Mere is cleaning up in the kitchen and asks Cowrie what she wants for dinner.

"A hug and forgiveness. I was truly stupid today."

"Yes, you were. But all's well that ends well, Cowrie. Be thankful Maata didn't panic too much."

"I am."

"She learned the lesson it took you most of your life to get, so she's well on her way now," offers Mere, hugging Cowrie.

"Reckon she'll be OK?"

"I think so. Ka pai."

"Since I didn't bring back kai moana and lost your kete to the sea, then I reckon it's my turn to cook. You relax while I prepare a treat." Mere sits at the kitchen table, while Cowrie fries aubergines dipped in egg and flour. Her mother tells her of the progress at Te Aroha and of plans to get a full time co-ordinator to run the sexual abuse programme since it has become a resource for all the iwi.

"Got anyone in mind yet, Mere?"

"'Ae. Kuini."

"Really? Would she give up her university position to do it?"

"We've already talked about it. She feels she'd be more appreciated for her work here and the university marae is just using her for all its official occasions to impress mostly Pakeha visitors. I think she's ready to make the break."

"She didn't whisper a word of this to me. Tainui trickster!"

"She was sworn to secrecy. We all were. We had to seek funding before we could make it official and that just came through this week. Then I had to make sure the iwi were happy with her as co-ordinator."

"And were they?"

"Mostly. A few didn't like it."

"Why?"

"Oh, you know. The usual problems. You'll never get full consensus on anyone."

"You mean some of them didn't like the fact she is lesbian?"

Mere is silent a for a while. "Yes, that came into it. But it wasn't the sole reason."

"Typical. She's far and away the best at what she does, but it's never enough when you're a dyke."

"Cowrie, you know I don't like that word."

"OK, Mere. I will honour that. But naming is a part of reclaiming what is ours, using the prejudice against us in a positive way."

Mere is silent. There are still some areas where they feel oceans apart. But Mere has fought to get Kuini as co-ordinator of Te Aroha and Cowrie knows it would not have been easy. "So what's the final outcome?"

"We met this afternoon and more people wanted Kuini than either of the other two. So, I thought we'd call her tomorrow and see if she's still interested and invite her up for the weekend to talk over the details."

"Great idea! I'll smoke some kahawai in preparation and we'll have a feast to celebrate!" Cowrie hums as she turns over the eggplant, excited at the thought of seeing Kuini again.

Maata stays at Mere's until the weekend so Cowrie can keep an eye on her and make sure she's recovering satisfactorily. Remarkably, she appears to have taken the incident in her stride and is actually milking it for all she can get at the kohanga. Cowrie wonders if the experience of watching abuse made her shut off to pain, and fears she will do the same now, masking it as an exciting adventure.

On Saturday morning, she is working with Irihapeti in the nursery, sorting the seeds and plants to take back to Tomales Bay for Clem, when a gypsy caravan draws up outside, spraying dust all over the shade house. "Bloody hippies," Irihapeti mumbles. The dust settles to reveal a beautifully crafted house-truck made of mottled kauri with stained glass windows in the side. Brightly coloured geraniums in red, pink, white and indigo fill the window boxes. The wheels have turned wooden spokes, and the outside beams display traditional Maori carvings. The door opens and a large woman carrying a kete bulging with taonga steps out.

"Kuini! I don't believe it! Where did you get this amazing truck?"

"Tena korua, Cowrie, Irihapeti. This, my sisters, is my new home, bought with my redundancy package from the University of Waikato, and hopefully to be set up over there between Mere's cottage and the dunes when I take up my position here at Te Aroha."

They hongi, then Cowrie hugs her friend, fighting back tears of joy. "Hey Kuini, you finally did it. Left the academy to follow your dreams. Mere filled me in on the background. Ka pai, sister, ka pai."

"So where's the welcoming committee then, eh?"

"Not so fast, Kuini. Due protocol and all that," replies Cowrie, grinning. "Besides, we didn't know exactly when you'd be arriving and I think Mere needs to talk you through a few things first."

"I know, Snapping Turtle. I'se just havin' ya on!" Kuini beams at her.

Cowrie feels a pang of nostalgia. The only other person who calls her Turtle is Peta and she hasn't had a letter from her in over three weeks now, which is most unusual. She fears the worst, but hopes it's just a mail strike.

"So how did ya come by this magnificent house-truck?" asks Irihapeti, apparently no longer worried that it blew dust all over her plants.

"I fell in love with her a few months ago when I saw her at Karioi. The owners were two women selling up to go overseas. They needed the money and I needed a portable home, so we did a deal. Then I got Apirana to do the carvings. We had a great time figuring out what we wanted."

"They're beautiful, Kuini. I specially like that double canoe. Reminds me of the Hawai'ian waka."

"'Ae, Cowrie, but this is a Tainui one. Among a fleet of about ten waka, there were single and double canoes. Hence Tainui—The Great Tide—commanded by Hoturoa. See, he's the dude out front here." She points to a strong warrior at the bow of the waka. "He's primal ancestor of Ngati Maniapoto and other Waikato iwi."

"I never realised how similar the construction is to the Hawai'ian canoes," says Cowrie, running her hands over the carved sides of the waka, admiring the intricacy of Api's work.

"This waka is called the *Tainui* and the original was carved with greenstone adzes by Ngahue, an early sea explorer and navigator from Hawai'iki. The *Tainui* brought kumara, gourds and other plants to Aotearoa and then took the shape of stone at Kawhia, to retain the significance of her journey for future generations. So here she is, sailing across my own travelling waka. I've named the housetruck *Tainui* to reclaim our ancestral journey."

"Whakamiharo! I love her, Kuini."

"Well, traditionally a *he* probably, but I felt enough poetic licence to have a transgendered waka for this journey," laughs Kuini. "So where's my cuppa tea?" Arm in arm, they walk over to the cottage catching up on news. Cowrie is envious that Kuini has had the courage to leave the university and, over morning tea, tells her of her own struggles at Berkeley and how she hopes to resolve them.

"Good luck, sis. If Waikato University can't get it together for local wahine, then I can't see the Yanks doing it! But if anyone can break the boundaries, it's you, Cowrie!"

"Gee thanks, Kuini! That really gives me hope!"

"Hey, don't take it to heart. It's just that universities are like any large institution. They look after themselves. Where we fit their grand plan, we're accepted. Otherwise, it's every bastard for himself. I'm sick of it. I'd rather work at Te Kotuku in Te Aroha than have to deal with idiotic administrators daily. At least I'll be able to effect change on our own terms."

"Kia ora, Kuini. You're right. But won't it be tough dealing with offenders daily?"

"You just watch me, sis. I've been waiting a lifetime to enact this utu!" Kuini poses as a warrior, using a wooden spoon as her taiaha. Cowrie has to laugh, knowing that Kuini is one of the most fair and gentle people she's ever met, though she never suffers fools.

Mere emerges from the wash-house to see Kuini thrusting a wooden spoon threateningly toward Cowrie. "So this is how the new Te Aroha co-ordinator resolves conflict, eh?"

Kuini looks sheepish until Mere smiles and gives her a hongi welcome. Then they settle at the kitchen table to talk over the details of the work at Te Aroha and plan a hui to discuss the terms of contract so that everyone is happy with the deal. Then Kuini will be officially welcomed on to the marae.

While they korero, Cowrie busies herself opening the fresh oysters Kuini has given them, dripping lemon juice on to their shells, savouring the treat to come. She remembers the feast of oysters she and Peta had at the Miwok Tomales Bay Oyster Farm and how they pitched their tent in the night close to a bin of empty shells. Then woke to oyster stench in the morning as the tractor came to take them away, nearly knocking down the tent. She smiles to herself, wondering what might have happened if Jake hadn't seen the tent in time. But the memory is tinged with anxiety. Maybe Peta and Nanduye have found more in common than their friendship? Maybe Peta plans to stay at Kahnawake Reservation? Maybe that was the significance of her dream, where Peta swam away with her dolphin mate? Mere interrupts her broken shell thoughts. "You gonna drown those oysters in lemon, or do we get a chance to taste them?"

Cowrie carries the first plate of oysters, decorated with edible nasturtiums growing within reach of the open kitchen window, over to the table. Mere takes a bright yellow nasturtium and sucks the sweet honey treacle from the stem hanging below the flower, then tongues an oyster from its shell. The mixed tastes are exquisite. She groans pleasurably.

Kuini steals a glance at Cowrie and whispers, "One of us, sis?"

"Maybe, but for a few generations," whispers Cowrie, smiling. But the oysters bring mixed memories for her and she longs to lie again in Peta's arms beside the waterfall at Yosemite, drinking in the roar of the falls, watching the bluejays titter with delight at their closeness.

Hopi Reservation,
Big Mountain, Arizona.

Haku, Cowrie,

Finally, a letter from me! Nanduye and I were
invited to Big Mountain, Arizona, to
celebrate the anniversary of the women
ripping down the federal fences erected in
the government's desperate attempt to try
to split Hopi and Navajo tribes and retain
their access to uranium on reservation land.
We've been camping with Uretsete and some
of the women in your storytelling group—
Ruth, DK and a large woman who reminds me
of you—Suzanne. Nanduye and I could not
believe that some of them hadn't heard
about the resistance movement at Big
Mountain before Uretsete suggested they
travel with her to mark the annual
remembrance. But it's great that they
came.

At night we meet to discuss resistance and
ongoing health and access issues that all
our tribes experience, each offering new
tales of struggle and hope. Afterwards, the
men go down into their sweat lodge and we
women light our fire above ground and tell
our own stories. There has been so much
intermarriage that these tales are
representing many other groups now. Mostly

170

Navajo, Cree, Hopi and Kahnawake talkstory—as you'd say—but on the third night, we convinced Ruth, DK and Suzanne to contribute. Ruth shared a moving story her grandmother told her and taught us a Yiddish resistance song. DK was unusually shy, after what you've said about her. Did you realise she had a Polish grandfather who survived the Holocaust? Fascinating details. She didn't even know much about him until the storytelling class, then she went back East, visited her family and asked awkward questions, finally breaking the silence. Suzanne admitted she felt out of place as a southern white woman, but told us what it was like growing up as a fat outsider in a thin-loving, redneck culture. The hatred she endured was familiar and touched us all.

You have been with us in spirit. One night Uretsete read us a poem you'd published in one of their texts, "Rainbow Warrior Women", about the women's resistance at Big Mountain and how Hinewirangi

> with her medicine bundle containing
> the dark, moist, sacred earth of
>   Aotearoa,
> placed it on the Navajo-Hopi border
> created by the united states government
> and sang her waiata of peace.

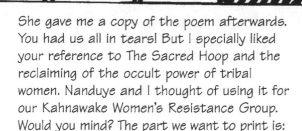

She gave me a copy of the poem afterwards. You had us all in tears! But I specially liked your reference to The Sacred Hoop and the reclaiming of the occult power of tribal women. Nanduye and I thought of using it for our Kahnawake Women's Resistance Group. Would you mind? The part we want to print is:

> Rainbow Warrior Woman, I hold you close
> in times of weakness
> remembering always that I have the power
> to kill at a glance;
> drop blood in my enemy's soup
> if I so desire.

Ok? Let us know soon.

En route to Big Mountain we flew into Texas, and Nanduye had a meeting with Chad's lawyer over Chad and Ela's custody case. He was one tough dude! However, we did some snooping and found out Chad has a fancy lady on the side—"a blonde barmaid with huge silicon tits" according to the PI—and he has photographic proof of Chad's adultery. So Nanduye believes Ela will get guardianship of their children. However, you never know in Texas, where the colour of your skin may prove you as unfit a mother as a married Texan cowboy with "a piece of fluff in tow" as the PI put it. But at least Nanduye now has evidence to build the case around. We phoned Ela—who was more relieved that she'd keep the kids than upset about the girlfriend. Sounds like she and Koana have formed a happy family unit with both their kids. Let's hope the Texan court don't decide to follow up that story and try to prove they are a gay couple. Koana assures us they are "just good friends". So keep your fingers crossed on that one.

So how are you, sweet Turtle? I've loved your letters and drawings from Te Kotuku and like to think of you back in the embrace of your whanau and the marae. Enjoyed the story about you and Kuini sending fresh fish through the fastpost service. You're incorrigible, Cowrie! But that's what I love about you. We could do with some of your wild ideas for our Kahnawake Women's Resistance Group! But I'm also coming up with a few of my own. I love being with Nanduye again. She brings out the warrior in me, but is soft and sensitive as well.

Will write again after we return to Kahnawake. Shall I send you out some more sweetgrass? Enjoy your summer. It's freezing back at the reservation now. But my work is exciting and challenging and I'm glad to be here. Finally able to do more for my people than back in Oakland.

Take care of yourself, Turtle—Peta.

Cowrie reads the letter three times, sipping her tea, relishing the thought of being at Big Mountain with all the women, glad her students have participated and grown through the storytelling classes. So wonderful to hear from Peta again. Even her handwriting has that soft familiar flow she has come to love. But beneath the joy, a niggling doubt. Peta seems to appreciate her still, but the bond with Nanduye is clearly growing. Will it remain a close friendship and work relationship or will it enter into sensual and sexual areas? The temptation must be there for them both. Even the thought pierces her soul. Maybe her dream of Peta swimming away with another mate was just her own fear, her own insecurity? The only way to fight this is to throw herself into her work and life at the marae and do the same on her return to UC Berkeley. If Peta falls for Nanduye, there is nothing she can do but let go and wish them well. But she prays the spiritual union she shares with Peta is strong enough to withstand that temptation if it surfaces.

"Tena koe, dreaming Turtle. Got a minute?" Kuini's face appears at the window.

"Sure. What for?"

"Well, I've just been through a thorough grilling from all the iwi involved in the appointment of coordinator and it looks like I will have the job. So I thought, who better to celebrate with?"

"Kia ora, Kuini. That's great! Come on in."

"Na. I think Mere will be bringing the elders back here after their meeting at the marae ends, so let's go to the Tainui and crack champagne on the side of my waka!" Cowrie grins. There's no alcohol allowed on this marae. Still, she imagines frothy wet sparkles sliding down the side of the house truck. She folds

Peta's letter, places it in her breast pocket, and exits out the porch window.

Kuini has been allowed to park the Tainui beyond the marae dwellings up in the sand dunes. She has a breathtaking view of the wild Tasman ocean breaking on to the West Coast. "Choice eh mate? All I need now to get famous is a bloody grand piano down on that beach!" Cowrie laughs. The success of *The Piano* has long been a joke among locals. While filmed here on the West Coast and evoking its awesome power, the colonial depiction of Maori in the film as noble savages, and thus unthreatening to overseas Pakeha audiences, especially Hollywood, riled more than a few feathers on the local marae.

"I reckon we could oblige, Kuini! I could get Eruera, Hone and the boys to drag that old honky tonk from the games room down on to the sand. We could paint our faces with moko and try to sail her out on our waka through the surf."

"Not bloody likely! Anyway, I wish Holly Wotsit had drowned with her piano. That's the only way the film could have retained its integrity. Resurfacing to live happily ever after with that pornographer really sucks!"

"Yeah, the only good bit was her tin finger. She could've poked him in the goolies with that and run off with one of the gorgeous local wahine."

"That's about as witchy as your poem dropping blood in the enemy's soup, Cowrie. Not that I haven't thought of it several times when entertaining the university chancellor's mates down at Waikato."

"Hey, hang on! I'll have you know that my poem has been read out at Big Mountain, Arizona, no less. Listen to this." From her breast pocket, Cowrie extracts Peta's letter and reads it to Kuini.

"That's great, Cowrie. You boomer! I've always

said the ripples from our work keep moving long after the initial creative process has ended. This proves it. But tell me more about the storytelling group. You only mentioned it briefly in letters. Sounds exciting."

Kuini fires up the gas stove on the bench for a cuppa while Cowrie explains why the group began and how it has come to mean as much as, if not more than, the literature classes themselves. How the students have relished it because of the predominance of secondary theory in all their other courses, leaving them feeling isolated and distanced from the women's lives they are studying.

Kuini agrees that it's an occupational hazard in academia. At least running the marae at Waikato she had a balance between that and the theory needed to work on her thesis and to teach mainstream courses. Between sips of tea and delicious strips of raw stingray Kuini has marinated in orange and mango juice overnight, they discuss the joys and struggles of university life, their hopes on entering the academy, its lack of responsiveness to different cultural needs in practice, despite the stated goals in theory.

As the sun sets, their conversation is broken by the singing of waiata up at the marae. Orange light enters through the lead and stained glass windows, casting a warm glow around the interior of the *Tainui*. Carefully carved kauri panels, each depicting different ancestral stories, seem to move with the reflected colours of orange shifting into ruby red then pale green pounamu as dusk encroaches. Through the swirling kauri waves, a waka named *Mangarara* appears out of the woodwork with Whaketoro in the shape of a crawling octopus at the helm. Perched on the bow of the mighty migration waka are pihoihoi and torea, pipits and oystercatchers, brought over by the Mangarara canoe to Aotearoa.

Outside the window, scanning the beach for kai moana thrown up by the tide, a lone oystercatcher runs toward the surf and grabs a half pipi shell flung on to the sand by the wave. Eagerly, it gorges on the sweet flesh, then flips the shell aside, diving its beak into the wet swirling tide, in time to catch a crab just before she re-enters her hole.

Te Kotuku o Hokianga
Tai Tokerau
Aotearoa.

Kia ora Peta,

Mahalo for your wonderful letter from Big
Mountain. Brought back warm memories.
Glad you enjoyed my poem. Tell Uretsete I
feel honoured she read it out. Fine to use
my words as you wish. I'm rapt the students
made it too. I can't wait to hear about it in
class. Good news about Ela. She and Koana
are close friends—but I think Koana
wouldn't mind it being more. Time will tell!

You and Nanduye are doing excellent work
together. Rapt it is so personally satisfying
as well. I realise Oakland was a compromise
for you. Better to be in the thick of the
action. Does this mean you'll be staying on?
Or will you return to Oakland after your
contract ends?

I try not to worry, but even in your tender
closeness I feel you swimming away from me.
I dreamed we were walking the Rainbow
Bridge from Santa Cruz Island to
Carpinteria and you looked over and
disappeared into the dark ocean to rise up
again and swim away with a beautiful dolphin
mate. Is this my fear or is it the future?

Kuini is now co-ordinator of Te Aroha and lives in a fantastic housetruck she converted which is by the sand dunes, with an exquisite view of the ocean. You'd love it. She calls it her waka Tainui, after her ancestral canoe. It's magic inside and out. Last night we had a ceremony officially welcoming her on to the marae and a hangi afterwards. Juicy pork, lamb, kahawai and kumara, topped with puha and pineapple! What a mixture! But delish. Our mouths could've make music together after that feast. Your fiery tongue on my oceans would be enough to make Pele sizzle into the sea. Hope you still feel that way about me. Can't help wondering, despite your lovely letter.

Only one more week here. Irihapeti and I have been sorting through the seeds and plants for me to take back to Clem and the Tomales Bay Nursery. We had to get clearances from government departments clearances first. Hope I'm allowed through customs in San Fran! Will miss you not being there to greet me—but Uretsete wrote a PC saying she and Ruth will meet me at the airport. Are they an item? That'd be fascinating!

Starting to get nervous about the new semester and thesis plans. Brief note from

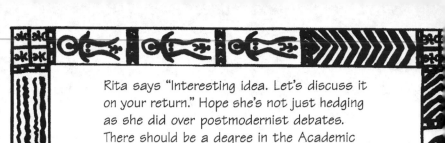

Rita says "Interesting idea. Let's discuss it on your return." Hope she's not just hedging as she did over postmodernist debates. There should be a degree in the Academic Art of Fence-Sitting. She'd be a contender!

Will make this brief and call you on my return to the Bay Area. It's so tempting to just stay here and get involved on the marae—but then I may not see you for even longer. Besides, I'm excited about possibilities at UC and the talkstory options.

Howd'ya like this paper? All images from Maori rock drawings on caves here and Hawai'ian lava etchings, from my notebook of sketches. I can't wait for you to come to Aotearoa. We have amazing caves which would blow your mind. At Waitomo, we can float over pitch-black water with glowworms guiding us. Always reminds me of our ancestors navigating from Hawai'iki to Aotearoa by the stars. And here in Tai Tokerau, we have limestone caves that are sculpted from dreams—like the tufa shapes rising out of Lake Mono. Remember that kiss under the waterfall? You still transport me to those magic places, Peta. It's the spiritual essence that fires the eroticism for me. You too?

I now have the abalone shell you sent me with the sweetgrass beside my hei matau and coconut turtle, so I can feel you next to my skin day and night. She was singed with fire—with your essence—and I licked her delicately and sensuously until all her rainbow colours shone brightly, like open paua under the ocean.

I miss you, Sacred Fire. Talk to you soon,

Kia kaha

Arohanui

Cowrie XXX.

I tetahi we, ka haere whakatonga mai a
  Brutus
ki te moenga o Marama
Katahi ka tino whawhai nga tokorua nei!
Ka tino mataku a Marama, ka peke atu ki
  waho o te wini
katahi ka oma.

Cowrie holds up the book so the children can see the black cat, frightened by the dog, fly out the window, knocking down everything in her way. The kids gasp collectively as she turns the page, waiting to see what will happen next. Maata bursts into tears.

"It's OK, Maata. She'll return," says young Rewia, putting an arm around Maata's shoulder.

Cowrie reads on, and sure enough, the little girl is reunited with her black cat which steals back into her bed at night. Maata lets out a sigh of relief, along with a few others. It's nearly the end of the day so Cowrie packs them off, after making sure Maata is all right. Maata promises she'll tell Irihapeti the story when she reaches the nursery and says she felt scared the cat would never come back. She's still missing her mother. The scars remain with her, even though she seemed to recover better than many imagined.

There's a strange line between seeing so much pain you get used to it, even shut off from it and responding to the grief and abandonment in the myriad other ways it manifests throughout life. Cowrie wonders why she omitted to tell Peta about nearly drowning Maata. Was it because the fear of abandonment is always so close to the surface in her, and Maata's experiences remind her of this? She has never fully recovered from being abandoned by her birth mother at the Rawene Orphanage, even though Mere gave her the best upbringing she could have had. Maybe she didn't tell Peta because she still feels ashamed for putting Maata at such risk? What if it had sent the child back to the shocked state she was in after her mother was beaten to death and her father taken away? Her dream and the fear that Peta will leave her have raised the issue again. Yet Peta's letter was so warm and caring. She must not give in to the paranoia that such premonitions awake in her.

Kuini pokes her head around the kohanga reo door. "So whad'ya wanna do for your last night in Aotearoa before you return to Great Turtle Island, sis? Irihapeti and I plan on cooking you some delicious kai since Mere is working late at Horeke. The night's all yours."

"Kia ora, Kuini. I'm in the mood for a quiet night actually, and I've still got to pack my bags."

"No worries. Why don't just the three of us gather a few mussels, roast them over a fire on the beach and indulge in talkstory? Time we shared our dreams for the next year or so. Besides, I want to know when you're finally returning home to Aotearoa so I can plan a trip with you in *Tainui*. Between all our Nga Puhi and Tainui rellies, we should have a few good hick towns to visit!" She grins wickedly.

Cowrie cannot help smiling when Kuini's around. "OK. I've got to talk to Iri anyway to get the details on the plants and seeds for Clem."

"So, let's meet at the nursery at five so we've got plenty of daylight to enjoy."

"See you then."

"You OK, Turtle? You look a bit down?"

"Ka pai. Just that Maata cried during a story this arvo and suddenly I found myself wanting to do the same. It's that old sense of abandonment resurfacing. Thought I'd dealt with it but it keeps returning when least expected."

Kuini walks over and hugs Cowrie. "It's like the waves, Cowrie. They just keep coming no matter what. But the sea's not always like that. Sometimes it's calm and peaceful."

"Not here on the West Coast. It's relentless surging energy, wave after wave."

"Yeah, but you've got a choice, eh? You can dive in and be swept away or fish in the calm upper harbour!"

"You reckon it's that simple?"

"It's about as complex or simple as you wanna make it, sis. I reckon you're pining over Peta and you're not quite sure if she's pining over you as much."

"How did you know?"

"Just your tone, the faraway look in your eyes when you read me that letter she wrote from Big Mountain, the sadness I've glimpsed around you every now and again."

"That transparent, eh?"

"Not really. You're so bloody good at hiding it, most would never notice. But not your old mate Kuini. I can tell when you're putting up one of your 'don't mess with me—I'll be OK' defences."

"I will be OK, Kuini. Besides, it's just my fears. There's no substance this time. Peta is still close in her letters."

"So there you are! No worries." Kuini hugs her close and whispers, "See you at five, darlin'."

Cowrie walks to the cottage to pack, but can't get in the mood. She's torn between wanting to stay and wanting to leave. Why does she always feel like this, stretched between the desire to be in two places at once? It doesn't occur to her, yet, that her genetic inheritance, the circumstances of her birth, will always return her to that space, that her role is not only to break boundaries but also to build bridges between isolated islands and the mainland.

After sorting through the plants and seeds, which Irihapeti has packed tight and stapled, the three women head out over the dunes armed with knives and backpacks. The roar of the ocean hits them as they reach the last dune and slide down toward the beach. This sound never fails to thrill Cowrie. She relishes its timbre, recording each note to recall when she is tucked up in her loft in Oakland.

As they pass the spot where Cowrie and Maata collected tuatua, a shiver enters her body. The memory of that evening will always mark this place for her. Thank Pele that Maata kept her cool, seemed to know Cowrie would be able to make it through the surf to reach her. Strange that she recovered so well from this, yet could cry at the thought of a young girl losing her black cat. Kuini notices she is deep in thought, knows this is the place where Cowrie nearly lost Maata. She takes her hand gently. "Hey, Cowrie, relax. Turtle Woman came to save you both that night and she's within you now. Just remember she's there and you'll never be alone again, even when we're thousands of miles away back here in Aotearoa."

Cowrie smiles, amazed that Kuini can read her thoughts so clearly. "Yeah, she seems to swim into me when I most need her."

"That's because she's a spirit guide. She's a part of you and you're a part of her. She just comes to remind you of the strength within," Irihapeti adds.

They walk in silence along the great expanse of

beach at low tide, watching the oystercatchers run across the wet ripples as if they are wearing stilts, then suddenly plunge their long beaks into the sand, pulling out a crab or a sea snail. Their movement is highly entertaining and they seem to enjoy the hunt as much as the catch.

Finally they reach a rocky headland where the sea crashes against the reef and the juiciest black mussels succulently feed on taonga the ocean so graciously provides for them. After stashing their clothes on the dry sand, they strap knives to their legs and clamber up on to the reef. It is slippery around the large pools that lie like craters filled with ocean along the reef surface. Large mussels rear out of the water when each wave recedes, their shiny surfaces revealing the obsidian and cobalt blue flash of a tui in flight.

Each of the women perches on the edge of her chosen mussel bed and begins the delicate task of choosing which succulent shellfish will be best to take, making sure the rock is cleaned after cutting so that new mussels can grow and the resource is replenished. Cowrie extracts her fish knife from its sheath. It glints in the sun, sending a sharp memory piercing through her. She is back at Puako, astride the struggling ika, about to plunge her knife into the belly of the fish to rip out its guts and throw them to the starving wildcats. The anger that urged her on, her desire to protect Peni after the fish had attacked him, merges with her anger against the sea, and herself, for letting little Maata be dragged out in the swell. She struggles to cut off the roots of two mussels joined together. The sun keeps catching the edge of the knife, sending sharp flashes of light back into her eyes. She curses herself for telling Maata to keep hold of the kete. If only she'd kept her digging in the shallows above the water line. What if she'd been dragged out and left to drown in the devouring ocean?

As she reaches for a large mussel hanging off the far outcrop, Cowrie loses her footing and is left hanging onto a ridge. The waves thrust at her back as she clings to the slippery rock ledge. For a moment she considers letting go, giving herself to the ocean, relaxing into its watery embrace. Another wave hits her hard against the rocks, pushing her face into the ledge, grazing her cheeks and nose, and shoving her eyes inches from the shining knife blade. Instantly, she throws the knife up over the ledge, away from her, and clambers slowly around the side of the rocks, being careful each toe hold is perfectly placed, until she reaches the top of the basalt shelf. She sits gasping a moment. Kuini and Irihapeti are both on the far rocks, filling their kete together. Cowrie picks up the knife, wiping its blade against her thigh, washes her face in a pool then begins working on the beds above the water line.

Kuini is first to leave the rocks. She gathers driftwood to light the fire for their dinner. Irihapeti joins Cowrie and they make their way back to the beach. By now, Kuini's fire is blazing and she wets manuka in the surf to lay on top so the smoky flavour goes through the mussels as they heat. They pluck each mussel from the fire as it sizzles open and lay it on a nikau tray from a nearby palm. Their tales and laughter are infectious and soon Cowrie is caught up in their mood of celebration and humour.

The women savour the succulent kai moana, letting the juice run down their chins, over their bodies, as each mussel slides off the shell and on to the tongue. Afterwards, Kuini produces marshmallows from her pack and they roast them in the embers, each trying to get the perfect mallow: brown on the outside but not burnt, and soft and dripping inside. Cowrie tells them how Peta tried to teach her how the do the perfect mallow on their camping trip to Yosemite and how Cowrie burned her first batches.

"Bet you were just wanting Peta to keep roasting and hand feeding you, Cowrie. I know you!"

Cowrie grins. "Well, I must admit, when she began serving them to me on her tongue, my motivation to roast my own completely lapsed."

They laugh and each recall the most erotic food moments they can remember. For Irihapeti, it was the first time she kissed a woman, at the end of the women writers' hui—the night after they sculpted the huge sand egg. Cowrie is surprised she has not heard this story and Irihapeti reminds her it was at the time of her leaving to take up the scholarship and besides, Iri didn't tell anyone. When pressed, she admits it was the gorgeous large Niue Island woman, Seone.

"So come on, Iri, tell all," urges Kuini.

"Well, you'll remember we worked together when we were editing each other's writing. I thought she was married with a bundle of kids. Turns out I was right but at the time she didn't mention it. Anyway, after everyone left the beach, we sat on the dunes in the moonlight and she produced an orange from her bag, proceeded to peel it into segments and fed me each piece by hand, then tongue, then..."

"Hey, kid, stop there. I have to work with her husband at Te Aroha!" Kuini interjects.

"Well, she's always had women lovers and he knows about it. After he first hit her and got convicted, he lost interest and so did she. The family pressure from both the Niue and Nga Puhi sides keeps them together, but they each have lovers outside the marriage."

"Unreal. So I wonder how many other married women live like this?" asks Cowrie, aware that it happens but never having thought of it in such a church-going family.

"A fair few from my experience, here and in the Waikato," Kuini replies.

"So do you still see each other, Iri?"

"Only as friends. I decided it was too complex. But I'll never forget her tongue on mine, the taste of orange, the juice running down my chin, the utter excitement of kissing another woman."

Kuini and Cowrie agree. Kuini tells them about the time she went eel fishing as a kid with Marama and her brothers. "Marama got the boys to lay the bait upstream and said we'd wait for the eels downstream. She took me to the pool in the nikau grove at Karioi,— you know, the one you love and wrote me about while in Hawai'i, Cowrie—and she said to put my feet in the water to attract the eels. I thought my feet would be more likely to repel them, but I reckoned she was choice so I did as she said. Then she got into the water and started playing with my feet. Said it'd attract the fish. Eventually, she tongued between my toes and I remember feeling these sweet shudders throughout my body."

"So what happened?"

"Well, it was quite funny actually. An eel did eventually swim downstream and it bit her on the foot which still had egg on from cracking them to use as bait upstream. I was entering seventh heaven when she screamed and jumped out of the water, landing on top of me with a thud!"

"I bet you hated that, Kuini!"

"Well, no, after we got over the shock, we did use the incident to do some exploratory kissing. So I guess Marama was my first girlfriend."

"You cheated, Kuini. The story had to include food."

190

"It did—the rotten egg bait on her foot!" They burst into laughter, until the tears are running down their faces, as Kuini adds scintillating tidbits to amuse them.

"So Cowrie. How about your legendary experiences with food and eroticism?"

Cowrie grins. "Hardly know where to start, really. You want the time Mere picked up my copy of Audre Lorde's *Zami* with the page opening at the bookmark on the well-read section where she goes down on Ginger with a mouth full of avocado, or…"

"No. It's gotta be your own experience."

"OK. Well, let me tell you how I seduced Peta into hours of lovemaking beside the magic tufa shapes of whales, dolphins and turtles at Lake Mono after showing her how to eat mango Pacific style…"

Later, they discuss their plans for the next year. Irihapeti has a scheme under review to train Maori youth in all aspects of the nursery business so they can work at the marae or take their skills and start a nursery for their own iwi. Kuini hopes to have Te Aroha centres established through Tai Tokerau and, in time, Aotearoa. Cowrie admits she'd like to see the storytelling component of her course set up in other learning centres and for the work to be recognised as a legitimate part of her thesis.

By now, the embers have burned down, so Kuini covers them in sand and they retire to soak in the deep pools scattered about the rock ledge like craters. Small octopuses and shrimps, rock cods and hermit crabs scuttle for shelter as the beautiful large brown naked bodies of three mermaids enter their sacred havens to savour the salt ocean under a moonlit sky. Lying in the ponds, they look up to see the Southern Cross beaming down on them, sparkling its fiery tail over the Pacific Islands.

Through the coal black sky, Cowrie can make out Orion but the Southern Cross has disappeared into the Pacific Ocean. She closes her eyes and imagines she is a navigator on a migration waka, with only stars to guide their way. Waves lash around the prow and she can hear waiata from the stern with the steady plash of canoe paddles providing the rhythm. At her feet, stores of kumara seeds, ready for planting in the new land. Spray splashes her face...

"Sorry, ma'am. The cart hit your shoe." The United Airlines steward beams at her, drawing her back into her current journey with a jolt. Another steward flicks the film screen up and a blanket of light appears, fading the stars outside.

An hour later, they land at San Francisco airport. Cowrie prays the plants and seeds with official New Zealand clearance will make it through customs. The officer in charge, a woman armed with guns and a baton, checks the documentation carefully. She asks Cowrie to explain why she is bringing in the seeds and when she finds out it is to replant the hills of Tomales Bay, she grins. "Good luck, honey. McDonald's'll love yer for replanting their farmlands. Try taking a few down to the Amazon rainforests as well. Haha!" She enjoys her joke and Cowrie thanks her and replies she will do so.

Emerging through the doorway, she sees Uretsete and Ruth, armed with frangipani they have bought from the Hawai'ian florist, waiting to greet her. They cover Cowrie in garlands of sweet fragrant flowers, known as plumeria this far north, and she feels immediately welcome. "Here's some sweetgrass Peta asked me to bring to you." Uretsete produces a bundle of stalks tied together, but this time no abalone shell dangling deliciously from the end. On the way home Cowrie tells Uretsete and Ruth about how she first arrived in San Francisco and was greeted by Benny in a camouflage suit holding a melting icecream, and how they had to cart all her cases and books on the rear of her old BMW bike. They both laugh, remembering Benny's films at UC.

The artist who was sub-tenant of the studio over the vacation has left the place clean and full of plants. Uretsete and Ruth help her unpack and then they relax with green ginger tea, while filling Cowrie in on all the latest, especially excited about their "mind-blowing" time at Big Mountain with Peta, Nanduye and the Navajo and Hopi women. As she listens, Cowrie feels a rush of desire for Peta, longs to talk with her again and decides to call her as soon as the students have left. They update her on progress with the storytelling group and also DK's discovery about her Polish grandfather and how she plans to go back East after the next semester and interview people who knew him. As well as telling the stories, they've decided to write some of them down and perform to others on campus and around the Bay Area, after they saw how powerful the Jewish Brown Bag Theatre Group was when Ruth took them to a performance.

Cowrie is proud of them for taking the initiative and developing the group in accordance with their needs. Maybe she should disappear more often, allowing them room to create? After all, her role as an educator is to inspire and provide them with the resources to expand their potential and apply their learning in such ways. Not that the university sees it in that light. Listening to their excited stories, Cowrie detects a closeness that has grown between Ruth and Uretsete through their work together. She smiles to herself. Each woman has a strong sense of her own culture and past and how to apply it currently. They have a lot in common, though their personalities are very different.

Uretsete stands, pulling Ruth up with her. "We'll leave you to recover from the flight. You're starting to look a bit jet-lagged. And we've got an appointment to keep." She winks at Ruth who goes bright red. Cowrie doesn't ask where they might be going at this time of night, and they hug and agree to meet on the weekend for a picnic with the storytelling group at Angel Island.

"We've got a name for the group now," adds Ruth. "Uretsete thought it up and everyone likes it."

"Siliyik," announces Uretsete. "It's the Chumash word for a sacred enclosure in the dancing ground, and we all felt that described the essence of our work well, especially now we are moving into performance."

"Siliyik. I like it," repeats Cowrie, rolling the word around on her tongue.

"The last *i* is like a glottal stop and kind of catches in the throat," explains Uretsete, "as in Hawai'i."

"Gotcha. Siliyi'ik."

"That's more like it. Pleasant dreams, doc."

"Steady on, kid, I'm not a doctor yet," laughs Cowrie.

"Yeah, but you soon will be, prof. So hang in there."

Uretsete and Ruth go out into the dark night, arm in arm. Cowrie grins. She closes the door, remembering she's back in the land of keys and locks, and latches tight the security bolts. Sipping the last of the green ginger tea, she wonders if it is too late to call Peta at Kahnawake, then gleefully remembers the Canadian east coast is three hours behind San Francisco time, so it'll be about 9 pm. She checks the list of numbers above the phone and dials, her heart in her throat. The voice at the other end is not Peta's and says that she and Nanduye have gone to bed because they had to leave early the next morning to take part in a land settlement dispute 200 miles north. Would she like to leave a message? Cowrie simply requests that Peta call on her return. She hopes that Peta will realise she's home and do so anyway. Did they mean Peta and Nanduye had gone to bed together, or simply both retired early for the night? Surely they wouldn't be so openly a lesbian couple on the reservation?

Cowrie refuses to let her doubts rule her. She climbs up the ladder and gratefully collapses onto her mattress in the loft, visualises the ocean lapping at the dunes, calling to her from Te Kotuku, soothing her.

Red, orange, yellow, green, blue, indigo...moving into violet. The road shimmers with heat and deep purple waves rise up around them as they enter the final stage of the journey, still ascending but nearly at the top of the bridge. They are suspended between golden struts and the painted wooden slats shake in the wind. Suddenly, without warning, she slips and is falling, falling, back through the rainbow, until she plunges into the sea. Cowrie watches, in awe, expecting her lover to rise up out of the ocean as a dolphin and swim away, but all she can see are dark shapes beneath the water...

Brrr...brrr. The phone. Peta! Cowrie slides across the mattress and is down the ladder by the fifth ring. "Haku Peta. I'm so glad you called."

There is silence at the other end. Then Rita's voice comes through. "Cowrie. Is that you? The line's not so good. It's Rita here. I need to speak to you urgently."

"Rita. Hi! What's up?"

"I can't discuss it now, but can you meet me at Mama Bears for lunch and I'll explain all then."

"Sure. What's the time now?"

"Ten. I waited as late as possible because I knew you'd have jet lag."

"See you for brunch in a couple of hours then."

"Fine." Rita hangs up. Cowrie rubs her head and yawns. She's not used to sleeping in this late but must have needed the rest. Still time for Peta to call. It's only 7 am over there. Mind you, the voice did say they were leaving early. Too bad. Wonder what Rita wants? Is it to reject my new thesis proposal, or something more personal? She seems really anxious. So unlike her usual cool, controlled self.

She showers, wraps her lavalava round her, then remembers she'll need to get milk for her tea and she's not back at Te Kotuku now. Walking the distance from her apartment to the corner liquor store for milk naked under a wrap-around is not a good idea in working-class Oakland with coke users and druggies living under the freeway viaducts. Not that she's ever been hassled. She walks as if she owns the streets and people respect her for it. Wonder if Lori and Squish'd mind if I borrow some milk from their shelf of the fridge? Surely not? They were all getting on OK after the farewell dinner for Benny, her landlady, and since she, Rita and Claudia had all attended Lori's art exhibition at Santa Rosa just before she left for Aotearoa.

Cowrie pulls up the bar on the back door and is nearly deafened by the noise of the freeways snaking above the apartment building. Such a shock after the marae. She shuts it a moment, then tries again. This time it's not so bad. Or else she's getting used to it. The fridge is making its usual grunting sounds and has been decorated with even more symbols and stickers since she left. Now a poster with different kinds of fruit hangs between the mountain nipples and the *Boys Beware* sign. Cowrie unlocks the door, and is about to pour some milk into her jug when she hears the stairs creaking behind her.

"Caught in the act! Welcome home, stranger," booms Lori. "Howd'yer stay in paradise go? Check out any mermaids downunder? Or didyer just do the family number?"

"Mostly the family number, but it was great to be back home, thanks Lori. Did your sculptures all sell at the exhibition? Looked as if there was a lot of interest at the preview."

"Na. The critics all love 'em but no one wants to buy 'em. Who'd want a nuclear weapon looking like the all-time erection standin' in the middle of their living room?"

Cowrie remembers the very piece, dripping with horribly life-like spermatozoa and powered by a throbbing machine beneath it, making it resemble a cross between a giant vibrator and a nuclear weapon. It certainly made its point though, as the *Santa Rosa Chronicle* had stated in disgusted tones.

"Well, maybe I wouldn't wanna live with that one, but I kinda liked the organpipe sculpture and the idea of playing nuclear weapons like a song, that it's all orchestrated in advance."

"Yeah. Thought you'd like that one. The most way-out of them all!"

Cowrie is never quite sure if Lori is joking or really means her digs. She decides to laugh at herself anyway. What the hell.

"So how come you've been reduced to stealin' milk from our fridge so early after your return?"

"I didn't want to disturb you, Lori, and I didn't think you'd mind since I've just got back. I'm gonna replace it, but didn't fancy venturing out to the liquor store with just my lavalava on."

"I dunno. You look quite cute to me, honey!" Lori guffaws, then adds, "lucky you're not my type" just as Squish appears on the landing.

"I'm glad about that. Stop teasing the Kiwi, Lori, and come back to bed."

Lori admits she couldn't give a stuff about the milk but enjoys seeing Cowrie squirm, grabs some OJ and climbs back up the stairs. "Catch up with yer later," yells Squish, as they disappear into their den.

198

Only in America, Cowrie mumbles to herself, pouring just enough milk for one cup into the jug and placing the carton back in the fridge. She slams the door shut and is clicking the padlock when she notices that the poster is not the Berkeley Bowl Market variety but a designer range of vibrators and dildos made to look like fruit. Obviously the SM trip has developed since she left. She's not so sure she wants to look at this every time she needs food or drink, but it is a communal fridge. It's not just a case of some brightly coloured fruit dildos. It's what they represent in terms of lesbian sexuality becoming more objectified and less to do with context, seeing the whole person. Then again, the Amazon Films bumper sticker, *We'll come in your face,* isn't much better. So Benny'd be in for it too. Where do you draw the line?

Brrr...brrr. Peta? Cowrie nearly drops the jug in her excitement to get to the phone, but it's Rita again, putting off brunch till one since something's come up. She sounds a bit of a mess. More than university stuff. Maybe she and Claudia are breaking up? Surely not. They've been together ever since their New Orleans days and as friends before that. The thought sends a shiver up Cowrie's spine and she wishes Peta would just ring so she could hear her voice again, feel reassured that all is OK.

She arrives at Mama Bears early to find DK serving the cafe lattes. "Kee-ah orrrha, prof. Didyer get my postcard OK? No zipcode. Felt I was sending it out in a bottle."

"Kia ora, DK. Nice to see you again. Yep—your PC arrived with all the details of you and Suzanne and your wild night exploits, which the woman with the pink hair-do at the corner store enjoyed very much, I might add."

DK turns a whiter shade of pale. "Really? You

mean those dudes got time to read all the mail that comes in?"

"DK, they get about twenty letters a week and postcards are especially welcome since they don't have to hold them up to the light or think about steaming them open to see the contents. So, you're famous back in the Hokianga, kid, and I can't wait till you visit in person so I can let them know the sex queen on the PC is you!"

"Serves 'em right for bein' so nosy! Anyway, Suzanne and I are still an item. She's real cute and we're very happy."

"Glad to hear it, DK. Now you gonna whip me up an espresso or do I have to come around that side of the bar and do it?"

"Sure thing. One espresso, double strength for the jet-lagged professor from the South Sea Islands, coming right up!"

"So what makes you get this special service?" Rita's voice whispers into her ear.

"Not what you think, Rita. Now, whad'ya having?"

"Same for me. I was drinking last night and I haven't recovered yet."

Cowrie sits at the round table examining nasturtiums in a glass bowl, wondering if she'll try sucking honey from the stem in front of Rita and deciding against it, while Rita launches into the events that have happened since the end of the semester. The university has questioned her ability to lead the department after she had failed to solve the debate about theory versus primary texts, and a letter-writing campaign to the regents hadn't helped. At this stage, Rita looks accusingly at Cowrie, suggesting she may have been behind it, but not actually saying so. In addition, the thesis review board had laughed at Cowrie's proposed storytelling component to the

200

doctorate, even though Rita put up a good argument. As if that wasn't enough, all this pressure has made her turn to drink again and now Claudia is threatening to leave her.

Rita gushes all this out, hardly taking a breath between sentences. Cowrie wonders why she is sharing it with her. After all, this is the land that invented and legitimised shrinks for everything imaginable. Surely Rita has closer friends than a colleague from Aotearoa? She does not want this to interfere with their work relationship and Rita's role as her supervisor, but also wants to respect her confidence.

"Rita, let's go back to my apartment where we can talk in private. I'm aware that DK is clearing tables around us and you look like you need a good cry and a decent cuppa herbal. What d'ya say?"

Rita appears close to tears, so Cowrie takes her arm and guides her to her car. On the way home, Rita cries as if she's been holding it back for weeks. Cowrie decides not to push the university issues right now, but to talk Rita through the relationship stuff and get that sorted first. Driving down Telegraph, she notices more street people than before, sitting in alley ways holding tins or still asleep on the sidewalk. It is bleak and the street is littered with scraps of paper, cartons, used glue dispensers and cans. The smell of gas fumes is strong and even the paint on the side of the Genova Deli looks as if it is flaking and abandoned. She feels a pang of longing to be back in Kuini's housetruck, looking out over the dunes to the clean green ocean.

Uretsete has the Red Nations van for the weekend and has agreed to drive Cowrie to take the seeds and plants from Te Kotuku to Clem, Tayo and the nursery workers at Tomales Bay. They head up the coast road, getting out of the Bay Area and away from the last few days, spent with Rita withdrawing from an alcohol binge which had made Claudia refuse to have her back in the house until she got her act together. Claudia had been through it all before and did not want to have to experience it again, since Rita has been a solid member of AA for the past few years and she feared the nightmare of her two-year withdrawal was beginning again. Cowrie's tolerance for alcohol abuse isn't so great either, but she felt for Rita and offered to have her stay until things with Claudia smoothed out.

Moana and the Moa Hunters blares from the tape deck while Uretsete taps to their beat with her free foot, telling Cowrie about a new lesbian Miwok band which plays at a local club, mostly a mixture of reggae with feminist lyrics but now they are starting to explore their own traditions. "You know, like Sweet Honey in the Rock did for African women? They've discovered instruments that are no longer made and they got the elders to draw them and describe the sounds so that they can make them and learn to play them. Siliyik are thinking of doing a performance with them at Mama Bears." Uretsete has become one of the key organisers of the storytelling group. Cowrie is impressed with their enterprise, commitment and confidence. The group has come a long way from the mixed bunch of students she tutored last semester.

They drive through massive eucalyptus trees that rattle their leaves in the breeze. The dry Californian landscape is so like parts of Australia that Cowrie expects a kangaroo to come bouncing out of the bush. She remembers she's got a copy of *Australia for Women* in her backpack and makes a mental note to present this to Siliyik. Maybe she could organise a South Pacific tour for the group, especially if the next International Feminist Arts Festival is being held there as planned within the next two years. She mentions the idea to Uretsete, who immediately embraces it and starts making wild plans for the group. "Maybe we'll leave UC and just perform. Get other Yankees telling their tales, finding out about their roots instead of clutching their breasts in guilt or remorse that they are white and privileged."

"Now you're speaking like a true Southerner! South Pacific, that is," adds Cowrie, amused.

The van rattles on with Uretsete humming to the music while Cowrie indulges herself in fond memories of her trip to Yosemite with Peta in this camper. She mulls over Rita's more than sober words about the responses to her thesis plan. It seems clear that the real intent was not conveyed clearly enough and she'll need to get back to work to make this come across effectively. If only she could present the idea in her own way rather than have it be discussed without her present to answer queries. These institutions guard themselves from discomfort by putting people like Rita between the students and the administration. And unfortunately for Cowrie, Rita was not at her best at the time of presentation. If only she could get the examiners to a performance by Siliyik, to see what potential this approach has to draw out previously unrecorded material from participants. Here in the States, they have so many opportunities for expression, but back in the South Pacific, we're so limited by our lack of resources, especially when some of our islands are just atolls, in grave danger of being sunk by the rising tides if they aren't nuked first.

"Hey, there's Tayo over by the barn." Uretsete swings the van toward the building and yells out "Haku, Uncle Tayo! Look who I've got here."

Tayo peers into the van and beams when he sees Cowrie. "Hi there, stranger. Glad you made it back. Clem tells me you've got some plants and seeds for the new nursery."

Cowrie gets out of the van and hugs him, unable to forget his words to her when showing her around the Miwok village and his wonderful tale of the little girl who spent several months under the blanket as training for her wisdom to be an elder. "Great to see you Tayo. Mere and the elders at Te Kotuku send their aroha to you and thank you for looking after their mokopuna on my last trip here. Mahalo."

Tayo smiles and invites them up to the nursery. He points to a grove of trees about a mile in the distance.

"Hop in, Tayo, and we'll give you a ride," suggests Uretsete, not about to walk up that length of dusty road. Cowrie moves over to make room and Tayo carefully clambers up into the cab.

"Just follow your nose," he nods to Uretsete in the direction of the trees.

They park at the entrance and walk through towering eucalyptus trees until they come to a clearing where a huge dome thatched with tule reeds sits. Around it are many more like the dwellings in the Miwok village, but larger. They enter the central dome and gasp with pleasure. Instead of a traditional shade house, the small plants and seeds are growing under thatched awnings with ventilation holes in the top. Twined tule mats cover the floor of the workspace, and red earth mixed with broken cream shells from the oyster farm forms walkways between the plants. Hanging from reed poles strung between the lattices are tropical exotics, exuding brilliant reds and oranges, purples and violets, as if an artist has painted splashes across canvas, capturing colours at their ripest. Uretsete nudges her gently, whispering, "Now you can tell Peta you've seen the Rainbow Bridge," speaking aloud the very thought that enters Cowrie's head in that moment. "Yes. And it's every bit as exquisite as I imagined," she whispers back. She won't let herself think about her nightmare of Peta falling off the edge.

Clem emerges from behind a vibrant purple bougainvillea with a shiny, deep red Hawai'ian anthurium for Cowrie. "Grew this specially for you." His eyes drop to the floor in shyness, then he adds, "Peta called to say she got your answer machine and you know how she hates those things—so when I told her you were comin' up this weekend, she made me promise to give you this plant." Clem then produces the anthurium in full bud and flower, an explosion of waxed ruby lilies poking out their tongues erotically. Cowrie is moved that Peta has thought of her after all, that Clem would care so much to go to this trouble. Peta would have chosen the anthurium especially, knowing how she'd drool over them at the flower markets in Berkeley, how they remind her of Hawai'i.

Clem introduces them to the Miwok nursery workers and they help unload the van with the pohutukawa and ohi'a trees, the small puriri and rimu, and finally, the minute kauri which will one day grow into a giant and preside over the forest at Tomales Bay. For each of Irihapeti's seeds, there is one plant to show them what it will be like.

They tour the main nursery and the smaller seedling dwellings with Clem, then adjourn for dinner, sampling the new oyster crop and catching up on news. Uretsete is in her element because she grew up staying with Tayo and Iyatiku in her school holidays. She tells them about the growth of the storytelling group, promising to bring Siliyik up for the official opening of the nursery in a few weeks. They eat, talk and laugh until late into the night.

"A pity Peta couldn't be here for this reunion," says Iyatiku, clearing up the dishes with Cowrie.

"Yeah. She'd've loved it."

"But I gather she's doing well at Kahnawake. That's important work for all of us. We're very proud of her."

Cowrie stacks the dishes, remembering their love-making in the tent beside the oyster shells at Tomales Bay, Peta stroking her face tenderly as the early morning sun came over the hill, blazing a fire around the perimeter of Peta's face, setting her eyes and tongue alight.

The morning sun slides in slits through the tent flaps, shining bars across Peta's face. Nanduye leans over to kiss her on the cheek. Peta moans, drawing her close, wanting her naked breasts, her lips on her skin. "Not now, Peta. We haven't finished preparing that lawsuit and we've still got to hear the other tribal claimants this morning. It's late already. Besides, weren't you gonna write to Cowrie today? You promised me you'd tell her. It's not fair to leave it until she finds out through someone else."

Peta rolls over, groaning. "I can't bear to hurt her, Nan. She's been so good to me and I still love her dearly, as you know. It's just that there is no future. She'll always be heading back to Aotearoa and I'll always be involved in reservation work here. We both know this."

"Then why are you putting it off? It's cruel Peta. Cowrie is intelligent and sensitive. She's aware enough to know the situation and it'll hurt more the longer you delay telling her. Do it today, or I won't speak to you tonight."

"Maybe that'd be OK. I could read in peace..."

Nanduye bends over and cuffs Peta across the shoulder. "You'd have a job keeping quiet. Now here's some paper and a pen. I'll catch up with you at the long house at noon."

She packs the last of her papers into her briefcase and disappears through the tent flap. Peta lies on her back, looking up into the roof of the tent, recalling

Cowrie's face in the dawn at Tomales Bay, when Jake nearly rolled them with the tractor. She lies legs astride, hands behind her head, remembering the rest of that trip, now so long ago, their kissing beside the waterfall, Cowrie seducing her beside Lake Mono with a dripping ripe mango. How could she let this woman go? But then Nanduye feeds her where Cowrie cannot. She instinctively understands the intricacies of tribal negotiation and will always be accepted by her people. Cowrie, despite her empathy and indigenous links, will always remain an outsider in Indian eyes. Besides, I've known Nanduye much longer, since our college days, and I'm sure we'll withstand the pressures, even within our own communities, of being gay and native. Most tribal elders are silently supportive. It's generally the heterosexual women who are threatened.

Peta stretches her limbs, suddenly screaming. A twisted knot of cramp has invaded her left leg and she cries out in pain, drawing it up under her, stretching her toes into the palms of her hand to pull against the tightening muscles, allowing her some relief. After a while she tries getting up, tentatively putting down one foot, then the other, until the pins and needles have subsided. Shit, I bet that's Cowrie warning me to be present, or Nanduye sending me a sharp message to get my act together. She picks up the pen and paper Nanduye had left on their mat, and starts to write.

Kia ora, Cowrie. No, that's too familiar. *Dear Cowrie.* No—she'll know something is up from the start. *Haku, Cowrie.* Yes, that's it. I need to assert my own language and identity. This is a part of what has drawn me back to Nanduye and Cowrie will understand.

Haku, Cowrie

How is life back in Berkeley? I hope you got the red anthurium I sent via Clem. It was to remind you of Hawai'i, your other homeland. I loved your letters from Aotearoa. You are so connected to nature there—the earth, the dunes, the sea. It feeds your soul and reminds me how much I miss my own land and ocean, how much I need to be out of the city. Luckily, our work takes Nanduye and I out often, so we get to light fires under the open sky, share tales with our people. This work is vital and we are thriving on it.

Cowrie, you know how we discussed the inevitability of our eventual separation, through our deep connection with our lands, which would always draw each of us home, despite our love for each other? Well, I've been feeling this pull back here, and especially with Nanduye. As you know, I felt attracted to her again, but resisted the temptation because of the strength of my relationship with you, dear Turtle.

However, I can resist the pull no longer. This does not mean I love you any less, that we cannot remain soul lovers, as we always declared we would, just that I cannot be physical lovers with you, that I am realising my work is here on the reservation and

Nanduye will work beside me, live with me.

Sweet Turtle, I still love you. I always will. How is it possible to love two women so deeply, want to be with each of them in different ways? But we both knew this might happen, that we are not into possession in relationships. I'm most concerned that we find a way through this, that we remain friends and soul lovers. Is this possible?

I expect you'll feel hurt and betrayed when you get this. I am ready for that. But please remember, Turtle, this does not detract from the quality of my love for you. It simply means it is growing and changing into something different. Please don't cut off from me. I need to hear from you, hear how you are. I remain committed to the work you are doing and want to support you in this— as a friend.

Nanduye and I are still working on Ela's case against Chad. It's been rocky but I think we'll win it so that she and Koana will keep the kids. They are coming over to the mainland for the court case next month, so maybe you'll get to see them en route? I hope so.

Write soon, Turtle,

Peta.

Peta reads her letter, then folds it carefully, placing it inside her pack. She decides to wait a few days before sending it, get used to the idea of it going, have time to change it if she needs to. She dresses, collects her gear and heads to the trading post to find something she can slip into the package for Cowrie, something that will let her know her turtle spirit is still alive and swimming inside Peta.

Peta's hand is in hers. The air is cool on the bridge, sending layers of coloured mist rising around their feet like a rainbow fog. Voices in front and behind. Suddenly, Peta's hand slips from hers and she falls down through the mist, turning red, orange, yellow, then green, blue, indigo, violet before she splashes into the black water below. A knife slashes through Cowrie's back, right through to her heart. As she bends over in pain, a sleek dolphin spins out of the water, joined by a mate. When they swim away, a haunting cry echoes in their wake, as if in farewell.

Ther is a hollow pounding. It crashes through Cowrie's consciousness, waking her with a jolt. She sits up, listening. The pounding again. It's outside her studio. "Open up, Cowrie. Rescue me." Then coughing, spluttering. "For God's sake, woman, let me in. It's freezing out here." The voice is slurred, distant and vaguely familiar. Cowrie drags herself down the ladder from the loft and pads across the film studio floor to the big latched door. She peers through the letter hole to see Rita leaning against the wall, hollering and coughing. She grabs the latch, opens the door, and Rita collapses into her arms. Her face is red and swollen, her eyes bloodshot. Looks like she's been drinking for a week.

Cowrie guides her across the wooden floorboards, each moment drawn out by her heavy weight, like crossing hardened lava, making sure the hot flow is not beneath their feet. "Fucking bitch locked me out of the house. My house paid for with my money from slaving at that fuck awful university. Locked out of my own house. And *she* works for the Oakland Housing Commission. Fucking bitch..." Rita's voice trails off as she collapses on to the sofa. Cowrie covers her with a blanket and fires up the stove to make tea. Rita's grumbling gives way to snoring before the kettle has boiled and Cowrie is thankful they'll be able to sort this in the morning. Trying to talk to a half cut person is a useless waste of time. She makes sure Rita is comfortable and warm, then negotiates the cup of tea up the ladder to her own bed, a skill she's recently acquired.

Fresh green ginger tea with manuka honey never fails to calm her. She can't avoid involvement now. It's strange that Rita does not have closer friends to give her support. Maybe it's easier to come to an outsider, a new person in town. Or maybe she's outworn her welcome with other friends. Alcoholics tend to do that if they don't seek help for their illness. Rita's snoring billows up from the cavern below, making it impossible for Cowrie to sleep. The nightmare returns to her memory. Peta falling from the Rainbow Bridge and swimming off with another mate. Is this a prediction or her own insecurity?

Gradually, the snoring from below lulls into a regular pattern and she imagines each breath drawn in and whooshing out is a wave breaking on her beloved dunes at Te Kotuku Marae. After a while, the ebb and flow becomes the swishing of the sea surging in and out. She dives into the belly of a wave and swims out through the breakers. But they are endless and she cannot reach calm sea. Waves are relentlessly breaking on the shore and her fins just keep her afloat until the next one comes, as if she is swimming against a current so strong that her

213

movement simply holds her suspended in the same place. She drifts in and out of consciousness, wakes to the roar of the freeways above, the snoring below, exhausted, as if she's had no sleep at all.

In the morning Cowrie fires up the stove and fills the old copper kettle, placing it on the fire. Her hand is singed by the flame. She quickly raises it to her mouth to quench the heat on her tongue, remembers Peta at the stove cooking their meal the day she came to rescue Cowrie from postmodernist boredom, feels her hot tongue sizzle in her mouth. She suddenly realises her own tongue is burning and thrusts her hand under the cold tap. The water gurgles as it gushes out over her flesh. She could be in the crater at Kiluaea, Pele sizzling up her arm, through her hair, warning her not to transgress her boundaries. Or maybe this is Peta telling her not to get too involved in Rita and Claudia's fiery relationship? She dives into a cold shower. The icy water flows over her breasts, down her hands and ample belly and her tongue is soothed by the falling liquid.

Rita is stirring slowly, groaning and begging for coffee, when Cowrie enters the room. She suggests herb tea would ease the headache but Rita insists upon caffeine and passes up a crumpled packet of Peets coffee from her bag.

They sit on the edge of the sofa all morning while Rita spills out the life story of her relationship with Claudia and how she's tried to give up booze but doesn't reckon it's fair because Claudia won't give up her dope. She reckons most of the Oakland Housing Commission survive on it and it buffers them from the pain of their work with the homeless. It sounds to Cowrie like the classic no-win co-dependant set up, but when she suggests this Rita erupts into expletives about how the shrink movement has stolen the heart from feminist activism and what harm did a few drinks do anyway?

What harm? Here's a woman out of control, in danger of losing her relationship, her home and possibly even her job, and she is still asking this question. Cowrie lays it on the line and offers to help only if Rita pledges to help herself and go to an AA meeting. Finally, through a morning of caffeine and a haze of tears, Rita relents and they make plans for her to attend meetings out of town where she's less likely to see friends and students or their parents. That's one of Rita's conditions. Eventually, they discuss the work situation. Rita is unwilling to budge. She knows she has been put in a fence-sitting position by the regents but she sees no alternative if Women's Studies and Gay and Lesbian Studies are to survive.

"But what's the point in maintaining a department that seeks to explore feminist theory and activist writings, but which is crippled because the establishment only allows certain viewpoints to be heard?"

"What's the alternative, Cowrie? I'm damned if I do and I'm damned if I don't."

"C'mon, Rita. You're more feisty than that. Why not break the mould, be the first to offer Pacific writing, bring in speakers from the outside, make storytelling a component for all groups? Admit oral literature is the base from which all our writing began, where women still make decisions, plan and theorise, whether it be around a fire at night or at the kitchen table or in the board room by day."

"But how can I justify this in a contemporary university context?"

"How can you justify not considering it? What do you think most people do in modern society? They go to work—if they have the luxury of a job—and then they come home and blot out in front of the telly. What's on the telly? A few newsbytes, but basically, it's modern storytelling. Albeit only a few storytellers and not representative culturally, but the tradition is alive and well, even in its muted and commercialised form. We can make it better by tuning in and having our say rather than denying it exists. And I mean that on all levels—not just TV and stage performances—but by making our own CD-ROMs, our own virtual reality. Otherwise, it'll be the porn freaks and sexist shits who control us all over again, just through different media."

"How on earth do you connect oral storytelling with virtual reality and CD-ROMs, Cowrie?"

"Well, look at the daily stories and retelling of tales that happens on email and the Internet now, the stories that make up vast sections of the virtual reality industry. The future of publishing lies with the electronic as well as the print industry and that includes our storytelling, our literatures. We must change and adapt to new forms of storytelling rather than pretending only one media version is politically correct. If we don't get in on the act now we'll be left behind again, and the survival of alternative cultures is once again weakened by our inability to adapt the media for our own ends."

"Cowrie, do you think we could make a case on this for the university? You know how they want to be seen to be world leaders, ever since they got attention for pioneering the free speech movement in the sixties? Maybe this is how we get them on board again? Make them realise Women's Studies and Gay Studies are crucial because not only do they embrace multiculturalism and gender alternatives, but they do so through using new technology."

"Precisely, Rita. If we don't, then we're doomed to

extinction. We can't just pine for the loss of our cultural and gender identities. We need to be right in there as the technology is changing. Already we are pioneers in gender and cultural terms, and you can see that we're regarded as really powerful by the backlash from university conservatives in the eighties and early nineties."

"This is the first time I've really seen a possible alternative, Cowrie. Thanks. Will you work with me on it?"

Cowrie pours milk over her muesli, layering slices of banana and a sprinkling of sunflower seeds on top. She hesitates before answering. "Yeah, but only if you include the students. They have a far greater knowledge of the new technology than most of us. Look at DK's work with CD-ROM already."

"Oh, no. I don't have to work with DK do I? She scares me some days with her rebellious and smart answers."

"Then give her something awesomely difficult to occupy her brain. She works with a team of computer hackers and she's likely to know the short cuts. She'll also be able to provide the appropriate jargon to get the regents on board."

"God, my head still feels so fuzzy. I hope this idea looks as good in the sober light of day." Rita manages a weak smirk.

"That's up to you, boss. Now I suggest you call Claudia and tell her your plans. See if she's willing to give it one more go."

"If she isn't, can I stay here a while until she's OK with it?" Rita reaches over to refill her coffee.

Cowrie hesitates a moment. The studio is hardly big enough for her, and she doesn't relish the idea of helping yet another friend or workmate through the maze of giving up addictions. But she also knows how hard it is to find that support and how costly housing is added to the shared mortgage Rita has already. "Only if you keep to our pact and attend regular AA meetings. No booze and no smokes in this studio. You're welcome to smoke in the back yard." She feels a bitch having to set these boundaries, but years of putting up with smoke filled-rooms has encouraged it.

Rita looks surprised. "I'd never have taken you for a health fascist, Cowrie."

"Shows how wrong you can be, huh?" Cowrie smiles. "Time for another cuppa. You on to Peets or green ginger?"

"I'll give that herbal shit a go. Might take away the withdrawal symptoms I'm feeling just at the thought of no G and T's and smokes."

"You could always smoke a hibiscus teabag and see if that fulfils your need for oral gratification."

"I can think of better ways to be satisfied orally."

"Yeah—but Claudia may not be into that right now. Take it slowly, Rita."

"Thanks, Cowrie. Jeez, I can't wait to feel my head clear again. Can't go on trying to lecture like this."

"You're lucky the establishment hasn't caught up with you before, Rita."

"Are you kidding? There was a printed survey in the *International Women's Medical Journal* last month that showed the pressure for women within university and teaching structures. Over half were regular smokers, alcoholics or took drugs."

"How does that compare to the national average?" Cowrie sips her tea.

"It's estimated up to two-thirds of the total work-force may be drugged by prescription or other drugs on any one day."

"Well, I guess you're in the majority then, eh? Still doesn't make it OK though, Rita."

"What about Pacific Island stats?"

"Not so high on prescription drugs, but yeah, the missionaries did their fair share of handing out tobacco and alcohol, and that's had enormous repercussions on indigenous people globally."

"So why don't we include this in our courses?"

"I do. Maybe you should drop in some time and listen up?"

"Touché. Point taken."

"Now, I'm off to the liquor store to get a paper. Why don't you call Claudia while I'm gone?"

"Thanks, Cowrie. I will. Take your time."

"Sure will." Cowrie hugs Rita, collects her pack and strolls off to the store. Rita nurses her sore head, weeping, then makes her way carefully to the phone.

The lens of the camera moves closer into the pupil of
the eye. Macadamia nut brown with a black centre.
As she bends her head to look inside, fire erupts from
the eye pit, forming a hollow crater where the eyeball
once was. The red and orange fireball gushes up from
the face and flows out over the body of land, down
toward the ocean. It passes over the thick black lava
sand, flows into a bleached bone lying naked on the
beach and disappears. The bone expands until red
fire explodes from its core, rushing out into the ocean.
A woman runs down the beach, wraps the remainder
of the bone in fresh lele banana leaf and holds it to
her breast, crooning. This way she can protect the
ancestors of the escaped spirit, prevent them from
disturbing the still living. But is she in time?

Cowrie wakes in a hot sweat, throwing the duvet
off her naked body. Someone has died. Whose spirit is
escaping? She immediately thinks of Mere, though she
left her mother safe and well. Then she worries about
Koana. After all, it was a Hawai'ian banana leaf in
the dream, not one from Aotearoa. She remembers
Koana telling her about the spirit or soul, uhane,
escaping from the dead body, kino, wandering about
as an apparition, hihi'o. It usually escapes through the
eye, lua-uhane, and often enters an object like a bone,
making Hawai'ians respect these carriers of the dead.
But what does this mean? Who is the old lady who
protects the soul by placing the lele banana leaf over
the bone? And who has died or is in danger of dying?

A cold wave surges through her and rests frozen around her heart. Perhaps it's Peta, sacred fire, escaping from her? Is she in danger, or does her soul need to escape? Cowrie shudders. She looks over to the once shining red anthurium Peta gave her. It had faded to dark pink in the dry heat of the studio, longing for the tropical moisture of its Hawai'ian home. Nearly two months since Peta's last latter. A rough two months after Rita had taken up residence downstairs. The saving grace was it allowed them to work closer together, though Cowrie was realising Rita's desire to please the authorities far outweighed her dedication to the students. Beneath her activist exterior lay a fiercely ambitious woman who would do anything to climb the career ladder. Cowrie had only seen glimpses of this before.

Peta, beautiful Peta. It's clear that something is wrong. A couple of faxes had arrived at work but that hardly counted for meaningful contact. They were mainly to outline the plans for Koana and Ela's visit, which had been delayed, and to make sure Cowrie would greet them at the airport *en route* and put them up for a few days. Cowrie was pleased because it gave her a fair deadline for Rita and Claudia to get their act together.

She'd been bracing herself for the final farewell letter from Peta, news that she and Nanduye were together, or she'd met someone else. But it wasn't like Peta to leave it this long. Maybe she's hurt? Maybe the dream was a premonition? Cowrie decides to call Kahnawake in the morning and find out. She tries to read the latest postmodernist text required for the general courses. It works. Within minutes she is asleep, albeit a disturbed and restless repose until the dawn light enters through the stained glass leadlights above the loft.

Rita is up early. She's alcohol free, but still into the Peets. The smell of freshly ground coffee filters up to the loft and Cowrie asks for one too.

"Have I succeeded in corrupting you at last?" Rita replies.

"Na. Peta beat you to it. I've always enjoyed freshly ground, but only every now and again."

"So what's the special occasion?"

"A disturbing dream and restless night. I'm worried about Peta. Think I'll call her today."

"About time too. It's not likely for her to be so lax. Reckon there's a reason, Cowrie."

"Bloody better be, eh?"

They celebrate Rita's last day with a mushroom omelette, fresh OJ and Rita presents her certificate of survival from AA. "Two months sober. Reckon Claudia will accept me back?"

"You gotta do it for you and not just her, Rita."

"Yep. Both. And to keep my job. Thanks for your support, Cowrie. I know it's been rough at times. But I'm alcohol-free now."

"Reckon you can stick at it?"

"Not much choice now. I have to."

"That's good enough thanks for me. Besides, I've managed to use the time productively to sway you into the CD-ROM and virtual reality universe for our Women's and Gay Studies courses, so it's been worthwhile!"

"Yeah—and you've enjoyed seeing me kowtow to DK also. Admit it!"

"It's kept DK occupied and less on to my case, true."

"To tell the truth, I'm getting to actually respect her. Who'd've thought the tractor driver would turn out to be a CD-ROM whizz?"

"Yeah, but remember she was an ace student before

driving tractors. Besides, one does not cancel out the other."

"Girls can do anything, right?"

"Everything—and better!"

"Agreed. I'll do the dishes while you call Peta. Good luck."

"Hope I won't need it. But thanks, Rita."

Cowrie walks into Benny's film studio to make the call. Once again, she gets the answer machine at the reservation number. Damn! I wonder if Peta's getting my messages? She tries again. Same response. She leaves a reminder for Peta to call her, then hangs up.

"Ko, I can't believe you wanna do this tourist number at Pier 39."

"Auwe, Cowrie, it's not that often we get to fly the mokulele to the mainland—especially to Kapalakiko. We wanna enjoy!"

"I know mokulele is the big bird, fly united and all that—but what's Kapalakiko?"

"You should know that. Your favourite city outside the Big Island and Aotearoa," Koana replies.

"San Francisco?"

"'Ae, hoahanau. Whatcha callit back home? Cuzzy-sis?"

"You're getting good at kiwiana, Ko. Can't wait till your Big Bird finally makes it to Te Kotuku Marae."

"One day soon. Next Indigenous Peoples' Conference. But let's get this damned court case outa the way first, eh?" Koana wraps a comforting arm around Ela, who is admiring a carved bone taniwha in the window of a jewellery store.

"Hey, Ela. That's from Aotearoa. Fisher's Custom Jewellery on Solano have even better ones. I'll show you tomorrow. You've gotta get one carved with soul. Many of the tourist ones are machine carved like this. Pure trash. Won't hum through you."

"I want one each for our kids. As protection. Whad'yer reckon, Ko?"

"Great idea, but let Cowrie take you to the authentic place."

"How come this Fisher-person has a line down to the source, Cowrie?" Ela asks.

Cowrie laughs. "You got it in one, Ela. I bring some over each trip to support the marae carvers back home. Mere inspects them all before I leave to make sure the quality is as perfect as possible since it reflects the name of Te Kotuku."

"Nice work, cuz," butts in Koana.

"Even better, and this may appeal to you both since you're here for the custody case, ten per cent of all profits go back into Te Aroha funds to support the survivors. The men carve, the women profit."

"Kamaha'o! But doesn't that assume that all the abusers are men and the victims women?" Ela asks.

"The stats show that's true in ninety-five per cent of cases," Cowrie replies.

"So it's the same all over the world, not just in our islands, then?"

"Reckon so, but the good news is that it's changing. Small efforts like this help."

"Can we swing by there on the way home?"

"Sure. We can take the Solano exit from the freeway and it's not far from Albany back to Oakland. Especially since I have the luxury of Rita's car today. Costs her less to lend it to me than pay parking fees at UC, so she's happy."

That decided, they sample fresh kai moana from a local fisherman whose trawler is tied up beside them at the pier. He cooks lobster on a gas grill on the deck of his boat and flicks raw oyster shells apart while his daughter cuts fresh lemon to adorn their paper plates. All for five bucks.

"Not bad, eh?" says Cowrie, handing them plates.

"Free back home," whispers Koana, "with a bit of fried honu on the side!"

"Don't tease me, Koana. I know full well you don't

eat turtle, and would never dare tell me if you did. Though Meleana remembers the days when everyone ate turtle. Not that long ago."

"Well, let's hope she's not feeding it to our kids right now, eh?" laughs Ela. "She, Hale and Ika'Aka have all four of them. I reckon they'll be needing a break by the time we return."

"Too right. And to think we're over here fighting to keep them," laughs Koana.

After kai, they stroll to the end of the pier where Peta took Cowrie to see the resident seals on their first date after watching the film about Hawai'ian sovereignty. Cowrie remembers it so clearly. The sound of the sea lapping against the pier, the freshness of the night, Peta's hand in hers, tongue on hers. The seals squabbling joyfully on the rocks below and the smell of seaweed.

Today, the seals are absent, and all she can smell is petrol fumes from a passing trawler. She peers down into the water. Not even a dolphin disappearing with her mate. An oil slick floats on the water, turning it silver grey. Maybe that's why the seals left? The air is moist and the stench of filleted fish fills the sky. Death hangs near the mooring ropes. She recalls Keo telling them how Koana's husband Aka was hung in the ropes off Ka Lae.

Sensing her coldness, Koana holds her hand warmly. Tears fall from Cowrie's eyes. Grief for Koana, Aka, letting go of Peta. Death of the Soul. For a moment she is back in her dream, the river of fire issuing out from the eyepit, being sucked into the dry bone. Pain enters her rib cage like a knife and she bends over, dry retching.

"Peta. Another message from Cowrie on the reservation answering machine. Did you reply to the last one?"

"Damn. I forgot. I figure she's got my letter by now and judging by the delay, her response is not good. So I thought I'd give it a couple more weeks for her to calm down and accept the changes."

"C'mon, Peta. That's not even logical. I thought you really wanted to work this through with Cowrie. Isn't our relationship worth the effort of you ending that one honourably?"

"Sure, Nan. But I really don't want to hurt Cowrie. I still care for her as a friend, in a soul way."

"Well, you sure as hell aren't showing it, Peta. Why don't you call her now, deal with it?"

"I will. Just give me a few more days and I'll be ready."

"You'd better be or..."

"Or what, Nan?"

"I dunno. But I sure as hell didn't leave guys to watch women fucking each other around like this."

"Steady on, Nanduye. That's a bit harsh. I've written to Cowrie. True, I held off a while before sending it, but I had to be sure."

"Sure of what? Sure of being with me, or not being with Cowrie?"

"Both, I guess. I can't get used to not having turtle in my life."

"Well, I'm not saying she can't still be in your life. If she's that important to you, then get off your ass and show her, Peta!"

"D'you treat all your lovers like this, Nan?"

"You should be asking yourself that question, Peta." Nanduye picks up her briefcase and heads toward the longhouse. "We'll be another two or three hours in negotiation, Peta. By then I hope you've called Cowrie and we can relax." She saunters off, leaving dust in her wake from the tinder dry ground.

Peta sighs, reaches in her pocket to check she's got her credit card handy, and walks slowly toward the trading post.

"Hi, Kushkut. Mind if I use your slot machine?" Peta holds up her card.

"Sure, Peta. Where's Nanduye?"

"Working, as usual."

"So you calling the other one, eh?"

Peta shoots him a glare. Damned Indian Internet. He shuffles back over to the buckskins and pretends to check the stickers. She pokes the thin piece of plastic into the machine and dials the number. Brrr…brrr…click… "You've reached Goddess Films. If you want Benny, call New York 212–343–7889 and we'll still come in your face." Guffaw. "If you want Cowrie, hold the line or leave a message after the beep." New music. Sounds like Moana and the Moa Hunters which Cowrie played on their Yosemite trip. Then the beep.

Peta clears her throat. "Cowrie, you there? Pick up if you're working. It's Peta. If not, I'll call you again in a week. I love you, Turtle. Remember that." Click. She replaces the receiver. Phew. Done it. At least that's broken the ice. Follow up to the letter. It'll give me a breather too.

"Thanks Kushkut. Just checking out my Turtle back home."

"You got turtle back home? In California? Strange place for turtle to live."

"Ah, this one's special. She comes from the South Seas—the islands of Aotearoa."

"Thought it would be too cold down there for turtles? Ain't it near the Antarctic?"

"Sure is, Kushkut, but this Turtle is one warm-blooded creature. She's migrated to the north and seems to adapt to all climates."

"I'll be damned. Didn't know they swam that far. Then again, we're not a coastal tribe. Now ask me about moose and I can tell you their mating cycles."

"Another day, Kushkut. I'm up to my neck in mating cycles."

"Ah, so I was right then, Peta?"

"Only if you include turtles in the overall picture. Hey, Kushkut, you got any more of that chewin' tobacco? Gave up smokes many moons ago but I sure could do with a good chew to ease the stress."

"Now you're talkin', girl. Want smoked or plain?"

"Why not smoked?"

"Sure. This here's bin aged like wine."

"Ta."

"Watcha sayin? That some Caleyefornikatin' term?"

"Na. Learned it from Turtle Woman. It means thanks, mahalo, gratias, tena koe."

Kushkut looks at Peta, squints his eyes, and mumbles "You gals ain't what yer used to be. Too complex for my likin'."

"Keeps yer on yer toes, Kushkut. Good for yer," chips in old Ma Kushkut from the door as she enters.

He grumbles as he wraps the chewing tobacco. "Women never chewed till recently, neither."

"Yeah, vulgar habit, eh? Wonder where it began?" smiles Peta.

Old Ma Kushkut guffaws loudly as she exits from the store and even Kushkut grins beneath his beard.

Koana and Ela offer to cook dinner because Cowrie is still feeling ill. The fisherman sold them some fresh dory which Koana has marinated in lime juice and coconut milk.

"You rest up, Cowrie. Looks to me like you've been working too hard. Just the thought of all those books makes me tired," says Ela.

"Yeah. I have been stressing out a bit and I've had a colleague at university staying the past two months so that's been fairly tiring emotionally."

"To say nothing of you missing Peta," adds Koana. "I know from your letters to me that you've both felt deeply committed and that kind of soul love mixed with sexual union is rare. Don't let it slip by, Cowrie. Call her again."

"Well. I'm not so sure. I think it might be over."

"C'mon Cowrie. It's not like you to be so negative. Call her."

Cowrie walks to the phone in the film studio and plays back her messages. Two for Rita, one for Benny, then a dry cough or throat clearing. She knows by the sound and pause afterwards that it's Peta. "Cowrie, you there? Pick up if you're working. It's Peta. If not, I'll call you again in a week. I love you, Turtle. Remember that." Click. The machine rewinds. Cowrie listens to the message over and over.

Koana slips in behind her. "You OK, Turtle?"

Cowrie spins around "Don't ever call me that. Only Peta calls me Turtle."

"Hey, calm down, Cowrie. I feel connected to the turtle in you. Remember Laukiamanuikahiki? The massage? I helped you recognise those powers within..." Koana pauses. "But it's not that, is it? It's Peta."

Cowrie nods, pushes the rewind button and plays the message back to Koana. She listens intently. "Cowrie, it's fine. The message is Peta in a rush—needing and hoping to contact you, but unable to. She's frustrated that's all. She does affirm her love for you."

"Ko, it's more than that. I didn't want to upset you on your trip here with Ela since we see each other so seldom. But I got a letter from Peta this morning. It should've arrived a couple of weeks ago but she put the wrong zip code on it. She and Nanduye are lovers. It's all over, Ko. I just don't want to face it."

Koana pulls Cowrie toward her, touches her cheek softly with the tip of her finger. Sobbing erupts from her friend, as if this small touch has released all the repressed energy that has built over the past few weeks, especially the last twelve hours. Between sobs, Cowrie apologises for biting her head off, says it's OK for Ko, of all people, to call her Turtle. Koana tries to lighten her up, reminds her one of Peta's most affectionate names for Cowrie was Snapping Turtle. She'd laugh at it usually. But the memory sends Cowrie deeper into her grief. Koana holds her, cradling her head to her breast, singing mele ho'ohiamoe keiki as she does at home to soothe the children, lull them into sleep when troubled. Ela pokes her head through the door to announce coconut and pineapple pre-dinner drinks, and Koana gently guides Cowrie back into the living quarters.

She weeps until it seems there are no more tears left, while Koana soothes her, reminds her that it is not over, that the relationship is merely changing. She wonders if Cowrie wept so deeply over her, whether the letting go had wrenched her at a gut level like this. She knew Cowrie was upset back then, but had never seen her in deep grief except for her anger as she watched her gut the fish that strange night at Puako. She'd never let on to Cowrie that she'd seen her take revenge on the struggling i'a when she got up for water at dawn, saw her friend kneeling astride the wriggling fish, taking life from its body after one of its mates had attacked Peni. It'd surprised her, since she knew Cowrie to be so gentle. Her reactions now have a similar force. They seem out of proportion to the change of pace in a relationship. From what Cowrie has told her, it may be the end of their sexuality, but it is certainly not the end of their friendship. How could lesbian sexuality be so intense? Koana embraces Cowrie until she is calm, then lays her gently on the sofa.

"Ela," she whispers, "let's leave dinner, let her sleep. I think this has been building a while. Cowrie needs some rest. Wanna come for a walk with me? Maybe we could find that store with the bone manaia in. Not that we'd know which to get without Cowrie, but we could at least look."

"I think it's too far to walk there. But the Genova Deli where Cowrie got us those fried artichoke hearts is just around the corner. Let's buy more to have with the marinated i'a."

"'Ae." Koana puts a top over her lavalava while Ela checks her bag for cash. They place a note for Cowrie on the sofa, then slip out the back door, leaving it unlatched so they can get in later. The street outside is littered with empty spirit bottles from the nearby liquor store, smoke butts and junk food wrappers. Kids are sleeping under the freeway struts, empty cans surrounding them. "Thank Pele we don't have to raise our kids here, Koana."

"For now. But ever seen Hilo on a Friday night after the pubs close? Even Kona, kept clean for tourists, is getting rough. Keo tells me they've approved plans for a McDonalds there. It's just time before the stores are stocked with junk food and liquor. It's beginning to happen already. Look at Oahu. More take-out bars per square foot than the rest of America. On our islands. It's already bad."

"Yeah, but at least the schools are still relatively safe and the kids still enjoy more than street life and TV."

"Maybe, for now. But Peni told me last week one of those haole kids offered him some dak. We know that the taking of our land has caused some to resort to growing dope to survive, so it's only a matter of time, eh?"

"I still can't see it getting this bad, Ko."

"Why? Because Oakland is full of dispossessed black working class? I can see Hilo like this in a decade. It scares the shit out of me sometimes."

"Me too. I just don't want to face it."

"You're as bad as Cowrie, Ela! That's what she said about Peta. Poor Turtle. I can't believe she carried that letter from Peta around in her pocket all day, not wanting to spoil our time here."

"It's strange coming from someone so assertive in other ways."

"'Ae. Cowrie never ceases to surprise me. She's so tuned in on the big issues, but still so shy and unassertive when it comes to matters of the heart. I reckon it stems from her being split at the root, growing up unsure of her identity. You know, she once told me she got attacked at school by kids throwing sticks and stones and calling her a 'fat coconut'. Local

233

term for islander, evidently. She was never sure if it was her physical strength or the mixture of haole and islander that most upset them."

"That's interesting. Neli's friend Kakana told her he reckoned the local kids hated him more because he was from a mixed-blood family. His father is Hawai'ian and his mother a blonde Amazonian Californian!"

"Yeah, well it's having dark blood mixed with their own which most pisses haole off. They can distance themselves from us because we look and talk and act so differently. But Cowrie can pass. And so can Kakana. They hate that because it reflects a part of themselves. Besides, he can look after himself with a name that means Tarzan!"

"That was his mother's choice, believe it or not! Then again, she'd make an OK Jane."

"You been studying her biceps, Ela?"

"No way! I remain 100 per cent heterosexual, Koana, and you know it."

"More's the pity, Ela. You have to admit we do make a good couple."

"Yes—and the kids like it." Ela smiles. "But I'm sure it's not for me, Ko, or for you."

"Don't be so sure. That's what I said before I met Cowrie. But since then I've thought a lot about my childhood feelings. I realise I suppressed my love for women. I used to be in love with Wanaka at school but never let on. Remember those pepe hauhau nights? We used to light candles and touch each other under the blankets. Meleana knew but thought it harmless."

"You still feel for her?"

"Not in that way. But I now recall the feeling with power whereas I kept it down before, pretended it was just childish pranks."

"I'm not there yet, Koana. Anyway, from the grief

234

Cowrie is feeling, it doesn't seem like loving women is any less painful than loving men."

"Sure. The feelings are deep wherever you go. I just don't think we should discount them."

Ela looks relieved when they arrive at the bright lights of the Genova Deli which appears to stay open day and night and is always full of people. They take a number and Koana eyes the smoked eel. "It's from Noo Zealand," the young Italian man tells them. "Best in the world. Mind you, you'll pay for it. Long way to fly it over."

Koana smiles. "We'll have some of that Ela. Might bring some warm memories back for Cowrie."

They spend half an hour drooling over a large selection of salami, fresh pasta, home-made pesto, and finally order fried artichoke hearts, pepper salami, olives stuffed with fetta and two varieties of herb bread to go with the smoked eel.

By the time they return, Cowrie is making green ginger tea and sampling the marinated fish. She looks better after her rest, but Koana is still worried about the depth of her grief. She hopes a good night's sleep will allow her to see that all is not lost, that Peta is still holding her dear, despite the change in their relationship.

The next two weeks pass by in a haze. Cowrie manages to enjoy her last day with Koana and Ela but finds discussing the court case difficult since it always brings Nanduye back into the picture. It wouldn't be so bad if Nanduye was a real bitch but by all accounts she is an extraordinary person, and Cowrie realises she should feel grateful Peta is with someone so nice and that they've both honoured their pledge to help Koana and Ela. It can't be that easy for them either.

If only I could get beyond this terrible feeling of falling flat of existence, skimming the surface but not reacting. Even when DK baits me in class I remain calm. Rita is drinking again, realises she's outlived her welcome at my place and is staying with other friends now. Peta failed to call back and it's been a fortnight. I feel as if I could fall down a giant hole and enjoy being swallowed up. Rationally, I knew Peta and I would need to face this some time, but emotionally, it's ripping my gut in two. I don't think I realised how much I missed her. I'd gotten used to her being around. Vowed I'd never do that. Play the marriage game. Makes people crazy, dependent on each other.

"Lesbians take over the Beehive," DK yells out from her screen. "Wellington, Noo Zealand." The class is riveted. She reads: "From sappho@victoria. To LesboInternet, date, etc...."

"Just fling out the goss," pipes up Suzanne, her face alight.

DK continues. "At 4 am this morning, lesbian pilots in the RNZAF dropped hundreds of kilos of manuka honey from monsoon buckets on to parliament buildings, known locally as the beehive, to protest the government's hypocrisy towards gays in the forces and the failure to compensate for the army's mistaken chemical poisoning of rural Beehives on a recent exercise. Kiwi beekeepers donated the honey."

"At least they're not afraid to take action," declares Ruth. "Imagine if that happened here? The President and FBI would be on the spot in seconds, declaring nuclear war."

DK goes on: "Parliamentarians were seen scrambling knee-deep through the treacle-like substance, trying to find the appropriate papers to enable them to take court action. All planes were returned to their hangars and the entire corps refuses to answer questions from their superior officers or the media."

"What a buzz!" adds Suzanne, getting into the swing of it.

Cowrie hardly looks up from her desk.

"C'mon, Cowrie. You can't be that used to activism that this ain't at least interesting," DK challenges, managing to get a wry smile from the tutor.

"Sounds like a prank to me, DK. Check the date," retorts Cowrie.

"March 31st today. Nothing unusual."

"Yes but Aotearoa is a day ahead of the USA. Check the date on the email."

"Aw shucks, April Fool's Day. If only…"

"Well," says Cowrie, looking a bit brighter, "I wouldn't be surprised if it did happen. Maybe not quite like that. Remember I told you about Bastion Point and the occupation of Moutoa Gardens, Wanganui, to protest the taking of land from Maori by Pakeha?

Well, Bastion Point was finally won back for the tangata whenua. Many people at the time thought they were just a bunch of loud radicals, but in fact they represented iwi and tangata whenua right across the board from the tohunga, kuia and elders through to kohanga reo educators and bikie gangs. We have a proud tradition of protest in Aotearoa."

"So what did it achieve in terms of race relations?"

"Some felt it widened divisions, but it succeeded in getting people talking, debating the issues wildly on talkback, in the streets, within family groups, Pakeha and Maori. It changed the whole consciousness of the country, made people more aware of the complexity of colonialism."

"So how come you've put a damper on our rebellion against the fucked politics at UC lately?" asks DK. "Once, you encouraged us to speak our minds."

Cowrie sighs. "Sorry DK. You're right. I haven't been myself lately. Personal reasons. And I don't think Rita is up to fighting for us at present. So let's just let it lie for a week longer and reconsider then."

"No. I think we should fight it now, while we've still got a chance of winning."

Uretsete, usually shy, enters the fray. "Stuff a rag in it, DK. Let it ride a few days."

Cowrie looks over, realising Uretsete will know about her cousin Peta being with Nanduye. Every day, Uretsete's face reminds her of Peta's, so much that it is hard to look at her and not feel like crying.

"Thanks, Uretsete. I appreciate it. OK. Term papers are due in a week, and then we'll discuss whether we should take the curriculum changes to the higher committees if our colleagues will not heed the results of our survey."

Cowrie picks up her books and smiles back at the

class on her way out. "I'll be in a better mood by then also. Bear with me."

After she has gone, Ruth admonishes DK for being so insensitive, yet again.

"So what's got into her? Bad PMT or somethin'?" replies DK.

"No. Peta has remained at Kawhnawake with her colleague," Uretsete offers. "She called me and told me to make sure Cowrie is OK. She's written and tried to call, but Cowrie won't answer."

"Shit! That means she's got it bad," mumbles DK. "Wonder what we can do to make it better?"

"Simply get off her case," suggests Ruth, and is backed up by the others. Reluctantly, DK agrees.

"And" adds Tanya, always one for hot gossip, "Rita's chick threw her outa the house last week. My boyfriend lives next door. What a scene. Yelling, screaming. She was as pissed as a newt. Rita sounded high on something. They yelled for over an hour and then out went Rita followed by all her gear."

"Shit a brick. Really?" asks Suzanne.

"Yeah," replies Tanya. "Doesn't say much for Women's Studies if our teachers can't get their act together in real life does it?"

"Aw, come on Tanya. You're always looking for an excuse to hang loose because you wanted to major in Media Studies and your radical feminist mother insisted you take Women's Studies first so yer wouldn't get brainwashed."

"Fuck off. How do you know?"

"'Cos you told us first day of the semester," giggles Suzanne.

Tanya screws up her face and manages a smile. "Well, it's not all that bad. Quite like some of that Pacific writing, actually. Least it's not as woosie as the Ivy League rich bitches in that *Women's Review of Books*."

"Hey, this is getting out of hand," insists Ruth. "We shouldn't have to all be examples. There are alcoholics, rejected lovers and people of all political persuasions in all groups of society. Don't expect individual women to always carry the can for all of us."

"Time to hit Michelle's Cafe," suggests DK. "Who's comin'?"

They clear up their work and head off down Telegraph Avenue. Cowrie sees them pass from Moe's bookstore and buries her head back in the pages.

Uretsete returns to the screen, thankful for the quiet. She finishes writing about Iyatiku, bird woman, then packs up her books and disks, walking down Telegraph Avenue toward the cafe. She pauses at the secondhand bookstore, wondering if they've yet got in her order for *The Sacred Hoop,* and decides to check. As she is inquiring at the counter, she notices Cowrie, her head down in a book, tears falling on the pages. She excuses herself from the desk, hesitating as to whether she should interrupt or allow her tutor her own space. Somehow she feels responsible for Peta, who has called every few days asking after Cowrie. Uretsete knows she is the only one who can reassure Cowrie of Peta's care. She moves closer to the large armchair Cowrie is nestled inside, waits a moment. Cowrie senses a presence and looks up, wiping the tears from her face.

"Haku, Cowrie." Uretsete touches her shoulder gently. Her voice and greeting remind Cowrie of Peta, and a new stream of tears swells behind her eyes.

"Haku, Uretsete. You didn't go with the others?"

"I'm on my way now, but I wanted to finish my work on Iyatiku."

"Great. Have you done so?"

"Yes, once DK left her sacred machine."

"Bit of a drag having to share computers, I know. But we're not usually all working at them simultaneously."

"It's fine. You OK, Cowrie?"

"Fine, thanks."

"Really?"

Cowrie screws up her nose. "No. I guess I'm still missing that wicked aunty of yours," she ventures, trying to force lightness.

"Yeah. I thought so. But she's still there for you, Cowrie. Holding you, even in your absence. She's called me several times to see if you're OK."

"Really? Why doesn't she call me?"

"She's tried, evidently, but only ever gets your machine."

"Fair comment. I let Orca answer these days."

"So when are you two gonna deal with this properly?"

Cowrie is surprised at Uretsete's forthrightness, ashamed to be caught mid-process, unable to articulate her emotions gracefully, deal with them as well as she'd like. It shouldn't be up to Uretsete to convince her to face Peta. "I guess it's time, huh? I just needed space to sort out my feelings. It's not just Peta but the disappointment, lack of hope I feel. In Rita, in the programme, in the thesis. Peta's rejection has just clinched it all at a bad time."

"C'mon, Cowrie. Out of death comes renewal, phoenix from the ashes and all that. You're always telling us about the power of death in symbolism, the opportunity for renewal it brings."

"Yes. But it's easier to deal with in literature and mythology than in life."

"What's the difference? One feeds the other."

"True."

"What about that dream you once told us in class, when we were all arguing from our different cultural perspectives and it looked as if Ruth and DK would kill each other?"

"What about it?"

"Well, you described to us a scene where all these women from different cultures were in a cave near

242

the sea and they were singing around a fire. Then a whoosh of wave and wind came in, nearly blew out the fire, bearing a force through the waves as if the energy of the women had combined to create a new power in the universe."

"Yes. I remember."

"Then it rose up into the sky, part fish, part bird, part woman."

"Ah, the fantastic dream bird. Maori call her hikioi."

"Yes. Isn't she a symbol of renewal in the dream? Didn't the fire nearly die under the wave, but was rekindled by the wind? And wasn't it a wave that took the new energy conceived and flamed in the cave back out through the water, letting the wind lift her into the sky to fly her way to freedom? Or did I misinterpret the dream?"

"No. That's exactly what happened."

"Then why is the death of one limb of the relationship with Peta not allowing you to rejoice in the renewal and birth of a new branch? Don't you still have your soul love together?"

Cowrie is stunned. Of course Uretsete is right. This is the heart of her relationship with Peta. Their sexual lovemaking always had a spiritual element and their spiritual sharing a sensual energy. By mourning the death of the sexuality, which they don't any longer share since they are physically apart, she has been killing the possibility of the spiritual connection growing to new heights, indulgently worshipping death at the expense of new life. It all seems so simple now, yet it still hurts like hell. She sighs.

"Mahalo, Uretsete. Of course you are right. I just need more time to take it in."

"Sure, but don't leave Peta out in the cold too long. She's not so good at being patient, take it from me."

Cowrie laughs weakly, "I know."

"That fantastic dream bird exists here too, Cowrie. It's about creativity, isn't it? In researching Iyatiku, I've been reading about Popul Vuh, the sacred myth of the Quiche Mayans. In the beginning the grandparents, creators, existed in water, covered over by blue and green sea feathers. They meditated in the darkness and were called Gucumatz because the light flashes around their meditative zones looked like the bright wings of the quetzal bird, which the ancient Mayans knew as gucumatz."

"Like the water birds that saved the Iriquois Sky Woman from falling through the void? Peta told me about them."

"Yes. And Iyatiku is often depicted with the body of a bird and the head of a woman. She's who I imagined flying out of the jade green ocean when you told us about the hikioi bird in your dream. She's the symbol of new hope for our work—and that includes your work with Peta. If we give up now, then all the energy that emerged from the cave and flew out of the water is negated."

"Phew. That puts a huge responsibility on Peta and I to get it right."

"Sure. And for all of us. Each time we embrace death and refuse to see the possibility of renewal, we return to old patterns of negativity. It's not denial of pain and death and new growth, but rather embracing its energy to move on and thus taking the energy with us. We have choices in how we deal with each symbolic death."

"Sounds a tad New Age for you, Uretsete."

"That's where you're wrong, Cowrie. Indigenous cultures recognise these powers. Whod'yer reckon the New Agers got it from? The more I study our own Indian myths and practices, the more convinced I am of this.

244

You know when you told us about saving Maata's life and how an almost superhuman force allowed you to get out beyond the breakers? Well, Peta later explained that was Laukiamanuikahiki, Turtle Woman, entering you to give you the strength to do her work. I had a similar experience abseiling at Yosemite when a safety rope snapped. I fell down into the gully but felt wings sweep me up and carry me to a rock ledge. Later, our guide said it must've been a lucky wind tunnel combined with the angle of the fall, but I know what I felt when those feathered wings embraced me. It was Iyatiku. I remember the softness of her wings and the look on her face as clear as light."

"You needn't convince me. Turtle Woman came to help me in dreams through my life, and in reality when I needed her to save little Maata. But why do you think these mythical women are speaking and acting through us now?"

"I think it's probably always happened, it's just that some people are more receptive to their help than others. And it's up to us to communicate these insights, work collectively for our future survival, just as in your dream."

"And I guess the moral of the tale is that if Peta and I can't treat each other well, still believe in our love even when it changes form instead of denying its energy, then we're not going to be very effective in our political work since the two are deeply connected, right?"

"Hole in one, Cowrie!"

"Didn't think I'd ever hear you use a golfing term, Uretsete."

"Well, I learned a bit about golf when protesting to get back land stolen from us for the white boys' golf course at Kahnawake. Grown men chasing after little white balls. Seemed rather pointless to me."

Cowrie laughs. "Well, teacher, thanks for the apt

lesson. I really appreciate your timing and your sharing of your knowledge and research, Uretsete."

"Ain't that what it's about, doc? So you want to come with me to join the others at the cafe?"

"Thanks for the invite. But I think I'll track on home. Got an important call to make to Kahnawake."

"Give Peta my love. On second thoughts, you'd better not tell her I intruded. She might think it's rigged."

"Sure, Uretsete. But I'll remind her of the dream. The part I didn't tell the class was that Peta was in the cave with me, then she disappeared. I think she might have swooped out of the water and flown away."

"Or she could've fallen off the Rainbow Bridge and been turned into a dolphin. Thank your stars you can still talk to her in the same language."

Cowrie remembers Peta telling her the Rainbow Bridge story, recalls her dreams. "I think she may be Dolphin Woman too, Uretsete. And I reckon I'll take more notice of my dreams in future."

"The best intuition comes from dreams. Peta always told me that when I was growing up."

"Well, she is one wise aunty, and I can't wait to talk to her. Give my best regards to the class. Oh, yes, and tell DK I'll try to contact Rita and get some sense out of her on the theory versus primary texts debate. I'll report back tomorrow."

Uretsete and Cowrie walk out on to Telegraph to be met by the bustle of students and hawkers. They part, and Cowrie invents conversations with Peta as she hums her way down the avenue, her heart still feeling a mixture of fear and rejection but her spirit rising to greet the carved taiaha Uretsete has thrown out to her. She recalls the hikioi dream vividly, wondering if Iyatiku, bird woman, looks like the rainbow-splashed taniwha flying out of the water streaking its coloured feathers into the night sky.

246

Brrr...brrr...

"Haku, Peta."

"Cowrie! At last! How are you, Turtle?"

"Surviving."

"Oh, Turtle, I'm so sorry to hurt you. I don't know any way to make this transition easier. I put it off as long as possible so I could be sure it was the right thing to do."

"And is it?"

"I think so."

"Well, I haven't been that receptive, Peta. I went into an old place. Thought I'd dealt with all that rejection stuff, but it comes back to haunt me every time."

"Hey, Cowrie, I'm not rejecting you. We both knew we'd need to adjust if I stayed at Kahnawake. The only unexpected part is Nanduye."

"I wasn't so surprised. There were signs, even in Aotearoa. I just didn't want to see them."

"Honestly, Cowrie, I worked with Nanduye and we knew each other so well I never dreamed we'd ever become lovers. It just evolved."

"So why didn't you tell me straight away instead of letting me suffer?"

"Wouldn't it have hurt as bad anyway?"

"Sure. But I'd still want to know so I felt I had choices."

"I guess you're right. I was selfish to hold back. I was scared too."

"What of?"

"You, Snapping Turtle. Of letting you down after all our powerful sharing. I never thought I'd ever meet anyone as compatible as you. And our lovemaking took us into sacred places. I miss that."

"But don't you have it with Nanduye?"

"It's different. Sharing work is the centre of our relationship and I know I couldn't stay here and work without her, or with you, for that matter. It's too complex to explain over the phone. I'll be back in the Bay Area next month for a Red Nations Benefit. Reckon you could spare some time to meet me so we can talk at more length, deal with this in person?"

"Sure, Peta. Hey—let's not fight. I do feel deep pain, and some rejection still, but I'd like to preserve the best of our soul sharing if that's OK with you and Nanduye."

"Nan wants that to happen. She urged me to contact you earlier, but you know me. I need time to mull things over in my spirit."

"I'm doing a performance with Siliyik—Uretsete's oral storytelling group—in three weeks. Will you be here then?"

"Sure will. Perfect timing. Book me a seat. Maybe we could do dinner as well?"

"That'd be great. Hey, Peta, do you still miss our good times?"

"Every day. You still swim inside me, Turtle. You always will. No one can replace that special place you have in me. Don't forget that. I love you, Turtle, deeply, tenderly, sacredly."

Cowrie's throat goes dry, then tears rush through her being, out and down the phone line, a tidal wave surging into the scorching fire coming down the cable from the other end. There is a moment's silence.

"Love you too, Peta. I still miss the tender moments,

the passion, your fire on my tongue, in my soul. Especially our last journey together. Kissing beside the waterfall at Yosemite, licking mango juice from your lips at Lake Mono, that tender night of lovemaking in the tent at Tomales Bay. But more than anything, your soul friendship."

"You've still got that, Cowrie, minus the mango juice! I keep thinking of the power of your poems, our discussions about oral storytelling, and I want us to continue to work together. I'd really like to get you and Siliyik up here for a performance to encourage some of the younger people on the reservation to get involved, reclaim their own heritage and stories. They'd really relate to the Hawai'ian and Maori myths you've shared with me."

"Now you're talking, Peta. I might just take you up on that offer. Have you spoken to Siliyik yet?"

"I've mentioned the idea to Uretsete, but she insisted I speak to you."

Cowrie laughs. "Reckon she was trying to get us to talk, Peta. Good on her. And thanks."

"Thank you for being so generous, Cowrie."

"You're just lucky I needed time to think. Besides, it's not just the changes with us that have been upsetting me. Feels like my whole world has crashed in. Rita tried to dry out but is back on the booze. Claudia won't speak to her till she gets her act together, so it's been awkward. Meantime my thesis is on hold and the students are rebelling against Rita's inability to make firm decisions regarding their challenge for more primary texts and less theory."

"So boundaries are being broken all over, eh Cowrie? Must be hard when Rita is your boss, your friend, your thesis supervisor, and answerable to both the students and the regents. Both of you are caught mid-stream."

"Yeah, but what worries me is that I fear Rita's final allegiance will be to save her own skin and her job at the expense of both the students and my thesis."

"Well, if so, you've got to go over her head or else cut your losses and finish your work outside the academy. Turn it into a book and video. Sell it to a groundbreaking feminist press. After all, you want to reach the widest possible audience, change attitudes, more than get three damned letters after your name, don't you?"

"Sure do. Bloody good idea, Peta. I'd miss the students though, deeply."

"Get Siliyik to go professional and tour with their work. That'd promote your book and video, which I assume they'd be involved in anyway. Then you'd all be employed doing the work you love."

"You're a visionary, Peta. I like it. But I'm sure some of the students will want to finish their thesis work first."

"They can do both if you handle it well. Let's talk more when I visit. Think about it in the meantime."

"I can assure you it'll be top priority."

"Good. It'll take your mind off the pain, Turtle. Remember to feed your soul too. I haven't seen any poems lately."

"I've got a few from the emotional deeps after you dumped me, but I doubt you'd want to see them."

"You're right. But send them if you feel strong enough. I think I'm ready to face it now. Maybe it'll help the healing process between us."

"OK. But I might update them with waiata for soul aroha, now we've got this far."

"Do me a tape, Turtle. I promise to do one back. So we can keep talking to each other through this time, not let bitterness set in. Promise me?"

"Yep. D'you realise we both got close to ruining our friendship by avoiding each other?"

"Yeah. We're wimps when it comes to fronting up. I've been thinking about that. Culturally, we learned denial as a way of surviving as kids. We've got an opportunity to change that now."

"I see Nanduye has been good for you, making you face up to things. I'm pleased Peta. I reckon we can help each other with that one."

"Sure thing, Turtle. Gotta go now. We're preparing for Koana and Ela to arrive. They're getting a full welcome at the longhouse. Should be interesting for them."

"Ko will love it. Thanks so much, Peta. I love you."

"Love you too, Turtle. Don't forget that."

"I won't. Mahalo, Peta."

"Bye." Click.

Cowrie stands in the studio, surrounded by Peta's letters which she's retrieved, finds a stalk of sweetgrass in the bottom of the box. She lights it and takes the letters into the kitchen to read. Tears of release, pain, grief flow from her over pages lit up by the moonbeam through the leadlights. The black ink runs on to her wrist and forms the curved shape of a canoe, a waka for the next stage of their journey.

Waka Tainui
Te Kotuku Marae, Hokianga.

Tena koe, Cowrie.

It's been ages since I wrote but so much has
happened here at Te Kotuku. I tried doing
you a tape but gave up when the bloody
batteries ran out. I hope all's going well for
you. You haven't been in touch in a while
either and that usually happens when you're
hassled or worried. Especially hope all is OK
with Peta. Write and tell me anyway. You
know I'm here for you.

Progress at Te Aroha has been rough but
satisfying. We've managed to get most of
the elders of local iwi on board with the
scheme to make sex offenders face up to
the harm they inflict and in many cases the
survivors find facing their offenders when
they apologise a strong part of the healing
process. It backfired in one case where the
offender broke his vows and started to heap
more abuse on the survivor. But the elders
silenced him immediately and the survivor
was given support and further counselling. It
put the whole programme in jeopardy for a
month while the issues were debated but
we've now got the necessary support to
continue.

There's korero about extending the scheme to take punishment for offenders out of Pakeha hands to be dealt with by local iwi where possible. Most of the elders now realise that clogging up the courts with Maori who just learn to reoffend in prison is useless and destroys our mana. So far, the justice system has supported us except in murder cases which are still dealt with by the crown.

However, I'm worried that Mike's attack on that ragged old pine at Maungakiekie turned previous supporters against us and the usual biased media handling of the occupation of Maori land at Moutoa gardens is turning the tide of opinion against us. But you'll be pleased to know the government put the screws on that Far North MP, John Carter, and sacked him as cheif government whip. He rang up old Banksie's radio show pretending to be a Maori dole bludger. Everyone knows he's been doing it for years. Hone Carter the locals call him. The iwi are divided. Some of the blokes think it's funny, and everyone else is insulted. At least it's brought the rednecks out of the closet—on both sides.

Following Moutoa, there was an occupation of the marae at Whakarewarewa which is tipped off to be the next government asset

sale. How dare they steal our land then sell it to foreigners? Some iwi are calling it Tokyo-rua already. Things are hotting up so you'd better not be too long in getting back home where you belong!

So how's that wretched thesis going? I must admit, I do not regret leaving the university at all, even the decent pay. Te Aroha and work at Te Kotuku keeps me working hard but it's more satisfying. Life's too short to waste our time on feathering the nests of the privileged at the expense of our people.

On the creative front, Irihapeti, Mere, Seone and I have introduced a mixture of storytelling and street theatre into the new kohanga programme at Te Kotuku, and the kids love it. We're touring Tai Tokerau in the nursery mini-bus, getting schools to participate, and the results have been amazing. Didn't know how many Samoan, Cook Island and Tokelau kids were up here. Also heaps of Yugoslav and Nga Puhi intermarriages. The family stories and myths the kids bring along are amazingly rich. Similar myths among many of the Pacific Islanders. If only their parents had experienced this at school, there might not be so much racism and fear of the different groups as now. It'll take years to break down the established patterns. But heh, it beats

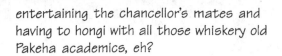

entertaining the chancellor's mates and having to hongi with all those whiskery old Pakeha academics, eh?

So what's your news? Has that Rita tart shown her true colours yet? I'd be wary, Cowrie, from the hints you gave out in that last fax after she went back on the booze. If she fence-sits on student issues, she'll do it with your thesis too. She's a pretender. Remember that Aotea proverb: "*ekore e piri te uku ki te rino:* clay will not stick to iron", in other words, don't pretend to be what you're not, because the clay disguise will fall off. That helped me through those empty days at Waikato University. I'll tell ya, though, wet clay sticks to yer face like shit to a blanket before it falls off! Haha! Get chipping away at that mask now, Cowrie, and know that whatever your final decisions, we're right behind you. Mere and Iri send their aroha.

Ka kite, arohanui

Kuini.

Cowrie folds Kuini's letter and places it in her breast pocket. Imagine the chief government whip being sacked for impersonating a stereotyped and insulting image of a Maori. Bet there'll be a redneck backlash to that one. But it shows there are some in government taking the issues seriously. The success of Te Aroha looks as if it'll be a pioneer for future justice cases. Good old Kuini. Wonder if she's right and I should just flag the university hassles and take my work to the feminist presses, do it on our terms?

Rita pokes her head in through the door. "Hi, stranger. Haven't seen you in a while. Is everything OK?"

"Rita, come in. I need to talk to you. But first, how's your own living situation?"

"Fucked. Claudia's given me an ultimatum. She's agreed to take me back in if I work in therapy. She knows I think the therapy movement has sucked the guts out of feminist activism, but I'm agreeing. It's our only chance. Went to see this shrink last night. She says I have a lot of anger. Tried to get me to thump a pillow. All I wanted to do was punch her lights out. Much more satisfying."

"So will you go back?"

"Yeah. In a way she's right, though fucked if I'll tell her. Last night I lay in bed and listed all the things I am angry about. Most of them are to do with the powerlessness I feel here. I'm caught between the students and the establishment, and my job depends on agreeing with the departmental line, so what choice do I have?"

"Rita. UC Berkeley was the beginning of the free speech movement in the sixties. What's happened?"

"One hell of a lot apparently. It's sort of OK for blacks to speak out, but it sure as hell ain't yet OK for radical women and dykes."

"Yeah, but it's a process. We need to form coalitions to get what we want, and I think we'd get further by aligning ourselves with the students and supporting their demands than sitting on the fence in between. What's there to lose?"

"Everything, for me. My last hope is to keep this job, my medical insurance. That pays for my shrink work, which seems inevitable for a while, and without Claudia, it's all I have to live for."

"But Rita, I know you privately agree that the predominance of theory over primary texts has become outrageous in recent years, that we have abandoned the activism and original creative writers for reactive theorists who earn big bickies for generating an industry around their own careers. How can you live with supporting the status quo?"

"It isn't that simple, Cowrie. I've seen your student survey and I'm going to have to oppose it. That's the end of the story."

"You mean you're not even open to negotiation or discussion on it?"

"Absolutely not. I've made my decision and that's that."

"At least hear the issues put forward by the class. Come over this afternoon at three and we'll devote a session to debate."

"No, Cowrie. That's my final word. The texts remain as is. It's too late to change them anyway. The deadline was last week. If the new students don't like it they can raise the issue again. It's a free world."

"You mean, by the time they figure it out, it'll be too late in the semester to change the text, and so on for every successive year. Nothing changes but the pointless ritual of wasting student time by letting them think they have a voice?"

Rita's face twists into an evil grin which Cowrie has never seen before. She snarls back, "Took you a while to work it out. Then again, islanders are known to be pretty slow." She exits, leaving a stunned turtle in her wake.

No wonder Claudia feels alienated. Maybe it's not just Rita's alcoholism that gets to her. Maybe it's the cleverly hidden racism that is only now beginning to surface? She thinks back to the night Rita arrived drunk on her doorstep, the abuse she piled on Claudia. Moments of Rita at staff meetings, her hedging the students, her inability to answer questions directly, flash back to her now, crowd in on her mind. She'd so much wanted to like Rita, to develop a strong working relationship with her from the beginning, that she'd ignored the signs, just as she blanked out the dreams about Peta, not wanting to know the worst. Time to get a grip. Time to plan and act.

Later, in class, DK asks what action they can take regarding the results of their departmental student survey. This is the moment. Cowrie tells them to listen up.

"Since our last discussion, I've been thinking hard. I've spoken to Rita and it appears that there is nothing we can do to change the texts for the rest of this year. However, since most of you will be continuing in Women's or Gay and Lesbian Studies, I suggest we follow up the survey with an analysis of the results, actually develop a balanced curriculum proposal. We'll then meet with students the first week of the new semester and explain the situation and options so that they get the chance to act early. I've checked the minutes of previous meetings, and some of the same issues have arisen year after year. It appears that the tactic is to seem to be listening to the students, but postpone action until it's too late and then a new batch of students has to go through it all over again. This time, we'll beat them to it."

"Now you're talking. Action at last!" DK is jubilant.

"But won't we be in danger of being regarded in a biased way by those marking our work for the rest of the year?" questions Tanya.

"Sure," responds Ruth, "But that's always the risk of taking action. Hell, it's not exactly putting your life on the line, as my ancestors had to do."

"Yeah, and what's the point of us studying writing and theory about political action if we're not willing to take it?" ventures Uretsete. "At least in Native American studies, we debate the issues and take action where necessary because we actually live the reality daily."

"Women's and even Gay and Lesbian Studies have been hijacked by the theorists. We need to reclaim our roots, restate the links between our studies and what is happening out there," adds Suzanne, who used to be fairly quiet until she took up with DK.

"Right. But we need to be very careful how we do this, so we are taken seriously and so we get what we want," asserts Cowrie. "I want us to approach this on several fronts at once. We need to produce analysis of the survey results, a balanced and viable new curriculum proposal, do it through the appropriate university channels, and plan alternative action to take place immediately if we are not listened to. Each one of you needs to think how involved she wants to get and how much she's willing to risk. Anyone not on board can opt out now."

"Count me out," says Tanya, packing up her books. "I want good grades and a perfect record. I want to have a brilliant career and make heaps of money. Then I'll be able to do what I want. That's the true road to freedom."

"Aw fuck off, Tanya. Get real!" DK yells. "People who say that usually take the riches and run. How many rich bitches do you know who come out as dykes, support feminism, put their money where their mouths are?"

"Tanya's entitled to her opinion. I trust, however, you will respect our right to act and not snitch on us, Tanya," adds Cowrie, as Tanya is about to leave the room.

"That depends on my final grades," smirks Tanya, exiting the class.

Another Rita, thinks Cowrie. She's welcome to her. The rest of the afternoon, which is their time to debate issues raised during the week, they plot a course of action with three prongs: the survey and curriculum proposal, an alternative activist plan, and incorporating the issues into their upcoming performance by Siliyik.

"I think it's time we considered the options of turning Siliyik into a semi-professional group to tour reservations and communities over the vacation," suggests Uretsete. "And we've had our first invitation to perform at the Kahnawake Reservation. We'll need to raise funds for it."

Ruth is enthusiastic. "Let's go for it. Siliyik represents our own ancestry, our own stories in action. That's another branch to our activism and it's also putting our lives, our theory on the line. We need to show others we can do it by example."

A heated discussion emerges, with the rest of the group getting fired up to the proposals that are now erupting from them. Cowrie recalls their first debates, where each came from such a fixed position, she could not even hear the others. It's been their work together in Siliyik, feeling heard and sharing their stories, that has produced such strong bonds between them, the kinds of bonds that theory alone can never achieve. Their combination is electric; it fires her with hope for their power to affect others, to reclaim their pasts, if not shape their futures.

Cowrie wakes to the smell of freshly perked coffee and the unmistakable aroma of cornbread heating in the oven. She must be dreaming. She drifts back into the reverie, indulging herself. Steam rises from the coffee, filters through her nostrils. The oven door opens and cornbread fragrance sails to her on the updraft. A crash as the tin is uplifted on the counter.

"Shit. It's split!"

She leans over the edge of the loft. Peta looks up sheepishly, as she tries to mould the two halves of the cornbread together. "I wanted you to wake to your favourite aromas. Uretsete picked me up from the airport late last night and we baked you cornbread this morning. Thought I'd heat it up for our breakfast."

Cowrie cannot believe Peta is finally here. Feels like old times. Or does it? There's a huge difference now. But at least Peta wants to stay close. She'd forgotten she still had the key to her studio. She's not sure whether she should feel invaded or delighted. "Haku, Peta. Must admit, I'm a bit stunned, but not so much that I can't eat your delicious cornbread. Be down in a tick." Cowrie splashes some frangipani essence over her steaming body, grabs her blue and cream hibiscus lavalava, and backs down the loft ladder into Peta's arms.

"So we're allowed to hug then, eh?"

Peta smiles back. "Sure thing, Turtle. So long as you're OK with it?"

"More than OK. Rapt." Cowrie knows so well the

feeling of wanting to be close to someone she loves, and having to hold back for one reason or another. She just hopes she doesn't get too sensuous, then the pain of the situation would return. It's like old times. They have been parted so long now that they slip into friendship easily. But the temptation to take Peta to bed is so strong, it rises in Cowrie almost immediately, flaming through her body. "Just let me have a shower, love. I think we need to talk after that."

In the shower, she realises that things cannot simply return to the old days, that she needs to keep some distance between herself and Peta physically, until she gets used to not wanting to hold her, make love to her. But she desires the comfort, the warmth, the aroha also. Fucking boundaries. Here we go again. When she emerges from the shower, the table is set, with fresh gardenias floating in a bowl. The fragrance sets her alight. Peta looks radiant, her eyes on fire, her hair now short and spiky. Together, they break cornbread and imbibe coffee as if they'd never parted. Cowrie has not experienced this kind of break-up before.

"Hey Peta, if this is what breaking up with you is about, let's do it more often."

Peta smiles. "Well, I hoped we'd be able to remain close friends. To be honest Cowrie, I still desire you, but I know I've made the right choice to be with Nanduye. It wasn't easy but I am totally devoted to the reservation work and even if I weren't with Nanduye, we'd only be able to see each other from time to time, and that would hardly be fair."

"But you are in love with Nanduye, surely?"

"Yes. But that doesn't cancel out my love for you, Turtle. If fantasies were possible, I'd want to be with you both." Peta leans over, kisses her softly, tenderly. Cowrie knows she must pull back. She doesn't. She lets her tongue dance with Peta's, feels her nipples harden, her whole body flow to the passion rising in her. She remembers the waterfall at Yosemite, experiences the cavern of Aotearoa open inside her, hears the whoosh as the wave takes their energy out into the open sea, watches as the taniwha streaks her coloured feathers through the water, skimming the surface, flying up into the sky. Peta touches her nipples, swelling them under her fingers, shaping them into mountains, licking the sea surrounding their rising cones.

They make love wildly, erotically, more urgently than ever before. Cowrie knows it is not right, yet allows herself to be swept along on a tidal wave of passion. But afterwards, there is a strange sadness, a knowledge between them that this is their final farewell to a part of their relationship they will never share again.

"I told Nanduye I'd have to farewell your body with aroha to let the soul relationship flourish. Finally, she understood why and that it did not threaten my sharing with her. But how is it for you, Turtle?"

"Strangely, Peta, I feel OK. My intellect tells me it's not right, but my body and emotions feel it honours what we've shared, brings the joy back as the foundation for this new growth and work between us. For the first time, I do not feel rejected by a lover making a choice to be with another sexually. I feel I'm now ready to accept that. But it will take time and space for me not to feel like making love to you when I see you."

"I guess my return to Kahnawake will provide that. It's redundant to feel immoral, Cowrie. Most of that comes from conditioning. We had to find our own way of performing a ritual ending. Out of the spent fire of our passion, a new creature will rise, one enriched by our sexual union even as it strives to exist on a soul plane. For me, it would have been less honest to pretend the passion did not still exist and have to go through that charade."

"I guess so. But now I'm going to feel the pain of missing you so powerfully in every inch of my body."

"I'll still be inside you, Cowrie. You carry me with you, and you are with me. That's the nature of soul love, whether it is or is not expressed sexually as well. We have and still share the essence of that power, and we'll be able to remain friends forever if only we can rise above the temptation to act out the jealous lover role. Nanduye has taught me a lot about that."

"She's a wise woman, Peta, and I liked her even when I feared you were together. This is a brave journey we're entering and it feels like there's new territory to be explored instead of hashing out past stuff. I just have to keep telling my body to behave."

"C'mon, Cowrie, your rising ocean always had the power to snuff my fire. Just let her fill you with aroha and know I am still inside you, always will be, I hope."

After Peta has left, promising to call later to arrange a time to meet before the Siliyik performance, Cowrie hums through the morning, amazed at the unexpected joy she feels. The difference is in embracing the changes instead of fighting them. Besides, she knows she has been secretly mourning the loss of a part of Peta to Nanduye ever since she let the sweetgrass blacken the abalone shell that night in Aotearoa, when Mere worried she was burning the house down.

In a way, this is a relief. The loss and grief has been in my body for months now, though I refused to openly acknowledge it. I've been weeping for this, allowing myself to be numb. Now I feel the fire in me again, the power of a new beginning. And maybe I'm finally getting over that endless repetition of childhood abandonment in my life. Maybe this is the turning point at last.

Siliyik gives the performance of the year. Uretsete tells the story of her birth, being sung into existence, and Ruth links this with an ancient Yiddish tale of naming which ends with a passionate song which she's taught the group in Yiddish, then DK recalls the survival of her Polish grandfather in the Nazi death camps, elements of the tale connecting to Ruth's story. Suzanne recounts southern stories her nanny told her, interweaving myth and childhood reality. After intermission, their humorous sketch denouncing university politics receives a rave reaction.

Cowrie ends with the tale of Laukiamanuikahiki, who was orphaned by her chieftain father who also left tokens to guide her home. She tells how Turtle Woman is sent up on a bamboo shoot by the grandmothers, to be dropped gently beside a pond where she makes lei with a beautiful woman. Finally, she is reunited with her birth family. They conclude with waiata celebrating the journey home to themselves created by the telling of their stories. Uretsete enacts a ritual to bless the land of Great Turtle Island they are performing upon, burning sweetgrass and handing sticks for the audience to pass on, each lighting the other's taper.

The audience is electric, elated. Peta feels a surge of energy flow through her, humming and murmuring after the clapping. Some even stand up in appreciation of the treat they have experienced. Above, the full moon and stars glow, lighting up the courtyard, shining the faces of the women with new hope. Many gather round the storytellers, eager to add their own tales, experiences, share where it touches them most. Peta is so proud of Uretsete for pulling this together, Cowrie for suggesting it in the first place. A pang of nostalgia returns, a longing to be back here in the Bay Area, connecting with women, motivated by the energy that surrounds her now. The moon catches the side of Cowrie's face and the reflection from her jade green and swirling blue scarf stirs the sea within Peta. She remembers their lovemaking this morning, feels a pang of regret that they can no longer share this, wonders who will next swim into Cowrie's ocean, be attracted to her turtle charms.

Finally, the crowd dwindles to a few who cannot seem to leave, and Uretsete invites them to join Siliyik for dinner. Within ten minutes, the largest round table at the Siam Thai restaurant on University Avenue is surrounded by women of different nationalities, all telling their stories, eager to explore the links that have been sparked by the performance.

They order a delicious banquet: Haw Mok Plaa; steamed fish curry; Kaeng Khua Sapparod Hoi Malaeng Poo, mussel and pineapple curry soup; and Cowrie and Peta's favourite, Tom Khaa Kai, coconut and galangal soup, slices of chicken floating in hot coconut and flavoured by the gingery taste of the galangal. Cowrie can taste the kaffir lime leaves even as she orders the dish. Kaeng Cheud Plaa Muk, stuffed squid soup; and Uretsete's choice, Tom Yum Kung, hot and sour shrimp soup—and this is just for starters! After these delicacies from the Central Plains of Thailand they move on to Bangkok delights for their second courses—favouring the Kai Phad series of chicken fried with ginger, basil, green peppers or cashew nuts. The roti is from the south and, unlike

267

Indian cooking, is used as a dessert rather than as bread with the meal. Thai rotis, the waiter explains, originates from Thailand's Indian population. The main courses are from the North East—Laab Kai, Kai Yang and Neua Yang with spicy catfish salad, Lap Plaa Duk.

Between the feast of dishes, the conversation ebbs and flows, turns tides and enters new estuaries, according to the whims of the women, the pull of the moon, the flavours and aromas of the food. More stories emerge, each threading into the other as seaweed swirls with the tide. By the end of the evening, the malakaw (papaya) and ma muang (mango) juices drip down the chins of the women, on to their plates, like tears from heaven. Peta glimpses stars sparkling in the ocean of juice below their plates as the lights shine down on them, weeps at the joy of their union, the tearing of their breaking up. Her thigh touches Cowrie's but she is so motivated in her laughter and conversation, she barely notices.

Later, lying in bed, Cowrie recalls Rita did not turn up for the performance even though she was given tickets. Claudia was there at the side of the courtyard and Cowrie bumped into her before the show in the loos. They talked for a while and Claudia explained that she could no longer live with Rita because of her politics as well as her alcoholism, that one fed the other, and the Rita she'd first fallen in love with was unrecognisable from the ambitious woman she saw revealing her true colours now. Cowrie simply nodded in agreement, then the lights went down to mark the performance about to start, so they agreed to stay in touch in the future, whatever happened with Rita.

Despite the warm glow in her from the wonderful day, beginning with Peta's appearance and ending with the performance and dinner, Cowrie feels a slight unrest, a gnawing doubt in her body. She's not sure if it is guilt at making love with Peta or a premonition of things to come with Rita. She dismisses the guilt, since it was the memory of the interaction with Claudia that brought the anxiety back to her. She reads until she is so tired she drifts into sleep.

Rita is flanked by two men from the English Department. One she'd told Cowrie she wouldn't trust with her life. The other is a known opponent of Women's Studies. The head of department now seems quite relaxed with these academics. Cowrie is walking up a long corridor but she struggles to reach the end. Before her, she can see into the room where others drink and laugh. As she approaches, Rita turns and a Hallowe'en hat with horns emerges from her head. The two men are dressed as rams. They poke out their forked tongues and dangle their drunken nakedness in front of the women. She vomits all over them.

Cowrie wakes with a start, images still swirling in her head. Yuck. She reaches for the water beside her bed and gulps it down hungrily, wanting to drown the taste in her mouth. Surely Rita would not collude with scum like them? She's just going through a difficult patch and I should support her. Can't be easy to be in her position or to be struggling so hard with her addictions. Mustn't let paranoia take over.

She turns on the light and reads the final draft of her latest thesis chapter. She has relied heavily on primary texts and there's bound to be a debate over this. But Pacific lesbian literature does not easily fit into the classical canon from either Europe or America. Its themes reflect those of other post-colonial nations more closely. Proving this to the academy may be another thing. I'll need to show a thorough knowledge of theory to debate that this work lies both within and outside its boundaries. What a drag. Sometimes I wonder if working towards a PhD is about showing off your knowledge of previous theory or about discovering original ideas and new literature. Ideally, it should be both, but in practice the theory game prevails. Cowrie works late, rewording her ideas more clearly, discovering new strands to her arguments. She's glad she'll have new material to offer at the supervision meeting.

Brrr...brrr. The phone wakes her with a start. She backs down the ladder and makes it just before the answer machine cuts in. "Haku, Cowrie. Peta here. It's a glorious day. Wanna come to Angel Island with me for a picnic? I've baked you some fresh cornbread."

"Tena koe, Peta. I'd adore to. But I've got a bloody supervision meeting today. Stayed up late preparing for it."

"But Turtle, this is my last full day here. Can't Rita and all those grizzlies wait another day?"

"No way, Peta. Took me three weeks to get them all in one office for one hour to discuss the revised proposal. I'm not giving in now."

"Fine. How about I meet you afterwards? You might need some kai and a good laugh."

"Sure will. What about Mama Bears at four?"

"Only if I can take you out to dinner afterwards."

"Yes. So long as I get home safe. No more temptation, or I'll burst!"

"My fiery tongue will only ever touch sashimi tonight. Salmon, kina, dory, tuna, with fresh raw sliced ginger and jade green wasabi flaming the roots of my desire..."

"I haven't even had my Vegemite and tea yet! You're such a tease, Peta. I'll see you at four. And yes, make a booking at the Mikado on Telegraph and tell them I'll be ravenous for raw fish by then!"

"Done. Kia kaha, Cowrie. Give 'em heaps!"

"Mahalo, Peta. I will. See ya later."

By noon, Cowrie has taught her morning class and is preparing for the thesis meeting. When she enters Rita's office an hour later, she is surprised to find her alone. She asks where the other advisors are and Rita gives a lame excuse about a regents' meeting and asks her to sit down. "Cowrie, I have rather bad news. The PhD supervision committee has decided that the frame of reference for your doctorate is too small. There is not enough gay Pacific Island writing to justify a PhD, and you must show a clear knowledge of the European theory before you embark on new material. They want you to rewrite your proposal and just include a chapter on Pacific literature at the end or in an appendix."

"In an appendix? We've been a bloody appendix to your northern hemisphere definitions for centuries now. That's the whole point of redefining our work within our own terms of reference. How can we define a post-colonial reality if you are still treating us as colonies of your academic system? The whole *raison dê'tre* behind earning a Fulbright, as defined by Senator Fulbright himself, is to question current thought. After all, he was a peace activist long before his time."

"We're not talking about Senator Fulbright here, Cowrie. This is about our rules. The committee has suggested that you realign your thesis within the auspices of the English Department and work with the Dutch lesbian scholar, Marlene du Fresne."

"Oh spare me! She's the epitome of postmodernist jargon from a racist Eurocentric perspective. I'd rather work with a decent post-colonial scholar who understands the terms of reference for our Pacific literature. Does this mean you're piking out on me?"

272

"Cowrie. It is crucial that I'm not seen to support your radical stance within the academy, even if I might inwardly support your position. It will make things easier for both of us of you work with Marlene."

"You can't be serious, Rita. This woman believes that indigenous cultures are *primitive*. Did you hear her last seminar? It was outrageous."

"Yes, but she's a fine scholar, Cowrie. I've shown her your chapters so far and here is her analysis. I think you'll find her very good on technique—and that's your weakest point."

Cowrie is stunned that Rita would arrange all this without telling her, and show her work to another scholar without her permission. She takes the papers from Rita's hand.

"Perhaps you should consider her comments and get back to me later," Rita suggests.

"Is there room for negotiation here, Rita?"

"I'm afraid not, Cowrie. If you'd stayed politically neutral, there might have been. But you have brought this on your own head. And the emphasis of the Siliyik performance crowned the decision."

"You weren't even there."

"Yes, but Marlene was. And she reported back on the piece which clearly attacked university policy. You won't get away with it, Cowrie. I suggest you don't try to."

Cowrie is astounded. Rita has really laid her cards on the table.

"So where's the free speech movement of the sixties, which made this campus famous—where is it now, Rita?"

"That was the sixties, Cowrie. This is the nineties. You'd better adjust if you want to survive."

Cowrie stuffs the report into her bag and walks back to her room. Inside, she opens it and reads:

This thesis is a primitive first draft. It shows a lack of knowledge of classical theory. The student has not set up the paradigm, discourse, or canon sufficiently. For example, where is George Mosses's concept of sexuality and nationalism, his socio-political analysis of German culture and nationalism? This is crucial to any notion of gay theory. Is homosexuality, as he argues, a late-nineteenth-century construct or does this student think it originated on some isolated Pacific Island? Perhaps too many sunny island days have eroded the intellect of this student since she won the Fulbright Scholarship? I'll need to reprogramme her thoroughly if she is to gain enough credibility to complete a PhD. She'll have to drop the notion of including oral literature. It's irrelevant by definition since it cannot possibly be part of a literary canon if it is not written down. Surely logic dictates this?

The arrogant comments go on for two pages. Then a hand-scrawled note attached by paper clip, which Rita has forgotten to take off: *Liebe Rita. Is this along the lines you want? You owe me one, darling. You can repay me after dinner tonight. M.*

So Rita is seeing Marlene on the side? Then she'll still be able to exert influence over me, thinks Cowrie, slipping the note into her breast pocket.

Later, she shows the report and note to Peta, who agrees it looks like a set-up. But what can she do to get out of it? Peta believes it's time for her to truly consider her options within the academy or outside it. She explains the vulnerability of the student in the PhD system: while there are official advisory groups, they always support the tutor or system, never the student—unless it's a clear case of sexual abuse, and even then, it's weighted.

Over dinner, they discuss the options in depth, with Peta urging Cowrie to sleep on it, take time to develop a strategy. As the wasabi creeps into her sinuses, tears flow down Cowrie's cheeks. She lifts her napkin to wipe them away.

"Let the ocean flow, Turtle. Let a tidal wave gather energy. Let the anger build. Use it creatively."

Peta stays the night with Cowrie, cradling her gently, encasing her with flame.

Nanduye, Koana and Ela walk out of the Texas courtroom triumphant. They have won the case for Ela's guardianship of her children, even though Chad's lawyer tried to implicate Koana and Ela in a lesbian relationship which he argued would have an "evil influence" on the children. However, Chad's battering of Ela worked against his case and it was felt the children would be far better off growing up in Hawai'i than on welfare in the States with Chad. He had been out of a job for over a year now.

They celebrate at the Raging Cactus—a local cafe run by gay Mexicans who pooled all their meagre resources to scrape out a living together. They work and live on the premises and it is now one of the most popular alternative venues, and one of the few not offering steak and chips on the side to quench the appetites of the Texans. Nanduye chose it because it was the most unlikely place to meet up with Chad or any of his mates.

Over tortillas, salsa and enchiladas, they discuss the case, recalling the most difficult moments with glee now they have won. "I'm still feeling a little shaken though, Nanduye. At one stage, when they raised the issue of Koana and I living together, I really thought Chad had us. It'd be so hard to prove one way or the other."

"But that's not the point, Ela. So what if you and Koana were gay? They still have no right to take your children from you on those grounds. The children should always be with the person who can best care for them, and in this case that is unquestionably you."

"I agree, Ela. I'd be proud to be your partner, and I am, in matters of co-parenting. I'm also relieved it turned out OK," adds Koana, squeezing Ela's hand.

"You know," says Nanduye, "despite all my legal training, the one image that always remains in my head in these cases is a scene from Brecht's play *Caucasian Chalk Circle*. In a child custody case, a circle is drawn with a line through the middle. The battle is between the birth mother and the adoptive mother. The judge says the child shall go to she who pulls the child out of the circle. Of course, the mother who most loves this child cannot bear to hurt her that deeply. She lets go, thus proving she is the true mother, the one who can best look after the child."

"So it was a trick set up to show the most caring parent?"

"Exactly. Sometimes, when I hear the dirt that clients dredge up in child custody cases, I long for a solution this simple, this effective, though I know it is really much more complex."

"Yes. I hated having to use Chad's adultery in this case. In fact, I was relieved to find he was seeing another woman. It took the worst pressure off me."

"I've heard that from so many women, Ela. Men think it's the worst thing they can do but, for many women under sexual pressure, it's the best, despite media claims to the contrary. If only they knew!"

Ela laughs. "Well, there was a stage where I really feared the children would go to Chad when that lawyer spoke about the evils of lesbianism and brought up satanic ritual abuse. What has that got to do with two people loving each other, whatever gender they are?"

"It's all confused in the minds of these Christian fundamentalists. They divide the world up into good and evil, and anything they don't understand goes into the evil pit. That means anyone who is different by race, class, sexual preference. It's a wonder they get it together to procreate with another gender."

"We've got a few fundies and missionary rednecks on the Big Island too," adds Koana. "They are the main force in opposing Hawai'ian sovereignty. They simply cannot understand the historical takeover of Hawai'i, when it's so blatant to the rest of us."

"That's because missionaries, throughout the world, have played a key role in duping indigenous cultures who by nature believed in spiritual forces. They knew it was the strongest way to get their land and resources, and unfortunately, it's worked. From our reservations to your Pacific Islands."

"Glad you see us as part of the Pacific and not just another US state."

"Koana, your issues are not so different from ours as Native Americans. That the United States has colonised both our cultures binds us together in many ways. But I also recognise you share other issues with colonised Pacific Islands from what Peta has told me of Cowrie's work. It's important we recognise our differences but work together where we can against the forces of colonisation."

"C'mon, you two. Let's use tonight to celebrate the times we do win out and feel recognised. It's all a part of the same struggle, and we've just made sure that two children get the chance to learn different ways from our ancestors."

"Make that four. I never want Nele and Peni to forget their island heritage. Television coming to the island nearly ruined them with its seductive US consumerism, but luckily it now bores them so much they'd rather be at Kanaka Maoli events. Much better for their self-esteem."

"Nearly losing my kids has made me treasure them even more. I feel a huge responsibility to give them the very best parenting I can, and with Ko it's finally happening." Ela hugs Koana.

They order another plate of tortillas and some Mexican beer. It's an excruciatingly hot night but this only makes Koana and Ela more homesick, as they describe to Nanduye the warm, balmy evenings over the hula festival, and how pleased they are that their children are now learning hula with the resurgence of traditional dancing that the sovereignty movement has inspired. Koana recalls how she once performed a seductive hula to tease Cowrie, how she remembers the fiery sunset that night. Afterwards she realised that she'd enjoyed tempting her friend, though the notion of being attracted to another woman was alien to her at the time. Ela is still a little uncomfortable around the subject, but Nanduye encourages Koana to reveal more. After a few beers, they are all laughing and telling tales of their most embarassing moments.

Peta stays a few more days to make sure Cowrie is all right before returning to the reservation. Nanduye calls with news of their success in Ela's guardianship case and Peta uses this as an opportunity to drag Cowrie away from her work struggles by planning a trip up to Tomales Bay, with Uretsete and Ruth, DK and Suzanne. They've prepared their sketches from the Siliyik performance to celebrate the opening of the oyster season and Peta hopes the distraction will provide a new perspective for Cowrie, allow her to see there are alternatives to working in the system.

By the time they reach the bay, Cowrie has begun to relax, and after her first batch of oysters and the new honey mead wine which Clem has made with the help of a local beekeeper, the merrymaking begins. Jake and the farm workers have built an extension to the nursery, like a modern longhouse, only this one is round and serves as a performance area and for local Miwok gatherings. Lush ferns dangle from the thatched tule roof like dreadlocks surrounding the edges of a gigantic head.

The ceremony for the new season begins, Siliyik rounding off the evening with storytelling. Children sit at the front with their parents behind them, the elders along the sides. Peta introduces the group in her native Chumash, and Uretsete interprets for Miwok and others. There is enough shared language for most to understand the proceedings. The Miwok elders are fascinated to hear Ruth's Yiddish, so she teaches them a song. Cowrie rounds off with karakia and waiata to bless the new oyster season. A fire is lit outside, around which they gather until the dawn rises over the hills behind Tomales Bay. Then they trail down to the ocean to begin the next stage of the ceremony, pulling up the first oysters of the season.

There are plenty of moments to laugh, cry and reflect on the nature of the ritual new beginning. Peta notices that Cowrie joins in as if she is at home, is less absorbed in the problems she knows she'll have to return to in her work. She's proud of Uretsete, who broke through another barrier in her performance last night. She read from Beth Brant's *Food and Spirits,* the story about David's plight at being Indian and gay: "In the city they didn't want me to be Native. In this place, they don't want me to be gay. It can drive you crazy! *Be this, be that. Don't be this way.* So you get to be like an actor, changing roles and faces to please somebody out there who hates your guts for what you are." There was a hushed silence after her piece, until David's refrain came through, hauntingly acted by Tayo: "I've always been proud of being Mohawk, of being from here. I am proud of being from here even though everywhere I turned, someone was telling me not to be either."

Uretsete had been clever to talk Tayo, who is well respected, into reading the part. At first he'd hesitated, but when they discussed it and he realised that the struggle for respect and rights is shared, he was eager to play his part. Slipping it into the Siliyik performance was an astute way to get everyone discussing the issues, through talkstory, in their own tradition, allowing others a way in rather than challenging an individual. Uretsete was learning a few of her own tricks! Nanduye would be proud of her too.

Cowrie looks radiant with the dawn sun glowing on her face. Peta remembers waking to her love that morning in the tent, not far from where they stand now. She has an overwhelming desire to hold Cowrie again, but realises it has smouldered into friendship, is not burning at her like the other day. Perhaps the ritual ending was needed for them to move into this new place. She notices the abalone shell she'd sent to Cowrie hanging from her neck, gleaming in the light reflected off the water. It sits next to the coconut shell turtle her grandfather, Apelahama, had left her, and the hei matau which received the fiery message from Pele in the Kiluaea crater.

Suddenly, she realises the vast amount of talkstory they have shared already, in their two years together, the way this infuses her now, enriches her own life. Cowrie so reminds her of a turtle, carrying the world on her shoulders, swimming with stories hidden in her mottled brown shell, stories which creep out over the land and gradually get under the skin, into the souls of people. Stories that carry the power to perceive life differently, to transform one's vision, simply by coming from another place. Stories that link us all, culture to culture, person to person, with their shared myths and symbolism.

Peta knows that this energy must be given freedom to flourish, that it cannot and must not be locked up inside a thesis or a university. It needs to swim further, reach a much vaster audience than just the academics. She trusts Cowrie will find a way to do this, will rise to the challenge that has been issued. The water is calm as Cowrie bends down to set the first oyster of the season free, floating back out to the ocean in the bowl of a carved kauri spoon from Aotearoa, in the shape of a whale, a frangipani flower cradling her shell. The group chant a blessing for the new shellfish season. Cowrie looks up at her, beaming, her face alight in the dawn. Peta wants to surround her with fire, melt into her soul forever.

Waka Tainui
Te Kotuku Marae, Hokianga.

Tena koe Cowrie,

You wouldn't believe the energy that's
hotted up in Aotearoa since my last letter.
The spirit of Hone Heke is alive and well and
cutting heads off statues honouring the
colonisation of Aotearoa by the Brits! It's
amazing. In some places, local iwi have
replaced their heads with carved pumpkins,
a Hallowe'en-mockery of the process of
colonisation. You'd better come back, Turtle.
I know you've been longing to knock the head
off Governor Grey for tearing down all that
native bush on Kawau Island and replacing it
with bloody Norfolk pines and squawking
peacocks! But our sacred dunes are safe—
only because the Brits couldn't get a
decent foundation dug in the sand for their
monuments of oppression!

I wasn't surprised to hear about Rita and
the Thesis Coup. Hang in there, Turtle! Devise
a counter plan, but if it gets too rough,
remember the soul essence of your work—
which is alive in Siliyik. Your task is to find a
way to nurture and let free this Pacific
energy, to draw the past into the future
through the power of storytelling—and by
nature a PhD is a British colonial construct.

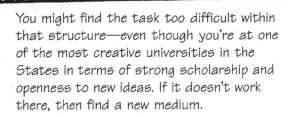

You might find the task too difficult within that structure—even though you're at one of the most creative universities in the States in terms of strong scholarship and openness to new ideas. If it doesn't work there, then find a new medium.

Irihapeti and I have been loving the Lesbian Review of Books you sent. Such a vast area of new and exciting scholarship. Maybe you should concentrate on getting your work out through some of those presses? In the end, ask yourself whether you want to be an academic, in which case you need the PhD, or a writer.

You once said to me academics just react to creative ideas of others, whereas writers are at the cutting edge of creating the ideas. Think about that. It seems as if Siliyik has been an earthing of the energy you've created there and will survive long after the PhD. I agree with you that we should be able to succeed, on our own terms, in all areas.

Don't be too hard on Rita. I abhor her behaviour—but remember she is a part of the whole pattern of abuse. Victims tend to oppress others until they face what drives them. But don't let her abuse you, either. You can't support her just because she is a woman and you felt so much hope with her

285

initially. We are all answerable for our actions. That's what Te Aroha abuse programme is all about. If we're going to force the men to face their abuse, then it stands for all of us.

I've been thinking a lot about this since your letter. Do you realise that the debate within your department about the heavy use of secondary texts over primary is symbolically linked to Rita's behaviour? One of the dangers of academia is that we can use it to challenge systems or to perpetuate old ones. In this case, the further you get from the primary texts, the further you move from the real lives studied. It becomes a game of literary critics speaking past the writers, to themselves, in jargon that deliberately excludes others. It fits the hierarchical system.

Women like Rita, who go into the academy as activists and with strong goals, often get worn down and end up capitulating to the system, taking the path of least resistance. This is linked with her refusal to face Claudia and her own pattern of addiction. The more we move away from linking how we treat people daily and what we study, the more licence we have to abuse or make excuses for our behaviour. They are connected. This work at Te Aroha has

convinced me that it all comes back to our ability to face and resolve conflict, whether this be Rwanda, Moutoa, or UC. Sometimes we need to remove ourselves from the conflict to see it more clearly. Think about that, Turtle. Return to Aotearoa, gather your strength and make plans for the future. Mere, Irihapeti and I are always here for you.

How's Peta, by the way? We got a card from Clem saying you were all coming up to celebrate the opening of the oyster season and that Siliyik was going to perform. How's Koana and Ela's case progressing? We did a beach ritual for them on the night of the court case opening.

Guess what? You know Mere's kete which you and Maata lost when gathering tuatuas? Well, it found its way back on to the shore further down the dunes. A bit worse for wear but still racognisable. Mere has it hanging out to dry and says she'll reweave the lost strands and use it for kumara. She reckons it's a good omen that it returned to us, and so will you soon, Turtle.

I don't like the sound of that Eurocentric supervisor. Keep well clear. I think you need to come up with a creative solution to the old structures, Cowrie. That's part of our

task on this earth. Look at how we've transformed a negative and punishing Pakeha justice system with Te Aroha.

Protect yourself against people who excel at working within such systems. Sometimes I worry because you are so trusting, Turtle. Be wise. Remember: "*He kokonga whare e kitea he kokonga ngakau ekore e kitea*: The corners of the house may be seen, but not the corners of the heart." Be wary. Tread carefully. Act always with aroha. And never forget we are here to challenge systems that are unfair—but also to replace them with creative alternatives. Your challenge is to work creatively within their system or find another medium for your work.

Had I remained at Waikato University I would have been safe on a good salary, but my spirit would be broken. That diminishes my power to work well and with aroha. You need to get your work out to a wider field than academics, and Siliyik is the first step. Move from there. We are all with you, Turtle.

Kia kaha, kia kaha, kia kaha! Arohanui

Kuini.

During the next few weeks, Cowrie works from home except for her lectures and keeps a low profile at the university. She's refused to minimise the Pacific input of her PhD, and asked for three more weeks to rework her proposal for Marlene du Fresne. But deep in her body, Kuini's letter has touched a strong nerve. She works also to secure the future of Siliyik with funding for them to tour over the next year. Uretsete and Ruth, who finish their degrees this semester, want to continue the group professionally and use it as a starting point to inspire other cultures to set up mixed storytelling groups to perform for their local communities. Cowrie helps them get a grant to establish themselves in business as a performing arts group.

At night, she dreams of Te Kotuku, the dunes, wondering if she should return and work with Kuini at Te Aroha or with Iri at the nursery. Completing the PhD on these terms simply seems to be a case of showing you know how to argue the work of other writers and reinforcing a northern hemisphere perspective.

Uretsete and Ruth have set up the Siliyik headquarters in Benny's film studio since she's accepted a position in Film Studies on the east coast for the next three years. They've worked out a deal with Benny where they get free rent in return for handling the distribution of her films to educational groups. Cowrie fears she might be a coward, helping

Ruth and Uretsete establish their creative work within a business, combining their learning with their dreams, while she still slogs away within the university structure, fearing to leave, fearing she will have failed her people back home in Aotearoa.

After finals, Uretsete and Ruth move into the apartment. Together, they collate the proposals for a new curriculum in Women's Studies and write their final report. Peta stays in touch, for she and Nanduye are helping organise a reservation tour for Siliyik later in the year. Rita and Marlene have booked a Club Med trip to the Caribbean during the vacation. Cowrie cannot believe their lack of connection between that mode of tourism and racism. They simply do not connect their actions to their politics and belief systems to their work.

Finally, the new semester begins. Cowrie carries her work up to the university on her back, like a turtle, humming through her shell, into her bones. Uretsete and Ruth cannot believe how elated she looks, after these weeks of struggle and depression, of debating the issues with them and over the phone to Peta, late into the night.

Carefully, she deposits the revised curriculum proposals and her own work in Marlene's tray, along with a copy for Rita and one for the departmental PhD committee. Singing waiata, she rides down Telegraph Avenue, stops off at the fish and fruit market, and upon arriving home announces she'll cook dinner for Siliyik tonight after their rehearsal. Uretsete and Ruth offer to help.

The meal is a wonderful celebration and everyone is pleased to see Cowrie back in her creative mode again. Over fresh green-lipped mussels from Aotearoa, cooked in their shells and hissing to be eaten, Uretsete's corn bread and Ruth's pasta, they excitedly

290

plan for the future, with DK and Suzanne announcing they'll be a part of the touring Siliyik group, the others joining in for local performances.

At the end of the evening, Cowrie proposes a toast to Siliyik and announces her plans for the future. She reads from the folder she has today presented to the university. They clap and cheer. The celebration continues until late in the night, with Lori and Squish coming downstairs to join them when the noise gets too much to take.

DK makes the final toast: "*Unuhia ki te ao marama*: Draw Forward into the World of Light!" Her accent isn't great, but Cowrie is deeply touched she bothered to learn the Maori off by heart for the occasion. Despite all the struggles, her efforts here on Great Turtle Island have been worth it. The chorus: *Unuhia ki te ao marama* is heard resounding through the streets of Black working-class Oakland as the Siliyik members wend their way back to their homes in the early hours of the new dawn.

Fresh from her trip to the Caribbean, full of good food and wine, and disgusted by the poverty and dirt outside the Club Med compounds, Marlene du Fresne collects her mail *en route* home. Rita meets her with a bundle of her own reports and they drive home to their new house near the Berkeley marina. Nestled comfortably inside bullet-proof glass windows looking out onto the bay, whisky in hand, Marlene comes across a folder from Cowrie.

"Dear God, Rita. What have you let me in for? Do I have to plough through another chapter of Pacific Island parochialism? When will these students realise this is an academy of learning, not a place to test out their political ideology? Most of them have no idea of classical scholarship. Personally, I'd have them all return to Plato, *Aeneid,* Latin, Greek, and a solid ground-ing in scholarship before I'd let them write a word."

"Strangely enough, Marlene, Cowrie did all that at university. That grounding was probably why she got the Fulbright Scholarship. Mind you, what's a university in a small island community got to offer? Probably about the standard of Cal State." The whisky crackles as Rita pours it over the ice in her glass.

"Yes. Ethnic politics rules, nein?" They laugh. Rita loves being able to relax with Marlene, not have to retain her political guard as she did with Claudia. She'll never be lovers with a black woman again. Too much hard work. Watching your words. Feeling responsible for the racism of others.

Marlene opens the package. Out flops the student curriculum report and a series of interviews with indigenous women of the Pacific on the effect of the nuclear industry in destroying their island lifestyles. A letter falls from the pages.

Marlene du Fresne, Thesis Supervisor
Rita YoungBlood, Thesis Co-Supervisor
UC PhD Committee.

Kia ora,

Please find enclosed my resignation as a PhD candidate at the University of California. Until Pacific issues are acknowledged within this university and more than lip service given to affirmative action policies and liberal rhetoric toward promoting cross-cultural studies, I have opted to work outside your system. I have filed a full report for the US Fulbright Foundation, documenting the lack of formal supervision received, the issues at stake, the work completed so far, with concrete suggestions towards a more useful approach, and included future networks for students coming from other cultures into this situation.

I firmly disagree that there is only one way to fulfil the requirements of a PhD programme and that this should necessarily involve a reinforcement of Eurocentric and northern hemisphere modes of working. Until there is such a system established which truly racognises alternative methods of academic work, than I choose to complete my work elsewhere.

I have signed a publishing contract for a text based on my PhD. You will note from the publisher's report that they wish me to extend rather than reduce the Pacific material and the press has agreed to the Siliyik CD and tape being produced as part of the final publication. They have also purchased the electronic rights for the project.

The Fulbright Foundation have accepted my grounds for a change of plan and are endorsing the revised proposal and publication of this material as falling solidly within the goals of a Fulbright Scholarship. I have now transferred to their Cultural Studies Programme. Their facsimile endorsing this is enclosed. You will note that they have initiated an inquiry into future university policy regarding their multicultural students.

Please address all future correspondence to:

Cowrie Honu Te Aroha
Te Kotuku Marae
RD 1
Hokianga
Aotearoa/New Zealand.

P.S. Thank you also for providing me with research for my first novel, which I will be working on while completing the Pacific text for the same publishers.

Darkness, chaos. Words fly at me on the wind, taunting me for using them, breaking my sacred pact to remain silent, to listen, to learn. Branches rip and slash my face. In the distance, my mother is calling. If only I can hold on. Will the branch take my weight? Voices soar from the black earth below, clutching at the twigs, twisting them in their grasp. She's nearly here. She reaches out her hand to rescue me. My limbs shrink into my body, become hard. A shell encases me. I am frozen inside a nut. Silent forever.

Tears slide over her cheeks as Cowrie finishes the last sentence. Tayo's story touches her own journey—but this is only the beginning. She will move this character beyond the words, beyond the silencing. Find words that fit her Pacific heritage. Words that have not yet been invented. Words that tell of the silent places where cultures mix and overlap, where loving can also mean letting go, where too much giving can oppress as much as no giving, where learning to receive is also a gift.

She will also tell the truth about systems women, systems thinking. She can't wait to get up to the chapters on Marlene and Rita. She'll change their names but keep the essence of the issues. She'll have to imagine their responses to the curriculum proposal and her letter of resignation.

Exhausted, but happy to have completed the first

paragraph of her novel, she blows out the candle. Through the window of her hut, built from flax and nikau, she can see the light flickering in Kuini's waka, *Tainui*. Beyond, the whoosh of the ocean surfing up the dunes at high tide. A lone torea digs deep in the sand after the water recedes, pulling up a tuatua just in time to fly away before the wave surges over her black back. As the bird soars across the waves, the tuatua pokes out its tongue, spitting juice into the bird's eye. The torea loses her grip on her prey and the tuatua plunges from her beak into the dark ocean below, burrowing its way back to freedom.

GLOSSARY

Legend

Chumash/Indian		= Chumash/Indian
H		= Hawai'ian
M		= Maori
NZ		= New Zealand
S		= Samoan
US		= United States
H	*'ae*	yes
H	*aloha*	hi, or dear
M	*aroha*	love
NZ	*arvo*	afternoon ie. time to snooze after a feast of mussels
US	*ass*	arse
H	*auwe*	yes
NZ	*bickie*	literally biscuit but used as slang for money (slang)
NZ	big bickies	a lot of money (enough to make robbing the bank redundant)
NZ	*bro*	brother (term of affection)
US	*buns*	arse (Americans are especially fond of these)
US	*cuz, cuzzies*	cousins (term of affection)
NZ/US	*dak*	marijuana; mary-jane; dope; extra income for those on social welfare
M	*haere mai*	welcome, come here
Chumash/Indian	*haku*	hi: hello, dear (in letter)
M	*hangi*	underground oven dug in earth, hot stones thrown in and a pig or two plus vegies
H	*haole*	pakeha or white person
M	*hei matau*	fish-hook (often bone carved fish-hook)
H	*heiau*	temple (usually made of stones)
	hoahanau	okay

M	*hokioi*	mysterious nightbird
M	*hongi*	rub noses in greeting
H	*honu*	Hawai'ian for turtle. Name of Cowrie's truck.
M	*hui*	meeting
H	*hula*	Hawai'ian dance, very erotic
H	*i'a*	fish
M	*ika*	fish
M	*iwi*	tribe
NZ	*jandals*	rubber slip on shoes, "slippers" in USA. "thongs" in Australia
M	*ka pai*	that's good; fine; okay
M	*kahawai*	delicious fish, especially, smoked over manuka on fire
M	*kai*	food
M	*kai moana*	sea food, eg. pipis, cockles, *tuatua*
M	*kai o te ata*	bacon and eggs
H	*kamaha'o*	good; great; okay; choice
M	*kanuka*	large manuka tree
H	*kapu*	sacred (M *tapu* sacred)
M	*karakia*	prayers
M	*kereru*	large green and white wood pigeon (extremely delicious)
M	*kete*	woven bag (usually flax)
M	*kia kaku*	stay strong
M	*kia ora*	greetings: hi; "goodaye mate"
M	*kina*	sea egg delicacy (best eaten raw from middle of egg)
NZ	*kiwi*	flightless bird; slang for a New Zealander
NZ	*kiwiana*	New Zealand kitsch
M	*kohanga*	literally nest (meaning language nest)
M	*kohanga reo*	literally language nest; Maori learning programmes for preschool
M	*korero*	speech
M	*kotuku*	wading bird like an egret (here it refers to the *kotuku rerenga*) *tahi*; rare visitor)

M	*kuia*	respected elder woman of tribe
M	*kumara*	Maori sweet potato: bright purple skin, yellow interior (very erotic)
M	*kumukumu*	gurnard—sweet fish, great marinated in lime juice and coconut milk and eaten raw
S	*lavalava*	wrap-around
H	*lei*	flower garland
H	*lomilomi*	Hawai'ian massage
H	*mahalo*	thankyou; thanks; ta, choice mate
M	*mamaku*	black tree fern (fern shoots taste delicious)
M	*mana*	integrity; charisma
M	*manaia*	carved figure (usually with head of bird, body of person, tail of fish)
M	*manuhiri*	guest(s)
M	*manuka*	tea tree (great for smoking fish)
M	*marae*	meeting place of *whanan* or *iwi*—family tribe people
NZ	*marram*	marram grass: coastal plant often found in sand dunes
M	*mere*	short, fat club
M	*moko*	tattoo
M	*mokopuna*	grandchild; grandchildren
M	*nikau*	palm tree—most southern in world
H	*ohana*	family
H	*ohelo*	berries from ohelo bush (usually thrown into Pele's crater)
M	*paepae*	orator's bench
M	*Pakeha*	white person; haole
M	*paua*	shellfish similar to abalone but with deeper blues and greens—stunning
H	*pepe hauhau*	card (card nights here)
NZ	*pikelet*	small pancake

M	*pipii*	delicious seafood, like an oblong cockle *(paphies Australis)*
NZ	*plumeria*	frangipani (Aus/NZ) sweet smelling tree with strong scented flowers
M	*poi*	ball used in ceremonial dances (often made from flax or straw)
M	*potae*	hat(s)
M	*pounamu*	greenstone (NZ jade)
M	*poupou*	posts
M	*powhiri*	greeting; welcome
M	*puha*	sow-thistle or fish gills (Great boiled up in a cauldron with Pakeha!)
M	*puku*	stomach; abdomen
M	*puriri*	large shiny-leafed, native, New Zealand tree (vitex lucens)
NZ	*rellies*	NZ for relatives
NZ	*squizzie*	look, as in *let's have a squizzie at ya new outfit* etc.
US	*sweetgrass*	dried grass sticks (used as a form of incense)
M	*taiaha*	long club
M	*tamahine*	daughter, niece, girl
M	*tamariki*	children, kids
M	*tangata whenua*	people of the land
M	*tangi*	funeral (literally wail, mourn)
M	*taniwha*	mythical beast; water monster
M	*taonga*	gift; sacred treasure
T	*taro*	delicious root vegetable
M	*te kotuku*	marae named after the Kotuku bird
M	*te reo*	the language
M	*te whenua*	the land
M	*tena koe*	hello (singular); hi; giddaye mate
M	*tena korua*	hello (to two people)
M	*tena koutou*	hello (to a crowd, more than three)
M	*ti*	cabbage tree
M	*tikonga*	customs; culture

M	*toe toe*	pampas grass (USA/UK); bush with tall furry, cream, feathery spikes
M	*tohunga*	expert; specialist, artist
M	*torea*	oyster catcher; bird with a connoisseur's palate!
NZ/Aus	*troppo*	mad; off ya rocker; crazy,
M	tuatara	ancient reptile, like a gecko lizard *(shenodon punctatus)*
M	*tuatua*	exquisite seafood in shell, related to pipi (excellent cooked over fire on the beach)
M	*tui*	parson bird (UK); native bird with white fluff under chin, also has an exquisite tonal range
M	*tukutuku*	ornamental panels (often on rafters)
Chumash/ Indian	*tule*	tule reed (used for weaving, making boats, etc.)
H	*unihipili*	spirits
M	*utu*	revenge
NZ	*varsity*	university or uni in Australia (ie. great place to hang out, drink coffee and debate issues)
M	*wahine*	woman
M	*wahine ma*	(song) gather around, strong women, be brave!
M	*wahine toa*	strong woman
M	*waiata*	song
M	*wairua*	spirit; soul
M	*waka*	canoe
M	*whakapapa*	genealogy; cultural identity
M	*whanau*	family (extended); *whanau ake-* close family
M	*whare nui*	meeting house

Other books by Cathie Dunsford

Cowrie

*Take a wonderfully-competent angling and
archeologizing lesbian who needs to know her roots:
take an attractive—because accurate—picture of
current Hawai'i ... and take the dignity and
irresolution of our lives ... Cath Dunsford's first
novel (of a series I hope) is a gentle, determined,
insightful and womanful book.*
—Keri Hulme, author *The Bone People*

ISBN: 9781875559282

Manawa Toa: Heart Warrior

Cowrie boards a ship bound for Moruroa Atoll
during the French nuclear tests. She is in for a rough
ride. As international attention is focused on the
Pacific and the environment, the stakes rise.

*The novel is suffused with Maori culture,
women's culture and a passion for the beauty
of Aotearoa, the land and sea.*
—Sue Pierce, *Lesbian Review of Books*, USA

ISBN: 9781875559695

Ao Toa: Earth Warriors

Ao Toa is that rare novel—an eco-thriller combining action and suspense with deep emotions and the sensual power of the natural world. This richly textured novel expresses fundamental conflicts over food security, the care of the environment and the morality of science. The writing is irreverent, funny and fresh, catching the authentic tone and flavour of today's global debates as they play out at a local level.

ISBN: 9781876756437

Song of the Selkies

The Edinburgh Festival brings together artists from all over the world, and Cowrie is among them, telling stories and giving readings. But even Cowrie can't anticipate the chemistry that will begin when a group of traditional storytellers sets off to the Orkney Islands with Ellen, to stay at her coastal family cottages. For Ellen turns out to be Morrigan, and Morrigan is a selkie, living in the sea and on land.

Read Song of the Selkies *as a guide to the Orkneys, a first class mystery story, a post-modern comment on lesbian feminism or just read it for fun. It is a visionary book and Cathie Dunsford is a writer whose visions begin with today.*
—Carolyn Firth Gammon

ISBN: 9781876756093

Car Maintenance, Explosives and Love and Other Contemporary Lesbian Writings

edited by Susan Hawthorne, Cathie Dunsford and Susan Sayer

What is mythic? / What is true? asks the opening anonymous poet of this collection. Lesbians have become cultural amphibians. This anthology reflects the varied tongues, the inventiveness of lesbian culture and the diversity of lesbian writing. It explores the mechanics of daily life, the explosiveness of relationships and the geography of love. Here is toughness, conviction, perseverance and passion: writing which makes a difference.

> *Definitely recommended.*
> —Jessica Hubbard, Critic, NZ

> *American lesbians should all be looking further west and south, if this Australian anthology is any indication of the overall quality of lesbian writing Down Under ... It's an unusually impressive collection, full of experiment and promise.*
> —Amazon Customer, Regina Marler

ISBN: 9781875559626

If you would like to know more about Spinifex Press,
write for a free catalogue, email us for a PDF,
or visit our website.

Spinifex Press
PO Box 212, North Melbourne
Vic 3051 Australia

women@spinifexpress.com.au
www.spinifexpress.com.au

Many Spinifex titles are now available as eBooks.
See the Bookstore on the Spinifex website for more details.